PENGUIN

MR. SCOBIE'S RIDDLE

Born in the industrial Midlands of England in 1923, Elizabeth Jolley was brought up in a German-speaking household, her father having met her mother, the daughter of an Austrian general, in Vienna in 1919. Elizabeth Jolley was educated at home and later at a Quaker boarding school. In 1959 she moved to Western Australia with her husband and three children; since that time she has been acclaimed as one of Australia's leading fiction writers. Among her books are *Five Acre Virgin and Other Stories*, *The Traveling Entertainer*, *Palomino*, *The Newspaper of Claremont Street*, *Woman in a Lampshade*, and *Miss Peabody's Inheritance*, which is published by Viking.

MR. SCOBIE'S RIDDLE

Elizabeth Jolley

PENGUIN BOOKS

PENGUIN BOOKS
Viking Penguin Inc., 40 West 23rd Street,
New York, New York 10010, U.S.A.
Penguin Books Ltd, Harmondsworth,
Middlesex, England
Penguin Books Australia Ltd, Ringwood,
Victoria, Australia
Penguin Books Canada Limited, 2801 John Street,
Markham, Ontario, Canada L3R 1B4
Penguin Books (N.Z.) Ltd, 182-190 Wairau Road,
Auckland 10, New Zealand

First published in Australia by
Penguin Books Australia Ltd 1983
Reprinted 1983
Published in the United States of America by
Viking Penguin Inc. 1984

LIBRARY OF CONGRESS CATALOGING IN PUBLICATION DATA
Jolley, Elizabeth, 1923 –
    Mr. Scobie's riddle.
    I. Title.
[PR9619.3.J68M7   1984]   823   84 -14890
ISBN 0 14 00.7490 2

Printed in the United States of America by
R.R. Donnelley & Sons Company, Harrisonburg, Virginia
Set in Palatino and Caledonia

For Leonard Jolley

Ille terrarum mihi praeter omnes Angulus ridet.

Horace with an explanation;

One could say there is a corner of the world which
smiles upon one but it is a little awkward,
what about ——

No cosy spot on earth caresses me more — or
words to that effect.

'the word killeth but the spirit giveth life'

Signed H. Hailey

A GUIDE TO THE PERPLEXED

NOVEMBER 1 NIGHT SISTER'S REPORT

ROOM 3 Mother vioded 4 a.m. Nothing abnormal to report.

Signed Night Sister M. Shady

NOVEMBER 2 NIGHT SISTER'S REPORT

ROOM 3 Mother vioded also Mrs Murphy Mrs Renfrew and Mrs Tompkins. Nothing abnormal to report.

Signed Night Sister M. Shady

NOVEMBER 3 NIGHT SISTER'S REPORT

ROOM 3 Mother vioded also Mrs Murphy Mrs Renfrew Mrs Tompkins Miss Hailey and Miss Nunne. Nothing abnormal to report.

Signed Night Sister M. Shady

Night Sister Shady: Please will you report more fully. Please report on the other patients. You are supposed to wash the kitchen floor too you seem to have forgotten this. I seem to have to remind you too often that if a patient upsets her tea in bed you are to boil up some water and pour on at once. All my sheets are getting ruined. Also my brother lt col. (retired) I. Price has something to add.

and Night Sister Shady please note spelling of void. V.O.I.D.
Signed Matron H. Price

ROOM 3 Mother vioded voided room three sponged slept well
4 a.m. kitchen floor washed as request sweet potatoes prepared also pumpkin please matron can I have a knife for the
veggies. Nothing abnormal to report.
Signed Night Sister M. Shady

Night Sister Shady: It is unfortunate that one of the patients
is your mother please will you refer to her in this book as Mrs
Morgan which is her correct name. Please bring your own
knife; it is simply not practical for me to provide knives as
all previous night nurses have left and taken them. Please
report more fully and why always 4 a.m. Is this the only time
you know? Please boil beetroots.

Signed Matron H. Price

ROOM 3 It's about mother I mean Mrs Morgan matron at
4 a.m. all patients voided and had terrible words. Sweet
potatoes have gone mouldy beetroots boiled as request. N.A.
to report.
Signed Night Sister M. Shady

Night Sister Shady: Please report more fully and please
explain why always 4 a.m. Surely things happen at other
times in the night. And what do you mean 'Nothing abnormal
to report'? Mrs Morgan's sheets were all covered in blood this
morning and why is her foot bandaged? You seem to have for-
gotten the kitchen floor, this is to be done every night. Mrs
Tompkins is complaining that she has not had a bath since
you took over night duty. Please clean thoroughly the sauce-

2

pan you ruined last night. Mrs Tompkins' bath should be at
10 p.m.

Please write a detailed account of what happened last
night. Write on a clean page in this book.

Signed Matron H. Price

NOVEMBER 6 NIGHT SISTER'S REPORT but first the Detailed
Account. First I am sorry matron about the time 4 a.m. There
is no clock here as you know and so when the milk comes
I know it is four o'clock as he is punctual and I hear his word
when he falls on the broken step out there. About Mrs Morgan's foot matron ever since you moved mother in with those
other patients they've gone for each other and at 4 a.m. she
got really wild with Miss Hailey because Miss Hailey kept
saying *mia culpa* in that loud voice of hers *mia culpa* over
and over and mother got wild also Mrs Renfrew and Mrs
Murphy and she slipped and caught her foot in the bedside
commode and the nail came off. Wound dressed p.r.n. with
menthol camphor. I could not change her bed as I used the
clean sheet matron for Miss Hailey's bed after mother tipped
the flowers all over. I am sorry matron about the saucepan
it could not be helped the beetroots caught while I was so
busy in room 3.

NIGHT SISTER'S REPORT FOLLOWING DETAILED ACCOUNT
Saucepan cleaned as well as could be expected. Bath prepared Mrs Tompkins 10 p.m. Mrs Tompkins came in 4 a.m.
she says she never in all her life asked for a bath and anyway
the water was cold by then. Mrs Tompkins and these two elderly gentleman was very noisy they said they had missed
their tea and wanted a snack but I explained to them the
fridge was locked and showed them your padlock, what about
a drink then they said and Mrs Tompkins showed us where
you keep the Hospital Brandy matron they all had a medicinal dose I hope this is satisfactory. Slept well. Dressed

3

mother's wound again p.r.n. with menthol camphor. Matron Rawlings I think I need some help in room 3.

Signed Night Sister M. Shady

Night Sister Shady: No it is not satisfactory the brandy is for my own personal medicinal use. Please remember this. Patients are to bring in their own brandy if required. Kindly note your mother's name for the purposes of this book is Mrs Morgan. Why did you use menthol camphor? And again the kitchen floor was not washed and the saucepan will not do.

Signed Matron H. Price

And, Night Sister Shady please note my name is not Rawlings. Mr Rawlings is my ex-husband and I do not use the name. Furthermore since we have Mrs Rawlings on the staff of this hospital it only confuses matters to have two of us.

NOVEMBER 7 NIGHT SISTER'S REPORT

Menthol camphor is the only ointment I can find. Bath prepared for Mrs Tompkins as request. Patient did not come in till 4 a.m. also Mr Boxer and Mr Rob. They said they had eaten but Mrs Tompkins said she had some cream and half a bottle of port somewhere and she would fancy asparagus sandwiches. In going along the passage to find the medicinal dose they disturb room 3 who was only just got off to sleep so I sponge all 4 a.m. Nothing abnormal to report.

signed Night Sister M. Shady

Night Sister Shady: Who is this Mr Boxer and what is his diagnosis? And Mr Rob ditto? There is no one of those names in this hospital. Please look on the list on the back of the bathroom door and see for yourself. Again you say 'Nothing abnormal to report' but what was all my linen doing in the passage and why was the door wrenched off the sideboard? Also the padlock on the refrigerator has been forced and why have all the contents of the cupboard in room 3 been put on Mrs Mor-

4

*gan's bed? She is quite unable to get into it. Please remember
she is 99. Menthol camphor is not the only remedy we have.
On the shelf under the sink is a tin of Epsom salts. In an
emergency why don't you use your eyes. Mrs Tompkins says
that it seems too much trouble for you to prepare her bath and
she did not like to have it because of this. Please remember
to boil the beetroots or they will go off before the cold trays
on Sunday. And, Night Sister Shady, Kitchen Floor.*

Signed Matron H. Price
My brother I. Price Lt Col. (retired) has prepared two notices.
Pin them up please.

TO ALL STAFF TO WHOM IT MAY CONCERN
IT HAS COME TO MY NOTICE THAT STAFF
ARE USING THEIR PERSONAL LIFE THIS MUST
CEASE IMMEDIATELY.

Signed I. Price (Lt Col. retired)

IT HAS COME TO MY NOTICE THAT ALL
JUNKETS ARE DAILY

Signed I. Price (Lt Col. retired)

NOVEMBER 8 NIGHT SISTER'S REPORT

Beetroots boil as request also bath for Mrs Tompkins 10 p.m.
Patient came in quite early also Mr Boxer and Mr Rob when
I ask her about the bath she says she never took one and Mr
Boxer says Betsy Tompkins never in her life took anything
bigger than a silver tea-pot and they roar their heads off
laughing. They make so much noise they wake room 3 and
there is another picnic here like last night and they play this
game matron where all hunt for the bottle of medicinal. That
is why all that confusion last night. I did not have time to

clear up. Really matron I think I need some help at night. Mr Boxer says he wants to be a patient if you will have him please also Mr Rob, he is Mr Shady I am sorry matron we are related. Mr Boxer is also called Mr Morgan so he is a relation too. I am sorry.

Mr Rob Shady medicinal dose 4 a.m. Slept well.

Mr Boxer Morgan medicinal dose 4 a.m. Slept well.

Mrs Tompkins medicinal dose 4 a.m. Also one medium pizza with cheese and anchovies (in a taxi) 4 a.m. Slept well.

ROOM 3 medicinal dose 4 a.m. voided. Slept well. Nothing abnormal to report.

Signed Night Sister M. Shady

Night Sister Shady: Who wants to read about junkets in the bathroom? In future please use your head for notices. Kitchen Floor please and Burned Saucepan.

Signed Matron H. Price

NOVEMBER 9 NIGHT SISTER'S REPORT Very sorry about notices matron but bathroom door is the only one soft enough to take a drawing pin. Bath prepared for Mrs Tompkins also kitchen floor and saucepan.

ROOM 3 very quiet all night. Nothing abnormal to report.

Signed Night Sister M. Shady

Night Sister Shady: Of course Room 3 was very quiet all night. Mrs Morgan, Miss Hailey, Mrs Tompkins, Mrs Murphy and Mrs Renfrew were moved to the District Hospital to have their injuries treated. Don't you ever read my day report?

My brother I. Price (Lt Col. retired) will be sleeping in Room 3 for the present. Please give him hot milk 10 p.m. also Mrs Tompkins bath and kitchen floor.

And Night Sister Shady, it has come to my notice that you are unregistered please note that your pay will be adjusted as from when you took up duties in this hospital. I shall be obliged, in future, to address you as Mrs Shady but for the purposes of the Good Name of this nursing home you will continue as Night Sister Shady brackett (unregistered) close brackett.

Signed Matron H. Price

NOVEMBER 10 NIGHT SISTER'S REPORT (unregistered)
ROOM 3 Hot milk prepared for Lt Col. I. Price 10 p.m. Lt Col. says why on earth Hyacinth because he never touches the stuff. Pat. very restless and disturbed. Mother came in 4 a.m. also Miss Hailey Mrs Tompkins Mrs Murphy and Mrs Renfrew discharged from the District. Satisfactory. Mrs Tompkins says what's the matter with this place these days there's never any food around and with what she's put into the place she should get a snack now and then what about sandwiches I said and she said yes but not beetroot. Could we have some bread matron please. Also Miss Hailey wants a word.

Quo Vadis signed Heather Hailey, patient in room 3. Milkman fell and bruise him in very awkward place dressed with menthol camphor 4 a.m. Lt Col. Price, Mr Boxer Morgan and Mr Rob Shady very pleased to see Mrs Morgan Miss Hailey Mrs Tompkins Mrs Murphy and Mrs Renfrew again especially Lt Col. pleased with Mrs Morgan. All pats. play cards in dinette Lt Col. brighten up but loose bad. Nothing abnormal to report.

Signed Night Sister Shady (unregistered)

Mrs M. Shady: Please note no Christian Names on duty. I refer, of course, to my brother's use of mine. What do you mean 'nothing abnormal to report', I never heard of patients being discharged from the District Hospital at 4 a.m. Please remember the milkman is not a patient here. And why only room 3? Please remember there are other patients. And what about the kitchen floor? What do you do all night?

Signed Matron H. Price
(please note spelling of lose)

NOVEMBER 11 NIGHT SISTER'S REPORT

Hot milk and bath prepared 10 p.m. Mrs Tompkins in early also Mr Boxer Morgan and Mr Rob Shady.

ROOM 3 All pats. play cards in dinette. They all play this game matron it's all raise a dollar kings on queens raise two dollars three dollars it's a real scream it's a picnic matron I don't think I ever saw mother enjoy herself so well. Lt Col. Price really enjoy himself but loøse lose bad. N.A. to report.

Signed Night Sister M. Shady (unregistered)

Mrs Shady: Your report noted. You realize of course that two packs should be used one pack for playing while the other is shuffled. Please see that this is done. Also what about the patients in Room 1? Don't you ever read my Day Report?

Signed Matron H. Price

NOVEMBER 12 NIGHT SISTER'S REPORT

Your instructions noted matron. All pats. in early. All play cards in dinette. Lt Col. Price lose very bad but enjoy himself. Also I am sorry matron about room 1 I did not realize there were patients in there.

Signed Night Sister M. Shady (unregistered)

Mrs Shady: What do you do all night don't you ever read the paper. It states quite clearly on page one of the Midwest Pullout that three ambulances (small ones naturally) on their way to this nursing home crashed right outside our front gate. We even have our picture in the paper. If you look back in this book you will see that in Room 1 there are three admissions. Mr David Hughes 85 years. Hemiplegia (left side)

8

multiple bruising and superficial grazes. Admitted 4 p.m. Condition satisfactory. Treatment prescribed: Epsom salts daily. Mr Martin Scobie 85 years. Hypertension. Transferred from District Hospital. Multiple bruising and superficial grazes. Admitted 4 p.m. Condition satisfactory. Treatment: Epsom salts daily. Mr Fred Privett 85 years. Hypertension. Altered mental state. Multiple bruising superficial grazes. Admitted 4 p.m. Satisfactory. Treatment: Epsom Salts daily. Religion and next of kin on bathroom door.

Signed Matron H. Price

NOVEMBER 13 NIGHT SISTER'S REPORT
ROOM 1 Very quiet all night I could not get in there matron as door stuck on chest of drawers.
ROOM 3 All pats. play cards in dinette Lt Col. Price lose very bad but enjoy himself and Mrs Morgan. N.A.D. to report.

Signed Night Sister M. Shady (unregistered)

Everywhere there was the lightness and the excitement of the coming summer. There was a warm garden scent of cut grass drying in brownish ridges. There was the fragrance of tall grasses, still growing, waving feathered heads. There was the perfume of unnamed flowers, the flowers of well-established suburban gardens, and the flowers of weeds and nasturtiums. It was not an accustomed sweetness of summer flowers but a penetrating freshness.

On all sides of the little hospital there was a piling up of colour. From the green and orange and yellow of the leaves and the brave trumpets of the nasturtiums, vivid splashes of colour climbed into the golden lantana and up into the scarlet bottle brush flowers. The pink and purple bougainvillea hung sprawling in one direction over neat brick walls and, in the other, climbed over garage roofs reaching still further up into the powdered rain cloud of cape lilac.

It was possible, from the verandah of the hospital, to look across the road into the thick glossy leaves of a Moreton Bay fig tree. In the twilight it seemed as if hundreds of doves were flying into the tree. Grey and silver pearled and pink edged doves, with tender feathers, disappeared into the dark branches.

After a time the big tree was quiet. All the doves disappeared as if absorbed into a thick dark-green silence.

There was not enough space in Room One for three people, not even when they were to be people with scarcely any possessions and one of them would spend most of his time confined to bed. One bed was opposite the door. The light switch could only be reached by leaning across this bed. To reach the other two beds a small chair and a bedside cupboard had first to be taken out of the room. A cheap wardrobe and a chest were huddled in the remaining space. The wardrobe, partly blocking the window, was inaccessible because of the third bed. The chest of drawers stopped the door from opening properly. It was possible, when in the room, with a flamboyant movement to pull out the chest of drawers, fling the door wide open and, in the same movement, quickly push the chest back against the now wide open door. It was not possible to close the door unless the action was repeated in a kind of reverse. Because of the difficulty, the door of Room One was kept permanently wide open or, alternatively, permanently shut.

A blind hung half way down the window. Immediately outside was a mass of dusty green foliage of the kind which grows outside kitchens and hotel toilets. The ragged triangular leaves on these vines shook in that restless wind which raises dust and causes doors to slam and windows to rattle. The leaves, moving in the endless trembling towards and away from one another, gave an impression of trying to speak or to listen but always turning away before any tiny message could either be given or heard.

There were flies in the room and the mingled smells of reheated food, stale tobacco and urine.

Mr Hughes was a tall man. He had a hemiplegia resulting from a cerebral lesion. It was, he thought, as if the whole of his left side was dead in advance. He could only drag his left leg. He could not use his left arm and hand at all; the forefinger of his left hand was always stretched out rigidly pointing at something. He hated this and felt he must say he was sorry about his finger pointing. He kept wanting to say he was sorry because of all the things which had to be done for him.

'I'm sorry – sorry – sorry,' he said to Keppie, his sister-in-law, who was too tiny to look after him. All the sisters-in-law, Heppie, Keppie, Annie, Elsie, Dolly and Florry wanted to look after him but they were all too small. They did what they could but they could not manage.

'I'm sorry, sorry,' he said to them.

'I think I'm going to need the toilet,' Mr Hughes told Keppie anxiously in the ambulance. Keppie, chosen by the others to travel with him, tried to comfort him.

'No, No David, it's just your imagination.' At that moment there was a severe jolt and Keppie was thrown off the little stool; her freshly baked cake flying out of its white cloth as her basket flew from her neat hands. Mr Hughes, being so heavy and held firmly on his stretcher, remained safely in position. Only his left arm, not by his own effort, moved wildly and the papery skin on the back of his hand was grazed. He bled badly from the graze.

Mr Martin Scobie, in his ambulance, coming from a different direction, was just explaining to the driver that all that was needed was a good hot plate of porridge.

No one, he said, at the District Hospital where he had been for three weeks, had done anything about his bowels and he was worried about them.

'Three weeks is a long time.'

'Too right!' the ambulance driver agreed with Mr Scobie and braked hard but too late. A driver from his direction was completely unable to see anything coming from the

12

other two roads. The corner was a meeting place of three roads.

'I'm perfectly all right thank you,' Mr Scobie said to the shocked driver, 'as I was telling you, porridge is the thing, hot porridge. In hospitals they never make things really hot . . .'

'Don't, but do not take everything I say *au pied de la lettre.*' Miss Hailey, towering in her formidable dressing gown, had additional height because of a round straw hat, Canadian Mounted Police style, with a narrow leather hat band, a badge and a leather chin strap. She stopped to address Matron Price who was at her desk writing her report. Miss Hailey's eyes glowed, the hat made her feel efficient and knowledgeable. She would be able to tell someone the way if someone asked her.

'It is simply my great love of *la petite phrase,*' she said, '*la petite phrase,* I . . .'

'Yes. Yes! dear.' Hyacinth Price had been matron of The Hospital of St Christopher and St Jude for thirty years and had had Miss Hailey for ten of them and knew her for many more. 'Yes, Dear!' She looked up with a quick frown. She, in spite of Miss Hailey's support and faithfulness to St Christopher and St Jude, did not enjoy being leaned over especially while concentrating on the spelling of diarrhoea and haemorrhage. Both words, though repeatedly occurring in her life, gave her trouble. It was a sort of mental blockage, she told herself, probably a daily reminder that she needed a holiday in a remote place, on a peninsula or, better still, an island where neither could exist. Though it was likely that some other difficult word would turn up even there, and she'd be unable to spell it. A word like archipelago for

13

instance. She was not sure how to pronounce it let alone spell it.

Here I am in the Greek Islands, the archipelago . . .

How could she even send a post card from her holiday if unable to write the word,

food good, weather splendid, the arkipalargo very lovely . . .

She began to try the word out on the blotting paper. Her pen hovered, caressing the fast-spreading ink.

'Yes, I'll go and lie down. I think I am a little tired,' Miss Hailey replied, from habit, to a suggestion Miss Price no longer needed to make aloud.

'She was only an undertaker's daughter but – wow – could she bury a stiff! – wow –' Frankie, singing, danced down the hall. 'Here's the Public Health to see you,' she stopped in the doorway of the office. Matron Price stood up. Later she would have to have a word with the girl about answering the front door in such a filthy overall. There was simply no need, either, to go to the door carrying a wet, dripping wet, lavatory brush.

Matron Price, with the benefit of previous experience, showed the Health Inspector the rather better spots in her nursing home. There was the magnificent front door with its polished brass knocker and the stained-glass tulips on either side of the door. There were the peaceful sunny places on the verandah for patients after their showers, and there were the shady corners so useful for the hot days. The hall of the hospital was cheerful with an autumn-leaf carpet. The medicine cupboard had an approved padlock. In the linen cupboard was the special lace-edged tablecloth, white, for communion. In accordance with suggestions made during an earlier visit the dinette was entirely covered in plastic, and curtains of flowered chintz screened occupants from

the hall during meals. Room One was neat with three unoc-
cupied beds.

'We are waiting for our new admissions,' Matron
explained. She went on to explain further that Room Three
was closed while afternoon sponging was in progress. 'They
would be very upset if a gentleman walked in just now,'
Matron said, her laugh silvery and fragile with caution. She
winked. The lavatories, she failed to mention there was only
one, were in use. One of the bathrooms, the only one – but
Matron Price often used the plural, sometimes even saying
kitchens – was free if the Inspector cared to look.

The Inspector glanced over the dingy room. It was all wet
with something strong smelling and slimy.

'You will need a different tap . . .' he began.

'Frankie has just been cleaning here,' Matron said. 'She
is a little too enthusiastic with the pine disinfectant. We
can't be too careful.' She laughed again like an excited horse
whinnying. Her laugh stopped her from hearing the Inspector. He repeated himself, making a note in his notebook,

'You will need a different tap,' he said, 'in this wash hand-
basin.'

'But that one's always been there,' Matron Price said.

'How can anyone scrub up?' he asked.

'Scrub up?' Matron said. 'We usually have to wash – er
– scrub down . . .'

'I mean to scrub up for a dressing, a dressing for a wound,
a surgical sterile procedure. Do you understand? The tap
has to be turned on with the elbow.'

'Ah yes, oh yes, I do see what you mean, but . . .'

'I'll be back later', he said, 'to see the new tap. It is essential to have one that can be turned on and off untouched
by the washed human hand. Turns on with the flick of an
elbow, and off of course in the same manner. Good day,'
he said, 'I'll leave by the back door, the dust bins, you know.
I'll let myself out thank you.'

Almost at once there was the crash in the street. It was so close to the front door, Doctors and Visitors Entrance Only, it could have been in the hall.

'Who the hells bloody bells left this mop and bucket here!' Matron's voice roused Room Three as she recovered her balance and made her way as quickly as she could to the scene of the crash. The walking frames, the sticks and the crutches, the flamboyant knitted shawls, the brushed-nylon pastel nightgowns and the burst open slippers of Room Three followed, with little moans of mingled excitement and pain, close upon her heels.

'It's all right, I think this one can walk.' Mrs Rawlings, the housekeeper, was already there. She was helping an old man out of the third ambulance while the three drivers, temporarily speechless, were contemplating the three squashed and disfigured bonnets and the three pairs of smashed headlights.

'Three ambulances ruined!' Matron Price said to herself. What was the world coming to, small ambulances only, not her property of course, but ambulances all the same. These young drivers, she reflected, they were too careless.

'Ambulances don't grow on trees you know,' in her mind she addressed the little group of shocked men. She had to, as she put it, keep her wits about her. It was not the policy of The Hospital of St Christopher and St Jude to take the moribund, the incontinent or the bedridden and it was possible that a patient, hitherto ambulant, may now, as a result of this crash, minor though it was, be thoroughly incapacitated and should therefore be despatched, with all speed, to the District Hospital.

She hurried forward, her white head-dress rising like a

sail behind her and the panels of her navy dress swinging with a clinical briskness.

None of the patients, apart from minor grazing and bruising, was badly hurt. Only one appeared to be bleeding. Mrs Rawlings was already leading one of them back along the path. He seemed nimble enough.

'Good afternoon Mr Privett.' Matron Price, aware in the back of her mind, of three substantial bank accounts, seized the folder from Mrs Rawlings and picked out his name quickly, a habit from long years of practice. 'Take Mr Privett to Room One, Mrs Rawlings, and we'll count up the damage eh Mr Privett?' Matron, at her most charming, hurried on to greet the others.

Mrs Rawlings proceeded with haste because of a premonition about a dried pea and lentil casserole. A side path led from the main one and wound beneath the lines of wet washing which crossed the back garden. Curious long garments and several sheets, dripping, slapped them as they made their way towards a collapsing trellis of vines which guarded the sacred regions of the kitchens. A stone-built wash-house and a shed, made of the same materials together with a collapsing fence of corrugated iron completed the fortification of this part of the hospital grounds. Weeds grew well and a kind of tough rough grass. A caravan, without wheels, resting on doubtful timber, stood a little further off in the shade of some cape lilacs.

'I told that Duck she was drunk. "She's inebriated," I told Hildegarde. "She's inebriated that Duck, she's on fifteen eggs. She's obstinate and she's pleased with herself." ' The short walk along the brick path between the few fragrant leaves of mint and spikes of lavender reminded the old man, Mr Privett, of his own scented path and of the half drum house where the duck fidgeted, knocking her eggs about, tapping against her tin walls. He told Mrs Rawlings, '"Listen Hildegarde," I told her, "you're a meat bird.

17

Chicken!" I said, that's what I said to her, "Don't yo' get to thinking yo'll get to lay eggs. Mind your manners!" I said to 'er. "Just yo' listen to that Duck, Hark at her!"'

'You kept fowls then?' Mrs Rawlings asked, propelling his lightweight bones and feathery memories over the bricks.

Mr Privett cackled and winked and cackled again, 'Yo' should 'ave heard her!' He began to chant in the reedy voice of old age and deafness.

HEP DUCK RATTLE DUCK TAP TAP HEP HEP DUCK
HEPPY DUCK
SHAKE DUCK RATTLE DUCK AND ROLL

The old man pranced on the path. Mrs Rawlings was out of breath beside him. They entered the nursing home through a maze of old-fashioned out buildings and were, almost at once, engulfed in a familiar – to Mrs Rawlings – black smoke.

'Ahoy there H.M.S. Casserole!' the old man said as Mrs Rawlings lifted the black oven dish to the table. She lifted the lid and, after standing back from the hot smoke, prodded the contents with a fork.

'Ahoy there!' Mr Privett cried and then said quietly, 'I'll have to be gettin' back home now. There's the poultry to see to, there's Hep Duck and Hildegarde. I usually have a bit of a smoke round about now – down in the shed – just about now.' He started for the door. Mrs Rawlings caught his arm.

'I'm sorry to have to be the one to tell you,' she said, 'but you're not going anywhere just now except the bedroom. After that accident, bed's the place for you.' Tucking his arm through hers, she drew him along the passage which led to the entrance hall. The door of Room One, about half way along, was open.

'What accident?' Mr Privett asked.

'Frankie! Robyn! Where the hell are those two girls,' Matron Price could be heard all over the hospital. 'Damn and blast and drat!' she fell over the bucket. 'Frankie! Robyn!' she strode across the patch of weeds and rough grass to the caravan. It was used for staff. During the years Mrs Rawlings had often slept there. Matron had suggested recently that she move in permanently. It would be useful, she said, to have her within reach. There was too the recurring problem of accommodation for Mr Rawlings which, when needed, was impossible to refuse. He was inclined to appear unexpectedly at intervals. When he came he was usually exhausted and in need of sanctuary. At the sight of the caravan she felt a curious pang somewhere beneath the covered buttons of the solid bodice of her uniform. It was hard to put into exact words, it was altogether too painful. In the extraordinary circumstances Miss Price felt it was hardly proper for Mr Rawlings, whenever he came, to sleep in her own house which was contained in the upper floor of the hospital.

She had earlier given instructions to Frankie and Robyn to move their things to a small room in her house. Ignoring the sudden arrival of Mr Rawlings, she had said, 'I can keep an eye on you both more satisfactorily. I can't have you out at all hours of the night. I do have the good name of this hospital to think of. I must remind you that we have two saints over our door.'

Of course, she remembered, the girls were moving. They should be finished by now. Both girls had a habit of never being where they were needed yet it had to be acknowledged that young Frankie was a good worker. One of the best the nursing home had ever had.

Matron Price could smell the fragrant smoke before she reached the partly open door of the caravan.

'It's this part that's the best,' Frankie's flat voice floated into the still air of the afternoon, 'this is the best part sitting here like this having a smoke and a rave, it's better than the climaxing.'

'I s'pose,' Robyn's lazy voice answered, 'I s'pose.' Words were lost in a confusion of soft giggles. 'I mean,' she said, 'you wouldn't feel, I mean you wouldn't feel like you do now, like we're talking now if you hadn't climaxed would you? You gotter have that to get the time after, eh?'

The two voices merged in lower tones and the sweetness from no ordinary cigarette hung between Matron Price and the torn net curtains.

Matron Price stepped back a few paces. There was a rustling in the bushes and Miss Hailey emerged. 'Hyacinth,' she said in her jovial way. 'You too! Visiting the *pavillon d'amour!* You are surely not allowing yourself the romantic emotions of demented wardsmaids?'

'No Christian names please, Miss Hailey. And please fasten up your dressing gown.'

'Oh yes of course, Hyacinth, I mean matron, it must be nearly tea time,' Miss Hailey said and hurried towards the verandah. Matron Price watched her disappear.

'Frankie! Robyn!' she called, 'hurry up and get dressed, the pair of you. Have you forgotten the three admissions? Didn't you hear the accident, the crash? Your belongings should all be upstairs in my house by now, and this caravan thoroughly cleaned out. Hurry up! I expect you in the Home in ten minutes.'

Before Mrs Rawlings could get away for her afternoon off Mr Scobie, Mr Hughes and Mr Privett had to be settled into Room One. They did not have many possessions but Mr Scobie had a cassette player which was put, with his Bible and some boxes of cassettes, under his bed. All their clothes were packed into ancient cases and put in the bathroom. There were some shelves stacked with suitcases behind the door.

Mr Hughes had a menthol camphor dressing bandaged on his lifeless hand. Mrs Rawlings took a lot of trouble propping him up in bed with five pillows. She was quite out of breath. She sat Mr Scobie and Mr Privett on their beds, their uneasy, thin knees almost touching. Perplexed they regarded each other in polite silence. Mrs Rawlings was pleased to have done with them, as she put it to herself, changing her shoes at last in the bathroom.

'It's my bowels,' Mr Hughes said in his sing-song voice to Keppie who was seated on the only chair wedged close up to the bed.

Keppie found Mrs Rawlings and asked her, 'Can Mr Hughes be taken to the toilet please?'

'It's visiting time now,' Mrs Rawlings said. She had done the cook's work, the pea and lentil casserole; and she had done all the work of admitting the new patients, single handed, while Frankie and Robyn were still slowly carrying their clothes upstairs and, even more slowly, mopping the caravan with far too much water and pine disinfectant. 'Almost out of the door!' Mrs Rawlings said to herself, and now this just when she had taken all that time getting him into bed.

'It's visiting time,' Mrs Rawlings said again, her mouth pressed into a thin line. 'Just look at the time,' she wanted to say, 'I've missed goodness knows how many buses.' She would have liked to explain that this was her only half day and it was more than half gone. She would have liked to explain that it was her only chance to get away from the place, to escape to the cinema for two hours of darkness and peace.

'I'm just leaving,' Keppie said with her comfortable little smile bulging her red-veined cheeks. 'I've told Mr Hughes

21

I will be in again tomorrow. It's his bowels,' she nodded, with a nod in the direction of Room One. 'Good afternoon and thank you,' she said.

Mrs Rawlings took Mr Hughes to the toilet in her good shoes.

'Take Mr Hughes back to bed when he's finished in the toilet,' she raised her voice in the direction of the uproar in the kitchen. 'I'm off now,' she called. To be a bit quicker she went out through the front door, Doctors and Visitors Only, slamming it behind her.

'I'll have to be getting off home now,' Mr Privett said. 'Good afternoon to you,' he said and, hitching up the overlong pyjamas, he slipped from his place on the bed and out into the passage.

Mr Scobie, having, temporarily, the small room to himself, groped under his bed and brought out his cassette player and his Bible. He selected some music, choosing because of strangeness in his new surroundings the first cassette he put his hand on.

Lord, make me to know mine end, and the measure of my days, what it is: that I may know how frail I am.

The sustained bass voice and the music swelled in the narrow room overflowing along the passage. Miss Hailey, walking carelessly to the bathroom, paused in the doorway.

'Normally,' she said, 'I don't have intercourse with men. I mean,' she said, 'I mean, in parenthesis you understand, I am adding a footnote – I mean not with any men here. Of course, you understand, I am using intercourse in its older and more dignified meaning.'

Mr Scobie immediately, out of politeness, turned down the volume. He was shocked to see a lady in her dressing gown and carrying intimate things like a towel and a sponge bag. His shock was increased as Miss Hailey had made no attempt to fold over and tie up her dressing gown. He was embarrassed too because the music had caused tears to fill his eyes, and his cheeks were wet with them.

'Oh! don't turn it off!' Miss Hailey said. 'I haven't had any spiritual refreshment for years.' She paused. 'I know that, in spite of my feelings about men, we shall be firm friends.' Her chin, bristling, squared on the words 'firm friends'. She leaned over Mr Scobie with a terrifying earnestness.

'I've brought you my ms,' she said gazing into his eyes, 'my manuscript. I'm a writer, a poet and a novelist. I concentrate on *la petite phrase*,' she said. 'Here, take it before the Muse insists that I make an alteration. Ah! the re-writing, the re-writing!' She dropped a floppy cardboard book into his unprepared lap.

'Everything's there,' she said. 'Birth, marriage, separation, bigamy, divorce, death – several deaths, all kinds of human effort, memories, joy, pain, excitement, transfiguration, love and acceptance.' Without waiting for a reply, she walked on down the passage with an admirable nonchalance.

Mr Scobie placed the untidy loosely bound papers on the chair. The whole thing was held together with bits of ribbon, some pages were not attached. The title, in green and purple ink was 'Self Stoked Fires'. There was also an illustration on the cover, a healthy but languid naked woman. Carefully Mr Scobie turned the whole thing over so that the title and the drawing did not show.

The Brahms was upsetting him. He tried Chopin instead but that was not any better. He began to think of Lina.

'Oh Mr Scobie,' Lina said, 'have you any Holy Pictures?'

'Holy Pictures Lina? Oh yes Lina,' he told her, 'Yes I have

some at home. I will bring them for you next time I come.'

Lina was fond of her music and he thought she was fond of him too. That was why he broke down when the music reminded him of Lina's fondness and of her gentleness.

Her sister was not at all like her.

He taught them both. His young ladies, he taught them both the piano. He went to their house to give them lessons.

'Do you like Holy Pictures Lina?' He asked her. She clasped her pretty hands together. Oh yes she did like them and she had some up in her mother's bedroom under the mattress. She led the way upstairs.

It was a large quiet house with the sun shining through a stained-glass window on the landing so that he felt they walked up a shaft of gold. He walked behind her short swaying fat body. She was Jewish and plump as Jewish girls so often are, and she wore rich clothes. A sweet warm perfume came from under them. She took him into her mother's bedroom and was, all at once, on the bed trying to turn up the end of the mattress. The silken covers made everything more difficult because they slid all to one side.

'It doesn't matter now Lina,' he told her. He kept telling her that it would be better to go back downstairs. 'Show them to me some other time,' he said to her. But no she would show him the pictures, she would hunt them out, she insisted, there was one in particular she wanted him to see. Perhaps he would be able to explain it to her.

Of course the housekeeper, Fräulein Recha she was called, came in then and asked Lina what she was doing on her mother's bed in the middle of the morning.

'And what do you think you want in here?' she asked him in a terrible voice . . .

'If you think I've overdone the superlatives and the hyper-bole please be quite honest. Say exactly what you think. Be cruel! Tell me honestly what you think of my Brain Child.' Miss Hailey was again in the doorway of Room One on her way back from the bathroom. 'Be cruel!' she said. 'I want your honest opinion. I know I'm a bit grainy in places. But with your love of music,' she gazed with reverence at the ceiling, 'you with your love of music will understand the rhythms and the choreography of my writing.' Miss Hailey smiled at Mr Scobie. 'Now do not and I repeat do not feel you have to utter a word at this moment. Digest what I have written. Digest and then spout,' she paused as Frankie and Robyn danced their way, disco rhythm, down the passage.

'*A lombre des jeunes filles en fleurs,*' Miss Hailey murmured. 'Proust in parenthesis excuse the footnotes,' she added with a little self-conscious laugh.

'Wake up Mrs Murphy here's your tray.'
'Wake up Mrs Tompkins here's your tray.'
'Wake up Mrs Renfrew here's your tray.'
'Wake up Miss Nunne here's your tray.'
'Wake up Mrs Morgan here's your tray.'
'Miss Hailey Miss Hailey tea time
Miss Hailey dinette Miss Hailey tea
MISS HAILEY HAILEY.'
'Here's your tray Mr Scobie.' 'Here's your tray
Mr Privett. Where the hell's Mr Privett?'
'Here's your tray Mr Hughes. Where the hell's
Mr Hughes?' 'He's in the toilet.' 'Put his
tray on his bed then.'
'Mr Privett! PRIVETT PRIVETT.'
'Say Robbo did you hear the one about the guy that fell
in a tank of beer?'
'Nah! Did he drown right away. Frankie? Huh?'
'Nah. He got out twice to go to the dunny. Yuk.'
'Aw Gerroff willya that's an old joke, it's got grey hairs
all over it. Haw! Haw! Haw! Greasy, eh?'
'This place, this place it's a real snakes' house.' Robyn
rushed from the kitchen with the trays of lentils, peas and
beetroot. Frankie, with her little transistor held close to her
head of shabby yellow curls, was still dancing up the hall
to the front entrance and back. Her mouth was open, her
thin shoulders poked forward, first one and then the other.
Her eyes were bright but completely without expression.
She stepped forward four steps and backwards four steps,
forward four back two forward four back one. She kicked
one foot forward and she kicked the other foot forward. She
stepped to the left and she stepped to the right. She
wriggled and swayed, her boyish hips twisting first to one
side and then to the other. She tossed her head; the curls
bounced.

'Anyways who the hell wants shithouse muck like this in
the arvo!' she said.

26

'Who wants lentils peas and beetroot any time!' The two girls enjoyed their profound remarks.

'You do the teas.'

'Nah. You do 'em I did 'em yesterdi.'

'I'll do Room One and you do Room Three Huh?'

Huh Huh Yair Yair Yair

Huh Huh Huh

Hula Rocky Hula

Let's get it together

Hula baby Hula rocky

Yair Yair Yair

Both girls, heads down, heels flying, danced down to the kitchen tapping the walls and the doors as they went.

There were not quite enough cups to go round and only three cups had saucers. There were no teaspoons.

'You can't give Ma Tompkins the cracked one nor the chipped one,' Frankie said as she tipped milk into the overflowing weak tea. Robyn, with a heavy hand, put sugar in all the cups.

'Here's your tea Mrs Morgan.'

'Here's your tea Mrs Renfrew.'

'Here's your tea Mrs Murphy.'

'Here's your tea Mrs Tompkins.'

'Miss Nunne here's your tea.'

'Miss Hailey TEA HAILEEE.'

'Here's your tea Mr Scobie.'

'Here's your tea Mr Hughes. He's in the toilet. Here's your tea Mr Privett. Where the hell is Privett?'

'Mrs Rawlings? Mrs Rawlings have you seen the new patient from Room One? Mrs Rawlings? Oh Shit! She's off.'

'Hey! he's taken his case and his clothes from off the bath-room shelf!'

'He only came in this arvo.'

'Well, he's gone.'

'Phone matron then. She's upstairs.'

'Nah. You phone her.'

For some time Mr Privett had been hearing a singing and a rustling in the next room as if someone was still there with a little brush and duster. An insect hummed alone and disappeared only to return reminding him, all the time, of a soft voice talking.

Twice lately he had stumbled though he was well acquainted with the little steps and corners in his own house. He forgot too that he kept the key in his front door and often he spent hours looking for it. For some reason he remembered other things instead; things he did not need, like the flash of green when the sun dropped into the sea at sunset.

He could not see the sea from his garden at home. His old house was surrounded by a ring of trees. Sometimes the cape lilacs, with their cloud-coloured flowers, a false promise of rain, annoyed him. From his verandah he could see the top of a Norfolk Island pine tree. He often shook his fist at it. It was like a clock for him. The changing light and shade and colour of the symmetrical tree told him what time of day it was. This tree bridged the middle distance between the earth and the sky. Long after the sun had gone, the top of the pine glowed. The tree simply stood endowed with this golden blessing. Every evening the old man watched the transfiguration of the tree knowing that the last rays of the sun would be caressing corner stones and cross roads making them noble.

Now, leaving The Hospital of St Christopher and St Jude well behind him, he hurried back to his house. He knew these streets well, he had been through them often enough. Hep Duck would be quiet, she was always quiet in the evenings and Hildegarde, curtained in jasmine, slept early.

The old man, Privett, sat in his shed to smoke. 'Help yourself,' the doctor had said to him, 'help yourself and I'll help you. Give up smoking.' He tapped the clean shrivelled chest with knowledgeable fingers. Mr Privett did not argue.

'Half head! Muttonhead!' he cackled when at last he was

sitting shrouded in smoke. It was no use to make life longer without life.

'Stop your snoring chicken,' he shouted up at the rafters. 'And don't answer back! Yo' was snoring. Meat bird! Don't get to thinking yo'll lay eggs yo'm a meat bird.'

The bluish-grey smoke crept through yellow and purple flowers and mingled with the subdued light and colour of the dusk.

During the evening meal Mr Hughes remained patiently on the toilet because he was unable to get off. Gently he kept calling, hoping someone would hear him. The din from the kitchen was ferocious. Someone was raking out the wood stove with an almighty strength. He imagined, with hope, the muscles of the cook but knew already that his need was not her prescribed work. At intervals he heard her powerful voice.

'It's not my job to get patients orf out the dunny. And as for baking apples, who do they think they are! This place ain't the Ritz. I'm not baking apples today for nobody. They can stuff them up their arseholes. Baked apples! My Gawd whatever next. There's no end to it . . . What's wrong with the junkets I'd like to know. There's some as don't know when they're well off.'

Mr Hughes listened for other voices. There seemed to be two girls who were carrying trays and cups of tea. He supposed there would be something for him.

'I don't feel at all hungry,' he said to himself, the words going up and down echoing like sad music, in the narrow place where he was.

He listened, still with hope, for a man's voice. He did not like the idea of those little girls having to help him off the toilet. The thought worried him.

ROOM 1 Mr Hughes taken off toilet 10 p.m. also Mrs Tompkins bath veggies and kitchen floor.

ROOM 3 All pats. play cards in dinette Lt Col. I. Price lose very bad. N.A. to report. Matron Mrs Tompkins says never mind about the bath what about a hot snack in bed.

Signed Night Sister M. Shady (unregistered)

Mrs Shady: Where were you and what were you doing at 4 a.m. when Mr Jack Privett who is Mr Privett's son brought Mr Privett back to St Christopher and St Jude? He had apparently gone to his old home where he disturbed the demolition and the neighbours. Mr Jack P. telephoned during the lunch hour to ask how his father was after being out practically all night to say nothing of the late afternoon and evening. After this how do you think I feel myself?

Signed Matron H. Price

And Mrs Shady suppositories.

Signed Mat. H. P.

Mr Hughes smoked and coughed and sighed and was only able to leave his bed when Mrs Rawlings had time to help him. She took him to the toilet, to the shower and, quite often, to the verandah where he sat looking out at the three-cornered crossing. The weeds and long grass of the hospital were fenced with pickets which had once been painted white. In places the fence was held up by loose-limbed bushes which, at intervals, bore a rash of dry-looking flowerlets. Pink climbing geraniums added a fleeting impression of charm. And, from an enthusiastic planting many years ago, the verandah rose from and seemed to rest on matted skirts of hibiscus and oleander. Sometimes in the right seasons, agapanthus raised bright-blue fragile heads, delicate china-like surprises springing from tufts of endlessly dreary, cockroach-ridden, dust-laden evergreens. Their appearance suggested a divine indiscretion perhaps from the second person in the Trinity. Across the road was the Moreton Bay fig tree. When Mr Hughes looked over there he could watch people walking or resting on the grass. In the evenings the doves came flying in from wherever they had been during the day.

From his chair on the verandah Mr Hughes watched the doves. He heard their tiny applause as they came, clapping their wings, into the tree. In the open spaces of the sky further along, a hawk hovered. The doves rose in a crackling cloud, agitated, disturbed, distressed, frightened. On all sides the magpies warned the drowsy world with their voices cascading.

Mrs Rawlings came out. 'Come along Mr Hughes,' she said.

'There's a hawk in the tree,' he said in his soft voice, the words sounding up and down like water in a brook. 'There's a hawk quite near.'

'Is there dear? Well never mind!' Mrs Rawlings, her

31

thoughts on other things, helped him to his feet. Slowly they made their way indoors.

When the old man, Hughes, drove his truck, the day unfolded in light and cool fragrance on all sides of him. Every morning his wife came out to see him off. 'Every morning, first thing,' he told Mrs Rawlings, 'I heard my wife calling to the fowls. There were magpies there too, like here, they swooped and called. Where they got all their energy I could never think. I went all over the place fetching and carrying. Sometimes it was firewood or empty bottles, sometimes loads of garden rubbish, sometimes small furniture bought or sold, secondhand. Sometimes I carried sand or crates of fruit and vegetables or poultry. My dog went with me in the truck. Once I had to take two live geese,' he said to Mrs Rawlings, 'two live geese. I had to put my wife, she's dead now, you know, in the back of the truck for the whole journey holding both the geese – '

'Did you now,' Mrs Rawlings steered him round through the door.

'They have long strong necks, geese have,' he said.

'Have they now?' Mrs Rawlings tried to hurry him along the passage. Though she was strong and stout it was hard for her to keep him upright.

'Yes,' Mr Hughes said, 'my wife sat there holding those geese by their necks.' He smiled to himself, remembering that a woman, years ago, had ordered some bricks. It was the first load of bricks in all the years of carting.

It could have been yesterday.

As he stacked them he counted them carefully, two at a time. They were rough and symmetrical; they had never been used. Red turning to purple at the edges. He marvelled, as he held them, at what could be done with bricks. The man in the yard, on his knees, peering under the truck said, 'She'll do. Mind 'ow you go. Brake slow. She's apples.'

Mr Hughes, nodding his head, had carefully reversed and, turning the loaded truck, had driven from the yard slowly. Uphill.

Almost at once the bricks fidgeted uneasily among themselves. He noticed that they were talking, quietly at first like people whispering in church, and then, with more noise, chittering and snittering together with occasional little squeals of brick laughter. Soft laughing, strange from hard things like bricks. The soft noise reminded him, at the time, of snow in the blizzard snittering on the window panes of the attic room he had shared with his brothers when he was a boy in Wales. Often, then, he heard the blizzard and was glad to be safe and warm in bed.

'The fine dry snow blew under the slates and settled in the loft,' he told Mrs Rawlings, 'and later, in the thaw, damp mouldy patches discoloured the ceiling.'

'Well I never!' Mrs Rawlings, red faced and breathing hard, undressed Mr Hughes and put him to bed. 'There you are!' she said rubbing her hip which was bruised from contact with the corners of heavy furniture.

'I used to work for Villiers,' Mr Hughes said. 'Whenever I passed their yards,' he gave a little laugh, 'I always raised my hat "Good-day to Villiers" I'd say though of course there was no one outside to see me and warehouses don't have windows. Villiers were good to me when I first came out here, see, from the valley, South Wales it was, we were very poor, you see?'

'That's nice,' Mrs Rawlings said, leaving the pattern of the comb in the strands on his head. 'Now just you sit tidy. Oh look at you! Tobacco and bits all down your sheet already.'

She brushed him with an impatient hand; licked her finger and moved grey wisps of strayEng hair to one side of his forehead.

'Just you have a nice rest now,' she said.

The bricks made more noise. The faster he drove the more they chattered and shuffled and pushed each other. He strained to try to hear what they were saying. They seemed to reach little peaks of excitement. Excited bricks. There was no need to take any notice of them.

When he stopped to cool his engine he went to the back of the truck. There was nothing strange about the bricks. They lay there cool and clean and new and quiet. He rested on the coarse grass between the road and the railway line. On the other side of the road were squat houses with concrete walls and flat windows. He paid very little attention to his surroundings being concerned mainly with his journey. There was always a hint of rain. He drove on. The bricks moving, scraping on each other, sighed and gradually first one and then another began to talk. All of them talking and talking subdued whispering and then louder but never audible. Little excited whispering voices their communication escaping him. It was the same when his wife and her sisters were all together. Seven sisters, like stars, six sisters-in-law. They chattered like the bricks never stopping busy, always telling laughing exclaiming, protesting agreeing endlessly . . .

The bricks shuffling rearranging went on talking . . . he tried to hear what they were saying . . .

. . . it was the whispering of the sisters, so much life they had – pinning dresses for fittings, the sounds and the odours of black for Chapel, the smell of roasting meat and the endless treadle sewing machine. The top left-hand drawer –

peacocks, carnations and roses on unfinished anti-macassars. An air letter explaining forty years ago that a thousand elephants would come from the Taj Mahal in a box of matches . . .

'Every so often you know,' Miss Hailey paused in the doorway of Room One, 'the blood in my veins turns into ink and my poems simply pour out of me.' She leaned on the door post. 'It's the Muse. A visitation,' she said.

'I beg your pardon?' Mr Hughes realized he must have been dozing. 'Is it visiting time?' he thought he might have heard Keppie's voice but perhaps that was in his dream.

'No, I was meaning my poetry,' Miss Hailey, towel over one shoulder and sponge-bag cord wound round her wrist, explained. 'I am, as usual, waiting for *la Salle de bain*. The Lt Col. certainly is taking his time. I've been out', she added carelessly, 'to a Poetry Reading. I read fourteen of my poems. They were very well received though I should not say so.' She laughed a little modest laugh. 'I am going again tonight,' she said.

'Oh I see,' Mr Hughes gave a polite cough. It was bad manners, he felt, to sleep in front of a stranger, a lady too. He wondered who she was. His head nodded forward, to try to hear the bricks talking. In wandering sawdust, they were off once more, he had never heard them so plainly. In wandering sawdust an embroidered camel sleeps undisturbed. Keys to pigskin and leather, three pennies and a florin, four farthings and a pearl nine hundred and ninety-nine pipe cleaners . . .' He snored gently.

'You write too I see,' Miss Hailey peered across the two beds to where Mr Privett sat.

'Yep,' Mr Privett said, 'it's a advertisement for . . .'

'Oh, What Fun!' Miss Hailey said. 'Ah! There is the Colonel. Yoo Hoo Colonel, bracket, Lt Col. retired, close bracket, bags I the bathroom. You have been an Age! Bongo, old chap.'

Mr Scobie, who was sitting on his bed reading, raised his

voice for Miss Hailey. '*And I heard a voice from Heaven saying unto me, write, Blessed are the dead which die in the Lord . . .* Revelations: Chapter fourteen, verse thirteen.' He tapped the open page with one finger.

Miss Hailey stopped just short of the bucket at the bend in the passage.

'I am writing,' she called back, 'but I'm not dead yet. Chekhov,' she continued as if making an announcement, 'Chekhov, in one of his less successful stories says something about the need in melancholy moments to inscribe one's name, as if to immortalize oneself, to be for ever remembered, on a tree or on someone's doorstep. Perhaps even on the back of the bathroom door.' She disappeared and, in the distance, the bathroom door slammed shut.

Mr Privett, pleased with his advertisement, put the piece of paper carefully in his pocket. When Jack and Lilian came to take him for a drive he would ask to call at the corner deli; he would ask the woman there to put the paper in the window with other mouth-watering descriptions of tricycles, dolls' prams, laying hens, golf clubs, houses, sheds, pianos and clothing. As far as he knew, no one else was offering what he was about to offer. He needed the money; he thought about the money and cackled.

'You'll have to turn that noise off now.' Mrs Rawlings, already in her good shoes, came to the door of Room One.

'But it's not a noise dear Mrs Rawlings,' Mr Scobie said, starting to rise to his feet from his place on the side of the bed. 'It's beautiful music, dear, it's the Brahms German Requiem. *Yea saith the spirit, that they may rest from their labours: and their works do follow them.* Revelations, it's Revelations . . .'

'Well I just hope my work doesn't follow me and reveal God knows what,' Mrs Rawlings said. 'Night Sister's here and she'll want Room Three to settle down. No one can sleep with that er noise er music, beautiful as it may be to some, I'm sure. So off with it, if you please.'

Suppositories given 10 p.m. Also Mrs Tompkins bath veggies and kitchen floor.

ROOM 1 Mr Hughes voided 4 a.m. Slept well.

Mr Privett voided 4 a.m. Slept well.

Mr Scobie voided 4 a.m. Slept well.

ROOM 3 Voided 4 a.m. All pats. play cards in dinette. Mother, I mean Mrs Morgan really enjoy herself and Boxer and Rob. Lt Col. Price enjoy himself but lose very bad. Matron I am sorry about Mr Jack Privett I hope you are feeling yourself again.

Signed Night Sister M. Shady (unregistered)

Also a note from Lt Col. I. Price (retired)

HYACINTH I WOULD LIKE MY POCKET
MONEY IN ADVANCE PLEASE

Signed IRIS PRICE (Lt. Col. retired)

Mrs Shady. Please note, No Christian Names on duty. I refer of course to my brother's use of mine. Also Mrs Tompkins says she has still not had a bath. What do you do with all my water? Kitchen floor not satisfactory. Also vegetables.

Signed Matron H. Price

In the days before Jack and Lilian came to live with him Mr Privett hurried down to the shed every morning. He always had several things on his mind. Mr Richards, the land agent, kept calling to see him. The gate would click and Mr Richards would, almost at once, be peering in through the ragged leaves and flowers.

'I'm not changing my mind,' Mr Privett was emphatic in the smoke-filled gloom. 'I've told you before, I like living here. That brick path you're standing on, my son, Jack, made when he was only nine.'

Mr Richards looked at the bits of path which showed through the weeds. He held out his large kind hand, feeling his way into the shed.

'Remember my offer? It's worth your while. It still holds,' his voice was soft. 'You remember don't you, there's enough land, we could build eight townhouses, remember? With balconies and carports. Remember, I've told you about the plan to pull down the old sub-standard homes . . .'

'There's nothing sub-standard here,' the old man Privett interrupted. There's not a drop of water through the roof, nailed every piece of tin myself. So I know.' Successfully smothering Mr Richards in a fit of coughing, he recovered enough to shout up to the rafters.

'Come down off there you lazy good for nothing meat! Hildegarde! I'm warning you!' he wiped his wispy-haired head with a rag, 'You nearly got our visitor here, only just missed him. I've told you not to do that!' He turned to Mr Richards.

'She's a sly one that one.' He turned to shout up to the roof. 'You watch your language!' He smiled at Mr Richards. 'Just you listen to that Duck out there. She hasn't stopped banging about her tin walls. She's Hep that Duck. Hep Duck, having her session,' he cackled, 'very fond of good music, both of 'em 'specially the Duck.'

HEP DUCK HEAR THAT HILDEGARDE
MIND YOUR MANNERS MEAT BIRD
COME DOWN OFF THEM RAFTERS –
– MEAT BIRD. HILDEGARDE THE MEAT
HEP DUCK HEP HILDEGARDE THE MEAT.

Mr Richards left as quickly as he could, closing the little side gate behind him.

'I'll be back tomorrow,' he called.

The light was out in Room One. A pale path from the electric light in the hall lay diagonally across the three beds. A tiny red glow brightened from time to time as Mr Hughes, with difficult slow breath, enlivened his cigarette.

All three men were perplexed at their unexplained closeness to each other.

'Goodnight Mr Hughes er David,' Mr Scobie said.

'Goodnight to you Mr Scobie er goodnight to you Martin,' Mr Hughes replied.

Mr Privett, coughing, said, 'I hadn't seen my son for twenty-three years when, one night, there was the noise of the key turning in the lock and I heard his voice in the passage . . .'

'Twenty-three years, that's a long time,' Mr Hughes said with his usual gentle politeness.

'Yes,' Mr Scobie agreed, 'a very long time.'

Mr Privett was pleased to have an audience. ' "You home Dad. Hullo there! You there Dad?" that's what I heard and the next thing there he was scraping up the kitchen lino with his boots.' Mr Privett coughed again and went on. ' "Dad," he said, "I want you to meet Lilian." "Pleased to meet you Lilian," I said. "We were married last month," Jack said to me. "Married," I said, "that's nice, very nice. Give us a kiss my dear," I said to her, "and are these your legs? Them very nice legs," I told her and I give her thigh a bit of a pinch, you know, just to see if she was as well made as she looked to be. "Married," I said, "that's very nice." I told 'em they could live with me, see. "There's plenty of rooms," I told 'em. "And I'll keep 'er company while you go to work," I told Jack. She was a sweet girl. I enjoyed having her about the house even if she did spend half the day getting herself dressed in nothing, and the other half in trying to think up new ways to arrange her hair. Gurls! "You mind!" I told 'er. "Yo'll get the cold, walkin' round the house with no clothes on!" '

Then he began to sing,

HEP DUCK HEP DUCK,
HILDEGARDE THE MEAT –
JEALOUS GURLS EH?
NO NEED TO BE JEALOUS
LILY DON'T INTERFERE
'ER LETS ME DO THE WASHING UP MY OWN WAY.
YOU STILL HEP HEP IN THERE DUCK HEP HEP?

Mr Scobie turned over in his narrow bed half listening to Mr Privett. Mr Hughes had slipped down his five pillows and was snoring in the regular gentle way which was to be expected, Mr Scobie reflected, from an elderly and respectable gentleman. Mr Privett's peculiar song ended in a fit of coughing.

'I thought,' he said when he was able to speak, 'I thought I'd make a dinner with roasted potatoes and plenty of gravy. I went out and fetched a half leg, shank end, from the butcher . . .'

'Roast lamb,' Mr Scobie felt hungry. 'Roasted meat,' he said, 'that's very nice.' It was just about dinner time in the outside world. Here in St Christopher and St Jude it was already night. The night-time was so early so that the night, without sleep, was long. He thought again about roast meat, perhaps with just a little well-browned fat on it. The lemon sago, burned, with a slice of bread and butter was not an adequate meal. The hospital smelled of the lemon sago which had spilled over and burned on top of the stove.

'When I came in from the shop,' Mr Privett's voice intruded, 'I could hear them in the sitting room, they were that excited. "Now what," I thought, and I went straight to the kitchen to get the dinner on, you know. "Dad! Dad!" my son, Jack his name is p'raps I've already told you, Jack was calling me, I took no notice, "Tek no notice," I said to myself.

' "Dad! Dad!" Jack came into the kitchen see. "Dad," he said, "don't just go banging about in the cupboard like that, leave the roasting tin a minute and come up to the front room." "I know your news," I told him. I'd heard that Richards man with them. I'd heard them all excited. "I know your news," I told my son, I told him straight. "I know what that half-headed old biscuit is on about. I'm telling you no one can live in a bank note. In any case, it's my place, it's my home and I'm not selling." I stuck to that and the outcome was a very awkward state of affairs. "Why's Lily sulking?" I asked Jack a few days later, he didn't answer, just shook his head. She never spoke . . .'

Mr Scobie waiting, because there was no alternative, for the rest of the story, heard the regular breathing of sleep from both the other beds. He felt wretched and cold. He wished for a hot water bottle; the nights, after the warm days, were cold. That morning he had asked Mrs Rawlings, 'Mrs Rawlings could I have a hot water bottle please?'

'But it's summer,' she replied, 'in any case Matron does not like you old folk to have hot water bottles. You old folk, you unscrew the tops and scald yourselves. And who gets the blame? Matron of course.'

The cost of the place worried him too. He was not at all short of money, not like in the old days, but it was a waste of money to spend it being in the hospital. He thought of his own house.

'I'd like to go back home,' he thought. At home he could do as he liked. A pain of longing for home, such as a young child experiences, engulfed him. He tried to change the intangible cause of the pain to ordinary things. 'Whoever heard of eating a chop with a steak knife,' he thought.

That morning when he carried his plate to the kitchen to show them the greasy sinews of fat, they, the cook and those two girls, Robyn and Frankie, had simply laughed.

'Aw, give him a steak knife,' the cook said. 'Have you read the latest bestseller? Mr Scobie?' Frankie said, *Hurry to the Washhouse* by Willie Makit and Betty Dont.'

'No I'm sorry I don't know the book,' Mr Scobie said. 'I suppose it would be in the library.'

'There's *Cats Revenge* by Claude Balls,' Frankie said, 'I don't suppose you know that one either.'

Mr Scobie, smiling to be pleasant, shook his head.

'Aw get on with them dishes,' the cook bawled from her place beside the stove. 'Robyn give us a hand here. And you, young Frankie, shut your gob for a minute or two.'

Back in Room One, sitting, crumpled, on the side of his bed, the plate balanced on his thin knees, Mr Scobie had not been able to eat the chop.

He turned over again in the narrow bed and wished for sleep.

The constant noise in the nursing home at night was incredible. From Room One he could hear, plainly, there was some trouble at the front door. Miss Hailey, having returned by taxi, seemed to be reciting verse. Mr Scobie, listening unwillingly, heard the angry voice of a taxi driver. The old women in Room Three were, as usual, ringing their bells and calling for the Night Sister.

NOVEMBER 16 NIGHT SISTER'S REPORT
ROOM ONE voided sponged slept well 4 a.m.
ROOM THREE voided sponged slept well 4 a.m. All pats. play cards in dinette.
Nothing abnormal to report.

Signed Night Sister M. Shady (unregistered)

Also note from Miss Hailey, *in parenthesis, bracket* 'Tout le trouble du monde vient de ce qu'on ne sait pas rester seul dans sa chambre.' Pascal. *close bracket.*

Signed Heather Hailey

Mrs Shady: Please report more fully. Mrs Tompkins says her bath was a holocaust (her word). Please write a detailed account of what happened last night. Write on a clean page in this book. I need a full explanation as to why Miss Hailey's taxi driver was in my office this morning. I have not been able to use my private parts all day because of him.

Signed Matron H. Price

NOVEMBER 17 NIGHT SISTER'S REPORT But first the Detailed Account and Full Explanation for the night of 16 November. I am sorry matron your privates was occupied. He said he would not leave till he receive his fare after bringing Miss Hailey back from her poetry 4 a.m. Miss Hailey told him she was a writer and she said he was so excited about her being a writer that her poems would do and she happened to have a hundred of them in her handbag which she gave him in the hall. Also she told him some. It was then I suggest he wait in the office matron for you. End of Full Explanation.
THE DETAILED ACCOUNT Mrs Tompkin's bath also hot milk

kitchen floor and veggies 10 p.m. Mrs Tompkins came in at 4 a.m. also mother I mean Mrs Morgan. Mr Boxer and Mr Rob did not come. Patient asked to have a water fight. As patient seemed disturb I said well just a very little water fight then. Mrs Tompkins loose fight very bad Mrs Morgan enjoy herself I don't think I ever saw mother enjoy herself so much except when she playing cards with Lt Col. I. Price (retired). Wounds dressed with menthol camphor. I think Miss Hailey's arm broke. Also.

REPORT ON CONDITION OF EQUIPMENT 1. Tap.   2. Curting 3. Requisition.

1. The shower tap broke off it is only banged on with my shoe matron so be careful or else loose all your waters.

2. The shower curting. Will you be able to run up the curtings matron? also there is a weakness in the bathroom wall near the shower curting.

And 3. please could we have another pane of glass in the bathroom window (3 is Requisition).

NOVEMBER 17 Nothing abnormal to report.

Signed Night Sister M. Shady (unregistered)

Mrs Shady: I seem to need to remind you too often that menthol camphor is not the only remedy we have. If you look back in this book you will find details as to where to find Epsom Salts.

Signed Matron H. Price

'What a nice view you have from your window Uncle,' Mr Scobie's niece Joan lifted the blind and stood staring into the dusty vines.

'I do wish, dear, that you would not wear such short dresses,' Mr Scobie said. 'Did you know, dear, that people can see all up your legs and down into your – er – lungs? That dress is cut very low for someone your size and age.'

'Breasts Uncle, Bassooms, Boobs not lungs,' Joan laughed. She let the blind drop.

'Joan, as I used to tell you years ago,' Mr Scobie said, 'you are built for child bearing . . .'

'Aw come off it Uncle,' Joan said, 'I'd have to get a man for that wouldn't I?' She sat on the foot of his bed showing more of her thighs as she did so. She lit a thin black cigar. Mr Scobie coughed and waved the smoke with his bony fingers.

'Shouldn't you have your hair cut, dear?' he said. 'I never saw hair like that on any woman before. It's all over your face. There's a nice barber's shop not far from here. He doesn't do women as a rule but I'm sure he'd make an exception . . .'

'How are you Uncle?' Joan asked. 'For Heavens sake forget about me and . . .'

'This morning I had a bowel action which left me stunned so to speak. All day I have been able to think of nothing else. It is something to thank God for.'

'How about I take you for a little drive before tea Uncle?' Joan eased herself off the bed. 'Come on I'll take you for a little drive.'

In the car, turning his eyes away from the fat thighs and flopping breasts of his niece Mr Scobie said, 'Joan dear, I don't think I want to stay here at St Christopher and St Jude. I don't think I can manage even to stay one day, not another day. I want to go home.'

'Why on earth Uncle?'

'There's no dignity,' Mr Scobie said, 'absolutely none whatever. You can't even shut the lavatory door, dear, and whenever I go down there someone else always seems to need to go, Miss Hailey you see, and then all the other old women, they call out for Mrs Rawlings to take them along to the lavatory and most of the time poor Mr Hughes is in there. There's only the one lavatory you see, dear. And the food, dear. I can't stand it! All those lentils and all that pumpkin, and all the noise at night, dear. There's always a terrible noise at night. There's always some sort of trouble. The food, as I was saying . . .'

'Look Uncle! School's out. All the little children are going home. See the little children Uncle? Wave to the children, Uncle. You always used to like children.' Joan lifted her hand and waved as if to show him what to do.

'Yes I do, dear, I think little girls adorn the earth. When I used to pass them in the street they seemed like little flowers waiting to be picked. When Lina played the piano she played with the whole of her pretty young body; you remember Lina Joan? I've told you about Lina haven't I? I'm sorry I can't help these tears, it's thinking about Lina. When she played the piano . . .'

'Uncle, how about I buy you an ice-cream? You'd like an ice-cream wouldn't you? Wait a minute, there's a shop. Now you sit here while I go in and get an ice-cream.'

'I must have been about four years old,' Mr Scobie took the ice-cream cone, 'my father put an old bucket in my hand and sent me to the slaughter house for a pail of blood. I suppose he wanted it for the garden. The butcher told me he was a very fine butcher and, to show me his strength and skill, he slaughtered an animal on the spot and said it was for my pail of blood. He had a loud laugh and very white teeth, very red lips and a black curling beard. I couldn't stand it, and I begged him, I implored him not to do it but he did and I watched it all against my will. Watching was like taking part in it.

Later when I got home I was trembling, all I could do was to kneel down in front of my father and say, "Never send me there again." Mother and Father, your Grandma and Grandpa Joan, stood there looking at me and then they went into the bedroom together . . .'

'How old are you Uncle Martin?' Joan asked.

'Eighty-five years last January dear, every bit of eighty-five – Mother and Father they went in the bedroom . . .'

'Well then,' Joan said, 'why are you thinking all that way, back to those dreadful times when you were a kid?'

'But it wasn't dreadful,' Mr Scobie said. 'Mother witnessed to the Lord and Father with her, they witnessed on their knees. There was just room between the bed and the chest to kneel side by side. On their knees I saw them . . .

'For all flesh is as grass, and all the glory of man as the flower of grass. The grass withereth and the flower thereof falleth away. 1 Peter, dear, verse 24.'

'Oh Uncle! Don't talk so much. Eat up your ice-cream. There's just time to drive you round the park. I can't spare too much time. Oh Uncle! Look at the children. Uncle. Don't cry. There! have your ice-cream.' Joan tried to pat his knee.

'Why do I mind the slaughter of the animal?' he asked. 'Why should I mind it so much?'

'Heavens Uncle I don't know. How can I know? But cheer up, do! Look, from up here you can see all across the river. I'll park for a while and you can watch the boats.'

'Whenever we look in the mirror dear we are looking at ourselves slowly dying. This, of course, isn't my own idea. I must,' Mr Scobie said, 'I must have read it somewhere, not just these words, but the idea. I think Sir Roger de Coverly said it but then he was only a made-up person wasn't he?'

'Oh! Uncle I wouldn't know! Just look at the mess you're

making with that ice-cream. Why ever I bought it I don't know. Why didn't you eat it up quickly. I'll bet there isn't a tap anywhere around here. I'll just see if there's a tap.'

Mr Scobie wondered how it was his niece was always so easily upset. He wanted to tell her that, in the violence of the slaughter, it is the ears with their soft edges and the black, tightly curling hair along the vulnerable part of the throat, exposed, taken by surprise when the innocent head is thrust back, it is the memory of these which is unbearable. After the slaughter no one would recall the animal and remember the hopefulness of life which accompanies every birth. It was the same with human beings.

'The butcher,' he said, 'and his victim are made up of the same colours.'

But Joan, her foot hard down, did not appear to be listening. She was in a hurry and seemed intent on the road. He knew from before that she could not bear to have her hands sticky on the steering wheel even for a short drive. She had told him so, often. He noticed, with shame, there was ice-cream on her dress too.

The days were getting warmer.

After their showers the old people were put in the sun, before it became too hot, on the verandah. Frankie and Robyn, seducing each other in plastic aprons, did the showers as long as, and sometimes after, the hot water lasted.

'Hey Robyn!' Frankie screeched along the passage. 'Why are nymphomaniacs like taxis in the rain?'

'I dunno,' Robyn's voice came back from Room Three. 'Why for Pete's sake? I give up.'

'OK. OK.' Frankie yelled. 'Why are nymphomaniacs like

taxis in the rain? When they finally come they don't stop! Hoola Hoola Hoola Baby Rock me Tip me Yair Yair Yair.' She danced, shrieking, tossing her head and waving her arms, all along the passage to collect the next patient.

The girls met, netted in a convulsion of laughter, at a bedside in Room Three.

'Say,' Frankie said in a low voice to Robyn, 'I think Rawlings' Old Man was over in the caravan last night. Need I say more!'

'I thought he was Inside.'

'Yep he is or was. Must a bosst out!'

'Ya don't say! Which one did he have?' Robyn giggled.

'Prob'ly both. D'ya reckon. Or just the one?'

'How ju know? I mean how ju know he was there?'

'Hoola Hoola Hoola Pat me, slap me Yair Yair Yair,' Frankie sang. 'Take a look at the caravan willya. It's tipped crooked offer the wood posts. Must a been some kinda night!' she said rolling and lighting a flimsy cigarette. After two deep inhalations she passed it quickly to Robyn who, after giving her entire attention to it briefly, passed it back to Frankie. The fine smoke drifted between them. Frankie nipped the burning end and carefully put the remainder of the cigarette in a little tin she had in her pocket.

'D'ya really think Matron? As well as Rawlings?' Robyn asked.

'Nah! He's Rawlings'. Married her *after* Matron. Anyhow Matron's hot for Hailey.' Frankie shrieked with mirth.

'Go on! Ya don't say!'

'Sure!'

Together the girls hoisted Miss Nunne out of her bed and trundled her, between them, to the bathroom.

Mrs Rawlings took the patients, one by one, as they were tossed from the bathroom and stuffed them into their clothes. She led them out, one by one, and stacked them on pieces of plastic, in cane chairs, along the verandah.

Once, safely in the chairs, it was peaceful, the voices of the doves sounding in the calm morning. To and fro the voices of the doves caressed the freshly washed row of old people. The hospital seemed, on these mornings, to be like a big tree with everyone resting in the branches.

Mr Scobie, sitting between Miss Hailey and Mr Hughes, felt rested, tranquil even. His thoughts were of leaving and of the place he wanted to go back to. It was his favourite thought and it consoled him. Perhaps tomorrow or even today he would go home. Slowly he allowed himself to think of the small house tucked away on a slope, partly in the shade of a row of pine trees planted by himself. Clearly, in his mind, he saw the white-painted weatherboard and he made a little mental journey round the verandah of that house. It would be in complete shade at this time of the day. The sun would move in slowly across the boards. Slowly he allowed his dream to continue, he paused, in his thoughts, at the delicious moment of opening the door. He stretched out his hand but did not turn the brass knob; rather he held back thinking about his rooms on the other side of the door; placing chairs, tables, saucepans, books, pictures, beds, clothes and other possessions in the places they were in before he was ill and taken away to the District Hospital.

Joan, he knew, wanted to sell his house and land. 'Prices have gone up as well you know Uncle,' he was accustomed to hearing her argument. 'It was land sales which brought you a fortune, Uncle, from land which, years ago, had no value. The place you're sitting on now is very valuable Uncle. It's selfish to sit on it all by yourself.' He remembered her angry face covered in tears. She had put tenants in the house now she told him on her last visit.

'To look after it, Uncle, while you are away,' she explained. 'After all it's a very lonely spot out there in the middle of the paddocks and that lonely scrub-covered hill right behind the house. You need someone there while you are away.'

'But I'd like to go back there Joan. I want to go home straight away.'

Joan was doing something to her face with things from her handbag. 'Not until you are perfectly well Uncle.'

'But I am well now. I must leave here at once.'

'Well you can't go yet,' Joan's mouth was in a tight line, 'the tenants have signed to stay for at least a year. I can't turn them out.'

'A year Joan, but that's impossible.'

'A year. Now Uncle don't be unreasonable, please.'

Mr Scobie's dream was losing some of its pleasant qualities. He began instead to think of the journey he would make, especially the last part of it. From the main road and the railway station there was a long, winding gravel track which went mainly through his land; it wound along the foot of the hill, and went on to other places. Thinking about this track he could smell the hay from the paddocks on either side. The hay would now be in neat bales scattered carelessly over the pale stubble. There was nothing sweeter, he thought, than the smell of hay from his own fields . . .

'Frankie! Robyn! Where ever are those girls!' All at once Matron Price was going around the rooms of St Christopher and St Jude like a bird of prey hovering, disturbing everyone, throwing up windows, pulling out beds and cupboards. Little weeping moans followed in her wake.

'Frankie! Robyn! hurry up both of you. I want these rooms thoroughly cleaned. Robyn you get the vacuum cleaner and Frankie you collect up all the jugs and glasses and wash them. Just look at this rubbish, stale cake, rotten fruit, dead flowers and who let Mrs Morgan have her case? Where is Mrs Renfrew's hair brush? Why hasn't Miss Nunne's wet bed been changed?' Her heavy step vibrated on the verandah boards.

'If you sleep all day Mr Hughes you'll never sleep tonight.' Matron Price nudged Mr Hughes who had slipped sideways in his chair.

'I think we'll have to cut out your afternoon cup of tea,' she said to Mr Scobie. 'We can't have you up at all hours of the night passing water can we dear.'

'But I like my tea Matron,' Mr Scobie said, smiling up at her. 'I do like my tea, it . . .'

'Well Mr Scobie you disturb everyone getting up at 4 a.m. and Mrs Rawlings says the light from Room One shines right into the caravan.'

'Oh I'm sorry,' Mr Scobie said, 'really, I had no idea . . .'

'Mrs Rawlings needs her Beauty Sleep like everyone else,' Matron Price said.

'Oh yes of course,' Mr Scobie said. 'But,' he added, 'the lights, all of them, not just mine, are often on in the night. There's quite a lot going on in the night, there's some kind of dreadful game they play . . .'

Matron Price, not listening, continued on her rounds, bending over some patients and ignoring others. She was, Mr Scobie reflected, big like Lina's big mother. It was possible that she had mottled breasts and enormous thighs. He sighed. Matron's visit was a nuisance, the peace of the morning was shattered. Mr Scobie thought about Joan and wondered how anyone as good and as beautiful as his sister Agnes could have given birth to anyone like Joan. And there was Hartley too, his nephew; Agnes had given birth to him as well.

He tried to change his thoughts. This might be a good time to ask his riddle. He often made up riddles and he felt an appropriate one forming in his mind. Matron Price made her way to the far end of the row of chairs. Mr Scobie looked along the heaped bodies and the red and yellow knitted rugs. One of the patients was sobbing. Matron was too far away for a riddle.

'What have you got there Mr Privett?' she asked.

'A advertisement.'

'Oh? Let me look. No? Well perhaps you'll let me see it later on eh?'

So many of the women were moaning or crying Mr Scobie thought better of his riddle. Instead he said, '*Here are words you may trust, words that merit full acceptance . . . Christ Jesus came into the world to save Sinners.* Timothy one verse fifteen.' He felt he should try to soothe the patients in some way.

'Listen to me Mr Scobie dear,' Matron had come back along the row of chairs. 'Listen to my wonderful lovely idea. You can tell me about the Sinners another time.' Matron eased an old lady out of her chair.

'Robyn!' she called. 'Robyn! Take Mrs Renfrew down to the lavvy. Robyn! Hurry!'

Miss Hailey peeped at Mr Scobie under Matron's large arm. 'I'm a writer,' she observed, 'nothing escapes me. All this is good copy you know. I don't like to ask you this really but have you read my manuscript yet?'

Mr Scobie, held fast by Matron's unmoving arm, was not able to answer.

'Frankie! Where the Hell are you?' Matron's voice rose to a screech. 'Frankie! Take Miss Hailey down to my office for her needle. For God's sake,' she added in lower tones, 'get her away from here.'

'Well, see you soon,' Miss Hailey raised her eyebrows and nodded mysteriously at Mr Scobie. '*À bientôt*', she said.

'Are you listening to me Mr Scobie dear?' Matron Price, pulling off the piece of plastic, sat down in Mrs Renfrew's chair. 'I want to explain how we do things at St Christopher and St Jude,' she said in her sweetest voice. 'We look after everything here,' she said, 'it's all very simple. All you have to do is sign a form and the hospital will take care of all your affairs. You will have no more worries. You take your money out of the bank and put it into St Christopher and St Jude. I can't think of a nicer fate for money, dear, can you? And it does prevent the nasty old Government taking taxes from you. This way you won't have any money for the Government, the naughty old Government, to take away. All you have to do is to pay it into the nursing home. Land too we can handle that.' She smiled her most comfortable smile at him. 'Here at St Christopher and St Jude we like to have everything under one roof so to speak,' she said.

'But my money is all right where it is, and my land.' Mr Scobie was surprised, shocked too, that such things could be known about and talked about by strangers. He wished he had not mentioned his land. He said, 'But how could I rest in my mind? How could I rest with God? What was it I was saying just now, *Christ Jesus came into the World to save Sinners . . .*'

'Oh never mind about Jesus just now,' Hyacinth Price was accustomed to initial opposition. 'He's been dead for years, dear. Now, how about if we go up, just you and I, in the morning, say tomorrow morning, to the bank and see to the transfer of your money. Get our act together as they say these days,' she laughed. 'We'll try to reduce it down, dear,

and it will be better too,' she gave him a look full of meaning, 'so certain other people won't get their hands on it after,
you know, after!' She laughed again. Her voice pealing
richly like a horse singing contralto.

Mr Scobie supposed she meant after he was dead. He, in
his mind, saw Joan, and Hartley too, stuffing notes and
coins into their pockets.

'What does it matter what they do after I'm dead,' he
thought. He was not dead and he felt he must help Matron
Price. Though she was a matron and no doubt very clever,
he felt she was mistaken in her attitude. In spite of feeling
shocked and suddenly very tired, he leaned towards her.

'Christ Jesus isn't dead at all,' he said. 'He dwells in the
heart. We are the Divine Image. Listen,

> For Mercy Pity Peace and Love
> Is God our Father dear,
> And Mercy, Pity, Peace and Love
> Is man, his child and care.
> For Mercy has a human heart,
> Pity a human face,
> And love the human form divine,
> And Peace, the human dress.

'Very nice Mr Scobie, I'm sure,' Matron said, 'but just you
get used to my little idea and tomorrow we shall sort it all
out. Ah!' she exclaimed, 'here comes Dr Risley. He's come
to see all the dear little old Uncles and Aunties. Good morning Dr Risley. Here we all are chatting on the verandah
when we should be working.'

The doctor tapped with experienced fingers on a few of
the shrivelled old chests. He recorded one or two blood
pressures. He exchanged a few jokes about racing the old
people to the cemetery. He cautioned Mrs Tompkins about
over-eating and told Mr Privett to give up smoking.

'What's all this about an advertisement eh?' the doctor, laughing, asked Mr Privett.

This lack of privacy in Mr Privett's intention was a nuisance. He knew it was not possible to prepare an advertisement without everyone knowing about it ultimately.

Matron Price, he knew, would declare at once that she would ignore any advertisements though it was quite clear to him that, swayed by the wish for dollars, she would leave slippery bars of soap all over the shower-room floor. People never ignored anything where money was concerned. Even Jack, taking him for rides in the car, would drive like a mad man, taking corners on two wheels, narrowly missing shop fronts, light poles and nuns pushing prams on cross-walks. Lilian, he was certain, would bake cakes with rat poison in them. Already he found himself, at times, fighting for air in cupboards or wardrobes among unwanted, heavy worsteds and bereaved overcoats. Twice he nearly suffocated because of the moth balls ... If you put a price on yourself, well, there were penalties ...

Dr Risley, with confiscated cigarettes squashed in one hand, spread out the crumpled advertisement with his free hand. He laughed as he read it.

```
┌─────────────────────────────────────────┐
│            FOR SALE                       │
│  1 old mans body with rare and            │
│  interesting condition only person        │
│  with established interest need           │
│  apply price reasonable                   │
│  will deliver   no dealers                │
└─────────────────────────────────────────┘
```

'So you're up for sale,' the doctor laughed again, 'it's a good idea but there's not really any money in it. You can't leave your body anywhere while you're still in it. You'll be with us a long time. You're very much alive.

'Old half-head!' Mr Privett, muttering, dismissed the doctor by taking back his piece of paper while staring straight ahead to the three-cornered crossroads. Folding the advertisement carefully, he put it away in his vest pocket. He knew that a man could not live on nothing, that was why the advertisement was useful. He would ask to be paid in advance and, with money in his pocket, he would be free to leave this place whatever it was, some kind of dump or loony bin, Jack and Lilian had put him into and he'd get himself a room opening on to a fenced yard where he could have a few fowls . . .

'HEP DUCK HEP,' he sang half under his breath, 'HEP DUCK RATTLE TAP HEPPY HEP DUCK.'

Once Hildegarde nearly choked trying to crow. She had to have a box put over her but she still stretched her neck and crowed, muffled in cardboard.

'What next mixed-up meat bird!' he muttered. 'Rooster!' he insulted Hildegarde. 'Meat birds is often Roosters,' he said. 'Who around here wants a young rooster!' He shook his fist and jumped up ready to fight.

'Steady on! Steady!' Miss Hailey, wearing, for a change, her pith helmet, was back walking on the verandah. 'Steady on old chap, it's only me, no need to make a fist at me.' Mr

Privett, not hearing, laughed his reedy little laugh. Remembering Hildegarde's attempts at crowing reminded him of his daughter-in-law Lilian.

'I suppose I could have a bit of a shed and a fowl yard on one of them new housing estates', he squinted up sideways first at Jack and then at Lilian. It was one night after tea in the shabby old kitchen.

'Oh yes Dad of course Dad. You can have anything you want.' Lilian jumped up and kissed the pointed top of his head. With judicious excitement she showed him pictures in her magazines. He turned the treasured thick pages carefully, gazing at feature walls, patios and bedrooms in white and gold with bathrooms to match.

'You're a good girl,' he said. 'We'll sell this old place if you like.'

In the new house the old furniture looked like rubbish. They had to throw it away and buy new things. Soon there was nothing left from the old house and there was nothing for him to do. He was lost in the new house, even in the kitchen.

He was lost in this place, hospital, whatever it was. Always, as he felt his way about the passages, he could not remember where anything was. When he thought about home it was not the new house but the old one he wished for.

'A cup of hot milk would be most acceptable,' Mr Scobie said in the evening when all three were in their narrow beds.

'Yes Martin it would,' David Hughes agreed in his sing-song voice. Mr Privett nodded his head as he saw Mr Hughes nodding. He had not quite heard what the other old man had said. All three men felt the cold air of the night as the day had been very warm.

Lying in bed Mr Scobie heard the sound of traffic in the distance.

Perhaps it was trains, he thought it might be a train. The distant echoing sound of the melancholy horn seemed to bring to his mind the railway lines, miles and miles of care-fully laid metal, gleaming in the moonlight, crossing the countryside, going away from the city, going out further into the fragrant stillness, on and on towards the place where his house was. Higher up the slope behind his house there was a scrub-covered hill. He had never walked there. Now, in the night, the hill seemed to possess mysterious qualities of invitation. In the cool air coming through the partly open window, Mr Scobie thought he could smell the hay, the almost overpowering smell of hay in the night dampness. The sweetness of the smell of the hay was intoxi-cating when it was still lying out in the paddocks. Poised on the edge of his dream, he thought he would not hurry to open the door, but simply think of the pleasure of being about to sit in the comfort of the familiar hearth. He listened for the sighing of the night wind in the stiffly bending branches of the pines . . . afraid to breathe, he caught fleet-ingly the fragrance of the pines.

'What's the time Mr Hughes, David? What's the time?'

'I do not know exactly, Martin, but from the noise along the passage, it must be about four a.m.'

'Is Mr Privett here, David? Is Mr Privett here?'

'I'm not sure, Martin, I'm not sure. I don't think he is. I think he left the room a short time ago. Very quiet he was.'

'Perhaps he has gone to the dinette . . .'

'Yes. Perhaps he has gone there. There's quite a racket from down there isn't there. Just listen, will you, to all that noise!'

Mr Scobie listened. How could anyone sleep with those voices, raucous, like black cockatoos arriving in a screaming flock to get what they wanted. Shrieking, laughing, insisting, crying, bullying voices.

'Are the blinds out?'

'I'm sleeping on Harry.'

'Throw!'

'The sleep has come off.'

'Play!'

'No.'

'Play!'

'Limit.'

'Play!'

'Play!'

'Okay I'll stay.'

'Three cards please.'

'One card.'

'Two cards.'

'Three cards.'

'Renfrew to bet.'

'Chip.'

'See the chip.'

'See?'

'Limit.'

'Throw!'

'Look!'

'I've got six tits.'

'Lucky Bastard!'

'Blinds out.'

'I'm over the blind.'
'Play?'
'No!'
'I'll defend.'
'How many cards?'
'Four now, one later.'
'One card.'
'Three.'
'Renfrew to bet.'
'Busted Flush. No.'
'Chip.'
'No!'
'See the Chip.'
'I've got two small pairs. Fives and Eights.'
'I can beat that. Midnight at Buckingham Palace.'
'Kings up Queens.'

'*Let all mortal flesh keep silence.* Hullo there!' Miss Hailey's deep voice sounded in the hall. 'Is anyone there? You there, in the dining hall. Did you know the hour is come? Advent is come. Advent. Join with me in the hymn number three hundred and ninety, Ancient and Modern er revised.' She cleared her throat and began to sing,

> Let all mortal flesh keep silence
>   And with fear and trembling stand;
> Ponder nothing earthly-minded,
>   For with blessing in his hand
> Christ our God to earth descendeth,
>   Our full homage to demand.

Mr Scobie, leaving his bed, went along the hall and saw Miss Hailey wrapped in a white sheet. On her head she wore the pith helmet she had worn all day. She was holding back the curtains of the dinette where a wild game was in progress.

Beyond the tangled heap of walking frames and elbow crutches discarded, a strange group stood and sat in the confined space inside the flowered curtains. They were dressed in an assortment of dressing gowns, night shirts and unironed tropical kit (the Lt Col.). With sunken toothless mouths wide open, and with grey-wisped heads trembling and nodding on scarcely supporting withered necks, with frail-skinned faces animated and with greedy groping hands they played their game with fierce determination. All were so intent they paid no attention to Miss Hailey's hymn and did not notice Mr Scobie standing, shocked and dismayed, looking on. Overcome by the sight of such wickedness he stumbled back to his own room. It was impossible to sleep listening to those evil people. He tried not to hear certain words which fell far too frequently from their foul mouths.

Then there was Matron's idea. Why did she want to take him out to sign papers? All his affairs were in good order. He did not want any interference. The thought worried him.

Mr Hughes, falling down his pillows, was dozing and snoring. Mr Privett's bed was empty. Mr Scobie, not deeply concerned, wondered where he might be. He had not been part of the dishevelled tattered group round the cards.

Kit floor, bath, hot milk veggies. 10 p.m. N.A. to report.
All pats. play cards in dinette. They all play this game Matron
it's all raise a dollar kings on queens raise two dollars three
bullets raise three dollars it's a real scream it's a picnic
matron. Mother I mean Mrs Morgan really enjoying every
minute. Lt Col. I. Price (retired) really enjoying himself but
lose bad.

Nothing abnormal to report.

Signed Night Sister M. Shady (unregistered)

*Mrs Shady: You realize, of course, two packs should be used.
One pack for playing while the other is shuffled. Please see
that this is done.*

Signed Matron H. Price

All pats. play cards in dinette Lt Col. I. Price lose. N.A. to
report.

Signed Night Sister M. Shady (unregistered)

Mrs Shady: Your report noted.

Signed Matron H. Price

Mr Privett frequently left his bed during the night. Usually there was so much noise from the dinette that he was able to walk down the hall and let himself out through the front door. He knew the opening and closing of the door would not be noticed.

It was the time just before dawn. Dark streaks of cloud hurried across the sky which was rapidly becoming light. The moon was transparent and, in the spreading paleness, trees and gardens began to appear as if freshly planted during the night. Mr Privett walked in the restless wind, his frail hair, lifting, made a halo for him. He stopped in a short cut, a back lane between two streets, for an old man's reason and hurried on without fastening his clothes. He did not notice the cold. He knew the way to his old house.

All these people in that Bin. They were nothing but a nuisance. He did not really need to place the advertisement or to rent a room. It was quite simple, he would go back to his old home. He began to leap and cackle choosing the middle of the road for his dance.

> HEP DUCK HEP HEPPY DUCK
> HEAR THAT HILDEGARDE
> HILDEGARDE THE MEAT
> HEP DUCK GUESS WHO'S COMING HOME

He could hardly wait to get home. Familiarity beckoned. The memory of the garden and the promise of the quiet seclusion of the shed made him hurry even more. He had to stop for breath. He coughed.

'Stop smoking. Give up smoking!' he mocked the doctor. He came upon his place, taking it by surprise. For a moment he thought he had made a mistake. Where his house had been and the neighbours' houses was a patch of ground resembling a newly ploughed field. The light from the unborn sun was not without sympathy. There was from this light a tranquillity. Mr Privett peered first in one direction and then in the other.

'Hep Duck?' he called before any birds were singing. 'Hildegarde? Where's your half drum house Hep? Where are you Hep? Hildegarde, you anywhere there?'

Then he began to remember. That was it. How could he have forgotten the day he fought the demolition single handed.

'We don't know how to handle him,' he heard the foreman saying to Jack. They must have sent for Jack that day.

'He's been sitting there on the path, in the middle of the old brick path,' one of the men said. 'We're scared he'll get hurt, see? I mean there's our trucks for a start. I mean, he gets under one of those . . .'

Mr Richards was there too. Mr Privett recalled his gentle voice saying to him to come and have a cup of tea with Lilian.

'Come and have your hand bandaged Mr Privett. You need your hand washing.' Mr Richards, for all what he had done, had a soft way with him.

The roof was off the house that day. The broken walls reared up, jagged in the sorrow of the bruised garden. As he looked at the flat neat paddock, for that was what it had become, he remembered the whole thing, even his own voice, screeching.

'Yo'll not take down this shed nor touch this path. And yo'll let them trees alone. Yo'll tek them ropes offer that pine or else.' All he could do that day was shake his fist. He was covered in dust.

Mr Richards was saying, 'There's tears and blood all over him.'

Jack could only say helplessly, 'Come along Dad. Come along Dad.'

He still had the graze scabs on the backs of his hands.

He stood gazing into the stillness where his house and shed used to be. He did not wonder about his neighbours.

The grey became a lighter grey. The sky was pink. The magpies and the doves, unconcerned, began to take possession of the street with their voices.

'Arra!' he spat on the footpath. There was nothing for it but to walk back to that Bin and have his breakfast and wait for Jack and Lilian to come.

'Like a ride in the car Dad?' he could just hear them.

'Oh, Ahrr, yes! That'd be nice.' He would ask them to stop at the delicatessen and the advert would be in the window the next day.

Ducking his head forward, he hurried back. The early morning walk had made him hungry.

Mr Scobie, allowed to take little walks, often passed by a bakery. Every day he stopped to admire the golden fresh bread displayed. In the window were trays of jam tarts and treacle tarts, there were slabs of fruit cake, on sheets of crisp white paper were currant buns with pink and white icing. The wholesome fragrance from the shop enticed him. He went inside. He bought a doughnut and carried it back to St Christopher and St Jude to eat it after tea.

As he entered the hall of the hospital, Matron Price and the cook, leaving the office together, came towards him. He hoped they would not see the little paper-bag with the doughnut in it.

'Oh, Mr Scobie, dear, you should not buy rubbish like that,' Matron said. 'It won't do your bowels any good.'

'What's wrong with the food you get here?' the cook said. 'Anyone 'ud think you didn't get enough to eat here. At least it's home cooking here and you know what's in it. That's what I always say.'

Not wanting to be discovered eating the doughnut, Mr Scobie tried to find somewhere to put it in Room One. There really was no hiding place. He put the paper-bag on the floor beside his bed.

Later, when he ate it, it was cold and heavy, lifeless. It tasted unpleasant as if it had absorbed all the smells of the hospital.

There was a young lady of Ealing
who had a peculiar feeling
She lay on her back
And . . .

Frankie was scrubbing a pile of false teeth in the bathroom.

'Frankie! Hurry up, girl, with those teeth.' Matron Price, with the help of Frankie and Robyn, was getting Room Three ready for the carol singers.

'Here's your teeth dear. You'll want your teeth in won't you dear. Well, let me know when you do want them. Robyn try these teeth for Miss Nunne, Mrs Renfrew says they're not hers. Teeth, Mrs Murphy? TEETH dear, open your mouth there's a good girl!'

The old women, gathered together, sitting in their cane chairs, were mostly dozing, even though it was only mid morning. Their cold feet, thrust into wrinkled stockings and felt slippers, were turned inwards. Matron was draping coloured shawls over the various hunched-up shoulders. Some of the shawls were pulled and tightly pinned across the narrow chests with large safety pins.

'There!' Matron was out of breath. She rubbed her hip. She had bruised herself badly on an enormous bedside commode. 'There! those red and yellow shawls do cheer things up a bit.'

Mrs Rawlings, in Room One, was dressing Mr Hughes. She needed Frankie and Robyn to help her.

'We're taking the dollies to the dunny,' Frankie called back along the passage. 'Be with you in a minute.'

'Leave me here,' Mr Hughes said in his soft voice, 'don't you worry about me. I'll be right here. I'll hear them from along the hallway.'

'Over my dead body you will, Mr Hughes,' Mrs Rawlings said, struggling to raise him to pull on his crumpled trousers. 'You must be there for the carols,' Mrs Rawlings said, 'there's little children coming this year to sing too. You wouldn't want to miss the ladies' choir and the little children would you.'

Mr Hughes sighed. Mrs Rawlings pulled on his socks and pushed his feet into his shoes. She sighed too. Her back ached. Not only was the caravan cramped and uncomfortable, it was precarious too.

From the kitchen there came a mounting crescendo of noise.

'I mean who, just WHO does SHE think SHE is!' the cook's angry voice voiced an opinion of Matron Price, of her hospital and all the people in it. Her words left nothing to the imagination. 'It's not my job to collect up crockery, cups or anything, and it's not my job to wash up either just because those girls are fooling about in Room Three.' Her sermon ended in a kind of scream, 'The conceited big-headed crab. Who the hell does she think she is – the bloody Queen?'

The old people, shuffling, trembling and unsteady, felt with old hands along the unfamiliar walls. In their minds they chased the vague possibilities of people no longer there for them and went, one after the other, with Robyn and Frankie, to the toilet.

Mr Hughes was half dragged and half carried down the passage. The girls shared the remains of a cigarette while they waited for him. Mr Hughes, embarrassed and awkward, was afraid they would hurt themselves moving him. His hand, flapping, caught the door post on the way back. The frail skin, brown mottled and paper thin, was grazed and broken.

'Oh my clean pinny,' Mrs Rawlings said as she helped settle Mr Hughes into a chair. 'I'm all over blood. My good pinny and the carol singers nearly here too.' Quickly she tore up a piece of old rag kept for padding up the old women and bound up the bleeding hand.

Frankie brushed Mr Hughes' hair. Mrs Rawlings sponged her apron with the corner of a damp towel.

'Here, this'll fix it,' Robyn shook lavender talcum powder over the stain. 'There,' she said. 'Whiter than White. A Miracle!'

'Surely it's far too early for presents and carol singers,' Miss Hailey's deep voice sounded along the hall; coming late from her shower she entered Room Three where Matron Price was arranging little parcels and balloons by every chair. She glared at Miss Hailey. This was no time to start discontent or troubles of any kind especially in Room Three.

'The carol singers,' Matron was purple from blowing up cheap sausage-shaped balloons, 'they have their work cut out for them, like the rest of us, some more than others. They have to get round to goodness knows how many places.'

'Oh Lord yes, of course, I forget these things,' Miss Hailey's voice dropped. 'Oh let's shake. Hyacinth, give me your paw. I'm terribly sorry for being gauche. Let's shake paws Hyacinth and call it quits. Please do forgive my gaucherie.'

'No Christian names in the wards please Miss Hailey, how often do I have to remind you.'

Miss Hailey, like a crestfallen school girl, sank into her chair. 'Can we look at our prezzies now?' she asked.

'Yes Hyacinth, can we open our presents now?' Lt Col. I. Price began to tear the red paper from the flat parcel. Unable to find his dressing gown, Mrs Rawlings had dressed him in an old button-through woollen dress which had been found in the wardrobe in Room Three. He was pleased with the dress.

'That's a lovely shade, Lt Col.' Miss Hailey, trying to be agreeable for the party, said, 'What would you say it was?'

'Oh,' he said, 'a sort of fraizey craizey, crushed strawberry, or do you think a dusty pink?' He pulled his present from the wrapping. 'Oh look! I've got a writing pad with a picture of a lady on the front.'

'Oh so you have, why I do believe it's the *Mona Lisa* in green, a sort of Mona lettuce salad. How lovely! Lines on the paper too. That'll keep you straight.' Miss Hailey, enjoying her own joke, laughed her deep laugh. 'Oh, Mr Scobie's got a writing pad too, so has Mr Hughes and Mr Privett. Four Monas in green salad. *With best wishes for a merry Christmas and a Happy New Year from Matron Price.* You lucky people I can never get enough paper. We writers never can.'

'What have you got Hailey, old girl?' Lt Col. Price, remembering ancient good manners, leaned forward to look. Several of the buttons burst off his dress.

'Why it's a little box of tissues,' Miss Hailey squeaked as well as she could. 'Just what I needed, thank you Hyacinth. I mean, thank you Matron. I keep forgetting I'm a patient.'

'All the old women unwrapped their tissues. There were so many tissues, enough for all the tears still to be shed in the finishing of a lifetime. Miss Hailey read out the accompanying messages,

To Mrs Renfrew with best wishes for a merry Christmas and a happy new year from Matron

To Miss Nunne with best wishes for a merry Christmas and a happy new year from Matron

To Miss Morgan . . . to Mrs Tompkins . . . To Mrs Murphy . . . Miss Hailey read them all.

They held their presents and their balloons on their laps.

On the mantelpiece, over the unused fireplace, there were a few Christmas cards from people whose names were not remembered by the people who received them. With some of the cards there were photographs, mainly of babies and children. No one seemed able to claim them either.

'Mrs Renfrew, dear,' Matron Price persisted, 'look at this

beautiful card, and see, there's a photo of your great grand-children. Aren't they gorgeous!' Matron moved to the next chair, 'Miss Nunne, dear, here's a picture of your sister's great grandchildren. See here dear, aren't they cute?' Matron read the Christmas card messages aloud. The old ladies gave little laughs and moans of affection and non-recognition.

'Well, I must be getting off home now,' Mr Privett made for the door. 'Thanks one and all,' he said. 'I've been here long enough. I've got the fowls to see to and my son and my daughter-in-law will be expecting me.'

'Now Mr Privett,' Mrs Rawlings held him fast by one arm. 'Just you sit down quiet. You can't go off out all by yourself. You'll be more comfortable here in your nice dressing gown. And the lovely church ladies are going to sing for you. You can't go off out when they are taking all that trouble to come here to sing.'

Mr Scobie thought he heard a noise. 'There's quite a com-motion,' he said, 'there's someone at the front door.'

The church ladies came along the hall rustling, whisper-ing, fussing and arranging. Behind them flocked the little girls from the Sunday School, full of life and importance, resplendent in white dresses, white socks and shoes and hair ribbons. All at once Room Three was filled with an intrusion and a reminder from the world outside. Soon they were singing with full rich voices of the hope and the youth and the health and the happiness which they knew was promised to them. The voices poured in praise over the huddled bodies.

They sang 'Oh Come All Ye Faithful', and followed it with 'Hark the Herald Angels Sing'. After a flouncing of full white skirts and a turning of pages they sang 'The Holly And the Ivy'. The room was full of the singing. Miss Hailey, moved by the voices, thought she squeezed Mr Scobie's hand but it turned out to be the arm of the commode. Mr

Scobie found he could not bear his thoughts. He, like Mr Privett, sat with closed eyes. The only difference being that Mr Privett's eyes were screwed up tight enabling him to squint sideways at the singers' legs while Mr Scobie's eyes were lightly closed being full with unshed tears, swollen inside the lids.

In the quiet moments of soft rustlings between the bursts of singing, a noisy crow, flying over the neglected gardens of St Christopher and St Jude, cried the tragedy and the gift of half-remembered places, of distant towns and villages, of mountains and rivers and of wharves and railway stations. The crow, swooping closer, still crying, brought to the doors and windows of St Christopher and St Jude the sound of the wind rushing across endless paddocks, the steady hopeful clicking of windmills and long country roads leading to serene crossroads. Another crow, in another garden, crying loneliness, seemed to answer the first one. When the crows were silent, the voices of the doves could be heard; a contented sound, perhaps a language of reason and of acceptance and of resignation.

Miss Parker, the leader of the little choir, asked Matron if any of the old folk would like to choose a favourite carol. The choir, she said, would be happy to sing an old favourite.

Miss Parker's clear voice rang out with her suggestion but no one chose a carol. Lt Col. Price, fidgeting, burst three more buttons off his pink dress.

'Good Heavens! Hyacinth,' he said, 'just look at this.'

'For Christ's Sake,' Hyacinth Price said in a fierce whisper to Mrs Rawlings. 'For Christ's Sake put a shawl or something over my brother's lap.'

Matron Price bent down over the old women in turn.

'Any requests dears?' she asked. 'The ladies want you to choose your very own favourite carol.'

Mrs Rawlings squeezed herself between the chairs with an apron for the Colonel.

Miss Hailey said, 'I must put on my thinking cap.' She rumpled her hair with both hands and stared at the floor. 'The mind boggles,' she said to Mr Scobie in her deep voice. 'Absooty blank,' she said. 'I must be quite bonkers, round the bend, not to be able to think of one single carol. What about you?'

Mr Scobie did not trust himself to speak. He thought he ought to make a request since none of the old ladies seemed to have anything they wanted to choose. Suddenly Mr Privett began to sing in his reedy voice,

> Won't you come home Bill Bailey.
> Oh! Ah! Won't you come home Bill Bailey
> Oh! Ah! Won't you, won't you come home Bill Bailey.

'I'll have "Won't you come home Bill Bailey",' old Mrs Renfrew said from her chair in the front row, 'that's always been my favourite.'

'Won't you – won't you – won't you come home Bill Bailey,' she growled. 'My husband was called Billy but not Bailey, he liked that one too.' She tried to sing again and choked.

'No dear!' Matron said as patiently as she could, 'something nice about Jesus today, dear, it's Christmas, dear. Lovely old Christmas!'

No one said anything. Miss Hailey remarked that it was, after all, still a little early for Christmas.

'What about "Away in a Manger",' Matron interrupted Miss Hailey. 'I'm sure we all like that one.'

The ladies and the little girls sang 'Away in a Manger'. When they had finished, Matron said, 'That was very nice wasn't it.'

Mr Scobie thought that the singing was beautiful. During the carols he had not been in Room Three at all but somewhere else and many years ago. He would have liked to say something about Agnes but Miss Nunne, who never spoke, was making one of her noises.

At first Matron thought Miss Nunne was crying.

'It's like her crying,' Matron said, 'but there are no tears.' She paused and everyone listened to Miss Nunne. 'I do believe she's singing,' Matron said. The carol singers, not used to small hospitals, stared at Miss Nunne and a faint sight of polite amusement rippled through their skirts.

'On behalf of myself and the choir,' Miss Parker stepped forward, 'I should like to wish all the Old Folk a merry Christmas and a happy new year . . .'

Mr Privett started singing,

> Christmas is coming,
> The goose is getting fat
> Please put a penny
> In the old man's hat
> Christmas is coming
> The goose is getting fat
> Please put a penny in
> In . . .

His reedy voice subsided in a fit of coughing. Miss Parker continued, lifting her rich voice above the noise. 'We have to be at the City and District by eleven o'clock,' she explained, adding that they hoped to get the Mental Institution done as well before lunch.

Quite suddenly, with rustlings and excited whisperings, they were gone, leaving in their wake a rushing of little draughts, recollections of vague unfinished ideas and incomplete thoughts.

'Hyacinth. Just look at this!' Matron's brother poked his fingers through the soft dusty pink.

'It must have got the moth in it,' Mrs Rawlings explained as the woollen dress, disintegrating, peeled away from the Colonel's bony body.

'She isn't singing,' Matron bent over Miss Nunne, 'her face is all wet. Robyn! Frankie! Get Miss Nunne to the toilet and back to bed. Look sharp now!'

'What about a game of draughts?' Mrs Rawlings said when Mr Privett and Mr Hughes and Mr Scobie were back in Room One. Red faced and out of breath, Mrs Rawlings propped up Mr Hughes with his five pillows. She placed the draughts board as well as she could between the three old men. She set the draughts out quickly.

'There,' she said, 'there's only two colours, black and white, but it'll pass the time for you.' The three men, wedged together, perplexed, regarded the board with conventional good manners and apparent thought.

'Miss Nunne's pillow is all wet,' Matron said later in her office to Mrs Rawlings. 'So it must be crying. But what in Heaven's Name is she crying for?'

'Search me,' Mrs Rawlings said.

Outside the window of Room One the triangular leaves were shuddering on the trellis-like little profiles of well-bred faces, agitated, moving one towards the other and away again. One leaf seemed to lean towards another leaf which, in its turn, leaned shaking, away from the first. Their sad outlines were tremulous. The light of the morning contained only vague hope. The sun, passing over, passed quickly. As the day passed, the leaves would be the first things to get dark.

The leaves nodded and waved and moved towards one another. They shook and trembled and moved away from each other. It was as if any messages they were trying to give would remain for ever ungiven.

Miss Rosemary Whyte, social worker in training, peeping

into the room as she stepped lightly on neat little feet along the passage, decided that all three old men were asleep. She consulted her watch. It was practically lunch time. She made a note on her folder to the effect that Mr Privett was asleep, that Mr Hughes was asleep and that Mr Scobie appeared to be about to sleep.

N.A. to report.

All pats. play cards in dinnette. Lt Col. Price loose bad. Message from Lt Col. Please can I have more money Hyacinth. Urgent signed Iris Price (Lt Col. retired) as instructed by himself.

Signed Night Sister M. Shady (unregistered)

Mrs Shady: Please note there is no report from Matron Price as for today. Signed Felicity Rawlings (hkpr)

When Lina played the piano she sat upon a little stool which had a seat made of red velvet. Mr Scobie, teaching her, sat close beside her. It was his privilege then to touch her smooth plump arm very lightly and, whenever necessary, to raise her wrist a fraction.

'Staccato Lina, staccato,' restraining her delicately. 'Adagio, Lina, adagio,' pressing a little more on her arm to indicate yet another musical instruction.

Some days had passed since Matron's little talk on the verandah. Mr Scobie was hoping she had forgotten his money and his land when Mrs Rawlings, after his shower, told him to sit by the front door to be ready to go out with Matron. Unwillingly dressed in his better suit he sat waiting, thinking about Lina.

'Piano, Lina, pianissimo Lina.' Whenever he said, 'Piano, Lina,' she bowed her head gravely, her expression tender and serious, her chin tucked down on her softly rounded neck and her, as yet, childish bosom heaving, an indication of the gentle heavenly transformation taking place within the bodice of her expensive but simple dress.

'When's Matron coming down?' the cook's raucous voice rose above a series of explosions from the slow-combustion stove. The question was followed by a fierce and terrible raking which seemed to cause large pieces of loose metal to fall about the kitchen floor.

'Eh? What's that? 'Aven't 'eard one word of what you're saying. I axed you, when's Matron coming down?'

The unbelievable silence which followed held the quiet answer from Mrs Rawlings, 'Matron's sick this morning. She's on flat lemonade. There's nothing to pass her lips but flat lemonade.'

'Seck is she? What's the marrer then?'

'Oh it's her old trouble. She'll be right as rain tomorrow. Any further conversation was lost in more rakings and the other wild and strange sounds which came from the kitchen in the mornings.

Mr Scobie, hearing enough, sank to his knees on the brown roses of the hall carpet to give thanks for Divine Intervention. He supposed Matron would be unwieldy to handle in bed. No doubt Mrs Rawlings, looking after her, would manage.

For a time Matron Price had to put aside Mr Scobie's money and his land and the getting of his signature. This worried her as one simply never knew, these days, about life and death. As Mr Rawlings said during the time when she was Mrs Rawlings, before giving up that title for someone surprisingly well known to herself, as Mr Rawlings said, 'here today and gone tomorrow'. She forgave him the cliché in the same way that she forgave him for marrying her friend while still being her own legal husband. Willingly she gave up her title, she was better known as Price anyway. But the title was given up by spoken word only, leaving no chance for the new Mrs Rawlings to be a real one and keeping Mr Rawlings bound to what is considered a crime. It was, Matron Price considered, only one crime among many.

'Here today and gone tomorrow' was a well-worn cliché, but it was a truth, Matron Price thought. She seemed to think nowadays entirely in cliché. It was worrying to be so banal.

There simply was not time for everything especially while Mr Rawlings was having a brief and secret respite from his normal routine in the caravan. There was no doubt he would be collected at some time in the near future. While outwardly showing no emotion, for he did belong by passion to Mrs Rawlings – who, in working without any time off at St Christopher and St Jude, took full responsibility for her illegal spouse and his expensive tastes – Matron Price did admit to herself and, when she had the chance, to Mr Rawlings himself, that she did love him still and always would love him.

Dismissing Mr Rawlings from her mind, she prepared herself to see Miss Hailey in the office. There seemed to be so many things to be thought about at St Christopher and St Jude. There was Mrs Morgan's hundredth birthday celebration. There was every indication that a surprise was called for. The biggest surprise would be to somehow get Mr Morgan, also about to celebrate his hundredth year, across from the maximum security hostel where he lodged permanently, for a surprise party. Matron Price sketched the possibilities on another neatly pencilled list.

There were problems too. Mr Privett's advertisement had caused some unrest. Mrs Tompkins, against all advice, had joined an over-seventy gourmet club and had to go daily for treatment at the City and District Hospital. And Miss Hailey had submitted an indecent poem to the Town Clerk.

'It's an ode,' Miss Hailey explained to Matron Price. 'I fail to see how the Town Clerk or anyone could be offended. It could,' she smiled, 'quite easily be set to music and it's very topical. And you'll see when you read it I have tried to look with renewed rapture and entirely new images at his water works. Well, I should say our water works. They are for everyone aren't they? You will see too,' Miss Hailey did not give Matron Price a chance to speak, 'you will see,' she continued, her dark eyes bright with poetic excitement, 'I have included the blessings of several saints, just to quote a few examples, there's Saint Cecilia, an ecstasy that conquers fear, there's Saint Anthony, you know the one who placed his sister in a house of maidens where . . .'

'I shall have to write a note and apologize to the Town Clerk,' Matron Price rose to her feet, 'Miss Hailey it is quite in order, naturally, for you to *write* poetry but that is where it must end.'

'But Hyacinth, you don't understand, it's a form of communication, it has to go somewhere. Do please read what I have written, or better still let me read it to you, the last stanza is devoted to St Theresa, the little flower, the perfume of sweet oils, it is deep symbolism . . .'

'No Christian names, Miss Hailey please. If I have told you that once, I have told you a thousand times.' She paused and then said, 'Now perhaps it would do you good to lie down for an hour or so.'

'Yes of course Matron,' Miss Hailey, adopting the expression of a reprimanded school girl, walked off down the hall.

'I'm on the mat again,' she smiled bravely in at the door of Room One. 'Matron's wiped the floor with me,' she said.

Mr Scobie, some time later, when the money subject was raised once more, sat again unwillingly in his best suit by the front door waiting for Matron Price and the promised unwanted expedition. He did not feel at all inclined to going with Matron. He tried not to have uncharitable thoughts about her. Rather he tried to see her as an individual trying to accomplish a difficult task.

Mrs Rawlings, her face pale and with her lips compressed in a thin line – perhaps the result of a sleepless night, Mr Scobie thought – was going to and fro on heavy tired feet even though the day had scarcely begun.

'Hallo there!' Miss Hailey sat on the chair next to Mr Scobie. She explained she was about to have a final check up at the City and District Hospital. 'It's my arm,' she said. 'It's nothing much, it was a small injury sustained during the water fight we had last month.'

A thin shaft of dusty sunshine came through the amber and purple stained glass of the front door. The tulips in the glass on either side of the door glowed. It was impossible not to feel caressed.

'*Ille terrarum mihi praeter omnes angulus ridet,*' Miss Hailey said. 'Horace, you know, with Hailey overtones.'

'Is it now,' Mrs Rawlings said as she passed them carrying a pile of sheets, 'and who's Horace when he's at home?'

'She seems to have a secret sorrow,' Mr Scobie said when Mrs Rawlings had disappeared into Room Three. He was pleased to have something to take his mind off the worrying errand Matron had in mind for him. 'She never stops working,' he said.

'Yes she does work hard,' Miss Hailey said in a low voice. Mrs Rawlings, going now in the other direction, had her back to them. Miss Hailey watched her with a surprisingly knowledgeable look. 'You are so right,' she said. 'She's paying back for her life, you know, how people have to,' she added.

Mr Scobie did not know. 'How do you mean?' he asked.

'Well now would you believe that Hyacinth Price and I were once close friends,' Miss Hailey said, 'we were at school together. Tin Tin sat behind me in class, you'll never guess, she used to copy over my shoulder, algebra, arithmetic, translations – everything,' Miss Hailey laughed in her deep voice. 'After leaving school we kept up our friendship. In time I had my own school, a boarding school for girls and Hyacinth had her hospital. We were good friends; we still are,' she said, 'but . . . well . . . except that Hyacinth and Iris have taken complete custody of all my lolly, I think that's what it's called, and I've gone out of my mind. I am not sure which way round those two things should be presented to you,' she said. 'Also, you might find this incredible, Mrs

Rawlings was at school with us, *Three little maids from school are we, Tra la tra la tra la,*' she sang.

'Tell me,' Mr Scobie said, 'how has Matron Price obtained this, er – custody you mention?'

'Don't,' said Miss Hailey with an air of mystery, 'do not on any account let Hyacinth Price take you on a visit to . . .'

'The ambulance is here Miss Hailey, and he doesn't like to be kept waiting,' Mrs Rawlings, grim, as if with some deep internal pain, stood over them.

Miss Hailey paused in the doorway.

'Farewell,' she said, 'I'll see you anon. I shall compose my poem on the way. I might try an epitaph.' Accompanied by Mrs Rawlings she left.

Thinking about Mrs Rawlings, Mr Scobie wondered if she too had troubles with her bowels. He went on waiting for Matron Price. He strained to hear her voice but all was quiet. Robyn and Frankie, in their shining plastic aprons, were leading people, one by one, to the bathroom. Gradually the row of wicker chairs on the verandah was being filled with bodies decked and wrapped in an assortment of hand-knitted woollens, red and yellow, green, violet and blue. Mr Hughes, in his dark crumpled suit, made a more serious spot in the variety of hideous left-over colours.

'There seems to be a kind of magic about the name of Rosewood East. Why can't I be there now,' Mr Scobie said to himself. He let his mind rest in his dream. In the mornings he remembered, the sun shone in heavenly peace on the little house. He could see his house clearly, hidden in the bush but with the pretty garden he had made. A lantana, with orange flowers like little lamps, was outside the kitchen window. In the mornings, just now at this time, the whole lantana bush would be alive with little birds. Silver eyes they were called. He often spent hours watching these birds.

'Anyone who has ever lived in Rosewood East would

never want to live anywhere else again,' Mr Scobie, without needing to convince himself, said aloud. Joan described his furniture as rubbish. He began to think about Joan. He seemed to hear her voice.

'Anyway Uncle Martin, I've got rid of most of the rubbish and . . .' He tried to stop thinking about Joan.

Matron was coming down the staircase. She was dressed for going out.

Someone was ringing the front door bell.

'It's a visitor for Mr Scobie,' Robyn said, water running in rivulets from her apron.

Matron Price, reaching the hall, said, 'Run away girl! Run along girl! You're ruining my carpet with all that water.'

'Hartley!' Mr Scobie was surprised.

'What Ho, Nunky, long time no see eh?' Hartley gave a long tremulous whistle and jerked his head, winking at the same time, in the direction of the retreating Robyn whose pink wet body was showing generously where not covered by the plastic apron.

'It's all the fair sex eh?' Hartley winked again, this time at Matron Price. 'All right if I take my Uncle out for a drive? I see he's dressed up to kill. Hows about a little run in the vehicle Uncle?'

'Oh yes of course,' Matron Price forced a smile to her mouth. 'I am just going out myself.'

'Uncle Martin,' Hartley said in the car. 'I want to come back to the Lord. I have seen the Light.'

Mr Scobie allowed a few tears to spill from his eyes. 'I can feel the Wonderful Presence,' he told Hartley. '. . . *the loftiness of Man shall be bowed down, and the haughtiness of men shall be made low; and the Lord alone shall be exalted in that day.* Isaiah 2, Verse 17.' he said.

'Too Right Uncle!' Hartley nodded wisely.

'You were born of Spiritual Seed, Hartley,' Mr Scobie said, 'your mother, my sister Agnes, was the most beautiful and gentle woman I have ever seen. If Agnes had not married,' he continued, 'I suppose I should not say this to you Hartley, if she had not married, she and I might still be living in my house at Rosewood East, happy and comfortable together. Free to come and go and to enjoy the sun and the air – not like it is in that dreadful hospital.

'When I was about fourteen, Hartley, I nailed some sheets of iron on our roof and I put the nails through the wrong part of the iron and, when it rained, all the water came through. Agnes, your mother, Hartley, pleaded with our mother not to be angry with me, and she paid for some fresh pieces herself. She was a teacher by this time and quite soon went away to another place to teach and was engaged to be married the next time she came home. Mother wept when Agnes married and I wept too.' Tears filled Mr Scobie's pale eyes.

'Amen. Hallelujah!' Hartley said, 'I'm getting the lingo Uncle. World without End. Amen. Arrr-Ah-menn,' he lengthened the vowel sounds.

'You came at just the right time Hartley,' Mr Scobie said, 'I want to leave the nursing home. I must get away. I can't stand it there.'

'The trouble is,' Hartley said, 'I still love Sybil. She's a lovely woman but she's got some very nasty ways.'

Mr Scobie was shocked. 'Oh, you mean That Woman. I thought you would have given her up, Hartley. If she is divorced wouldn't you be better to leave her alone? Have nothing to do with her.'

'No worries Nunk,' Hartley lit a cigarette while his knees took care of the steering wheel. 'Sybil's seen to all that,' he said.

'Hartley. You're driving too fast.'

Hartley laughed blowing out smoke. 'Here today. Gone tomorrow,' he slowed down and parked the car outside a large house. In front were well-shaved lawns and formal flower beds. On both sides of the drive were roses of all colours. There was a lily pond and a fountain. Hartley described in great detail the large rooms and the expensive carpets, the furniture, the ornaments and the original paintings. The back of the house, he said, had windows and glass doors overlooking the river. 'There's a path leading down to a private beach and a jetty,' Hartley said, 'you can approach the house, if you want to, by boat.'

'Is this your place Hartley? You seem to know it so well.' Mr Scobie imagined the Divorced Woman brushing her hair, or worse, in one of the upstairs rooms.

'Oh No Nuncle, my place is on the other side of town. Only I am not allowed there. Sybilla won't have me. She'll not have anything more to do with me. She's got the house and everything and yours truly got his marching orders.' Hartley paused. 'But say, Uncle, I like this house. How would you like to live here?' he said. 'If you lived here, I would have a reason, an excuse to come here.' Hartley seemed excited.

'Leave her alone Hartley,' Mr Scobie said. 'Evil can only bring about Evil.'

'But I love her Uncle. How can I leave her? I want to live. It's not evil is it to want to live?'

'I wouldn't want to live in that house,' Mr Scobie said. 'I want my own home back. Do you remember my dog Peter, Hartley? He used to lie on the sunny places on my verandah.'

'Animals have more sense nor humans,' Hartley said. 'Well Uncle, there's a rich widow here in this house. She wants a lodger. She loves the Bible. You could talk your head off, Bible stuff all day and she'd love it. How's about we go in there and see her. Talk your head off over the Scriptures.'

'What else is there about this widow?' Mr Scobie asked.

'Nothing except that she wants a Christian Gentleman companion. It was in the paper, Sunday.'

They were both silent.

'Are you sure this is the right place Hartley?' Mr Scobie said after the short silence.

'Well, yes Nunks. I haven't got the ad on me though,' he patted empty pockets, making as if to search the thoroughly known emptiness.

'It looks very grand. Far too grand for someone like me.' Mr Scobie looked at the house, 'far too grand for anyone to want to take in a lodger.'

'Too right Unks! But in the ad she said she wanted someone mature. You know. Mature Lady Bible Basher would like to meet similar opposite sex conversations and outings. Not exactly those words, Uncle, but that sort of thing.'

'Oh I see,' Mr Scobie said, 'I suppose it is possible well, perhaps we should, as they say in the criminal world, perhaps we should case the joint.' He gave a little laugh.

'Righty O Uncle,' Hartley drove up the drive and stopped outside the front door with a neat gravel skid.

'Is the Lady of the House in?' Hartley asked when the door was opened. 'Or', he corrected himself quickly, 'I see you are the lady. I beg pardon. My uncle and I have come in answer to the advertisement in the paper. I am sure you will find my uncle is the answer to your most ardent prayers.'

The woman, in a garden hat and gardening gloves, stared at Hartley and Mr Scobie from the threshold. Her chins quivered. Hartley, in his most refined and charming voice said, 'Perhaps I have made a dreadful mistake. If that is the case, Madam, please forgive me.' He bowed, 'I apologize to you too Uncle.' He caught hold of Mr Scobie's arm.

'I wonder, Madam,' he said, 'if my uncle could sit down a moment in your cool hall and perhaps, seeing as how your maids is out, could I perhaps slip to your kitchen and get him a drink of water?'

Together, they helped Mr Scobie on to a chair.

Hartley seemed to be away a long time.

'What a beautiful home you have,' he said when at last he came back with a cup of cold water. 'It took me quite a while to find your kitchens. Very cunning the design of this place, the arkiteck must have been a interesting man.' His flattering looks travelled towards as many corners of the house as possible, quickly taking in the wealth of possessions in knowledgeable glances and coming finally to rest, in admiration, upon the woman herself.

'My husband designed the house,' she said.

'I knew it!' Hartley said, 'what a man!'

'Thank you,' Mr Scobie handed back the empty cup.

'The only thing is,' Hartley said when they were back in the car, 'she is so terribly big, terribly fat, I never saw such a fattie.' He shook his head. 'I mean a rich widow and all, I mean some men like 'em big, a rich widow but, as far as I'm concerned with a big disadvantage so to speak.' He nudged Mr Scobie with his elbow, 'Eh, eh? big disadvantage eh? How do you feel Nunks?'

'Why were you gone so long, Hartley?' Mr Scobie said. 'I thought you must have gone. I thought you were never coming back.'

'Me? Lost? Never! I was like you said casing the joint. I got a good sighting of what's needed.' Hartley passed his cigarette to Mr Scobie who said, refusing the cigarette, 'Oh Hartley I thought you'd given all that away.'

'Needs must Nunks,' Hartley laughed.

'I can't stand a fat woman Hartley,' Mr Scobie said when Hartley's mirth had subsided. 'That's part of my uneasiness at St Christopher and St Jude. Sitting on that verandah I am surrounded, surrounded Hartley, literally, by fat old women. Matron Price and Mrs Rawlings, too, they're so big. Enormous. I must get away.'

'My real trouble,' Hartley interrupted, 'my real trouble is, I still love Sybil, that's my trouble. Love.'

'It can't be Spiritual Love Hartley,' Mr Scobie said. 'Forget her. Put her out of your mind.'

On reaching the hospital Hartley accompanied Mr Scobie, helping him up the uneven steps to the front door and along to his room. Mr Scobie's lunch was on a tin tray in the middle of his bed.

'Mawnin' all,' Hartley said cheerfully to the empty beds.

'The other two will both be in the dinette,' Mr Scobie said, 'the meal is usually served there at half-past eleven. Mrs Rawlings helps Mr Hughes.'

'Mmm! Smells good,' Hartley eyed the greenish plate. 'That'll be good for a growing boy,' he said looking away from the plate quickly. 'Look Nunky, I'm sorry I don't get round here very often, truth is I've a lot on my mind,' he whistled and winked and whistled again, following the whistle with a throaty growl, as the long legs and boyish hips of Frankie flashed by. She was racing to bring in the trays. 'It's the Fair Sex Nunky. They don't give a man no peace. But I tell you what Nunks, I'll keep my eyes peeled for a piyade ah Turr, pardon my French, for you. I'll be back. So long. Be good. Keep well. Orrivoire!'

After Hartley had gone Mr Scobie could not help thinking about the divorced woman, Sybil, and all the dreadful things she must be acquainted with in her life. He supposed she painted her face and went swimming without clothes.

He recalled an incident when he had suggested to Joan that she wash her face.

'Why ever Uncle?' Joan laughed full of surprise.

'Because it's not natural, all that red and black . . .'

'Uncle!' Joan interrupted him, 'if I wasn't bigger than you I'd slap your face. What I do with mine is my own business.'

He tried not to think about Joan. Quite recently he had read a paragraph in the newspaper about a mixed bathing party. He knew, without reading to the end, that all the guests had been naked.

He thought he saw something in his soup, something white floating in the thick lentil soup. He carried his tray carefully to the kitchen.

'I think the lentils must be infected,' he said to Mrs Rawlings and the cook.

'Aw what a shame! What 'ave they got the pore things, measles?' The cook nearly burst, she laughed so much. Mrs Rawlings took the dish and scooped out the dead maggot.

'It's only the one,' she said to Mr Scobie. 'Now how would you like to sit in the dinette to finish your lunch,' she said. 'I'll bring your lemon sago in there.'

'Tell me something about yourself Mr Privett.' The young social worker, on her second field-work assignment, sat down by his bed.

'Yo've got very nice legs my dear,' Mr Privett said. 'Are these your legs?' He gave the social worker's neat thigh a little pat. He would have liked to pinch her. He knew women always enjoyed being pinched, but this one, she was all sewn up in sail cloth or something very like it. Very smooth and quite unyielding.

'These are your legs I suppose?' he asked squinting up at her with a quick sideways turn of his head. Miss Rosemary Whyte thought he looked positively wicked and quickly she turned to the next bed.

There was so little room between the beds, it was not a question of moving, simply she had to twist round in her chair. She wished the old men were in separate rooms. Better still if they were young men, but then, she supposed, sensibly, they would hardly need to be interviewed.

Mr Hughes told her in his pleasant sing-song voice that he had been a coal miner in South Wales many years ago and that he had come out to Australia as a young man to take up farming.

'I got my own farm after a time,' he said, 'and quite soon after that I got my wife. She was one of seven sisters on the next property. There were dances every week in those days and that's how I met her.' He explained that, later, when his family were grown up he sold the farm and lived in town finishing up with his own carting business.

'My truck was too big for the shed,' he said with his little laugh. 'I used to have to take the doors off the shed to get her in there and then put the doors back up in front of the shed. I daresay the shed's still there,' he said. 'My wife died,' he explained, 'quite sudden it was. We were at Sunday roast dinner at Keppie's place. After dinner Sarah said she would lie down for a while. She went into the front parlour, right

92

on the street it was, but cream lace curtains, beautiful curtains, for privacy, you know.' An hour or so later he said, when they went in there to take her a cup of tea, they found she had died in her sleep with the quiet, front room, best furniture all round her and the photographs of all the family looking at her from the mantelpiece.

'She was tranquil and beautiful in death as if all care and sorrow were wiped away,' Mr Hughes said. 'All the sisters wanted to look after me when I had the stroke the very next night but they're all very small women and, as you see, I'm very tall. I'm helpless,' he said apologetically. 'I did not value my wife enough while she was alive,' he added after a pause.

Miss Whyte nodded. She was not sure what to say. She wanted to ask him, she was supposed to, a few questions about his financial state. But, how could she mention money straight after his last remark. Awkwardly she thanked him and moved herself round further.

'Mr Scobie?' she questioned, showing her pretty white teeth. 'I see you like music Mr Scobie,' she said with her accustomed brightness, noticing the cassette player and the little stack of cassettes. She picked up a few cassettes and studied them to show how friendly she was. Mr Scobie was eager to talk to her.

' "Mind how you go out of the door Martin Scobie," my school teacher called to me. You see, dear, in those days we were poor people and the school teacher, Miss Joseph, knew this. On wet days, because I had no coat, she would call, "Martin Scobie come out here." And she would have me stand over near the fire-place. I'll never forget the wonderful warmth while my clothes were drying.'

'Why did you have to be careful going out the door?' Miss Whyte asked forgetting that she was supposed to be asking him about medicines and pensions and any domestic arrangements which might be worrying him.

'Yes well,' Mr Scobie smiled and his light-blue eyes were shining with the happiness of his memory, 'you see dear, as I said, I came from a poor household. I longed to have an apple turnover like the other boys had. There was a shop near the school. All the children went there and I used to hang about the door wishing I had some money.

' "Mind how you go out of the door Martin Scobie," Miss Joseph called out to me. I was the last to leave as I had been putting the benches by the wall. I always tidied up for Miss Joseph. She was like a beautiful queen. I did not know what she meant, you see, dear, but as I went through the door I saw four pennies placed in a line on the floor. So that was what Miss Joseph meant. She had put the fourpence there so that I could buy an apple turnover for the next four days.' Mr Scobie smiled again at his visitor. 'The apple turnovers,' he said, 'were the best I ever tasted, crisp golden pastry, they don't make them like that now, and each one was filled to bursting with sweet syrup and apples and raisins. You should just have seen those raisins and with . . .'

Miss White surreptitiously looked at her reliable wrist-watch. No wonder she was exhausted, it was practically lunch time. The old people, she knew, lunched soon after eleven. Matron Price had explained that the early lunch enabled the girls to get the trays in early and everything cleared up.

'I'll come back when you have had your nap,' Miss Whyte said inspired suddenly with a method of escape. She rose quickly.

'Yes, of course,' Mr Scobie said, he tried to stand up too, out of politeness, but there was not enough room. He plucked at her sleeve.

'Dear,' he said, 'can you possibly get me away from this place? Please.'

'Perhaps we can talk about that next time.' Miss Whyte made a note on her file 'Mr S. wants to leave.' 'I'll be back in about four weeks,' she said. 'We have two weeks swot vac and then,' she made a face, 'and then exams and after that . . .' she backed out of the room and hurried to the front door.

Thank goodness she had mother's car today. She was famished.

Mr Scobie put on some Mozart. He turned the volume down. As he listened to the soft music he began to think of Lina.

Sometimes Lina asked him to play the piano so that she could sit and listen to the piece in all its perfection. They had to change over seats. Mr Scobie sat on the little velvet-covered stool and while he played Lina sat in his chair with her clean pretty hands folded in her lap. He played well, feeling her attention and admiration.

The house, in those days, was always quiet. The rooms were large and tranquil, polished and illuminated with pools of coloured sunshine. There were blue and green and red glass ornaments and splendid light fittings, heavy brass fire irons and candle sticks and whole sideboards shining with Georgian silver and expensive china. The room where the piano was was not very large. Folding doors led into a more spacious room. Sometimes Lina's mother sat behind the doors listening to her daughter's progress.

Mr Scobie always tried his best with all his pupils, but he loved teaching Lina. Next to the piano he loved Lina best.

Sometimes Lina's mother was not at home. She went out in the mornings to drink tea, elegantly, with other rich ladies, friends of hers.

'What do you do in the evenings Mr Scobie?' Lina always wanted to know. 'What is your house like?' 'Do you live by

yourself?' 'Tell me about your house Mr Scobie.' Was he
in love, Lina wanted to know. Had he ever loved anyone?
Did he love someone now?

When Mr Scobie looked at Lina as she asked her questions he felt he knew the true meaning of and the answer
to her questions.

'Yes.' He answered 'Yes' to all the questions and felt his
answers to be both honest and pure.

'Have you any Holy Pictures Mr Scobie?'

'Yes I have Lina, and I have brought them for you as I
promised. Do you like Holy Pictures Lina?'

Lina clasped her hands together. Oh yes she did like
them. And she had some too. They were up in her mother's
bedroom, under the mattress.

Lina led the way upstairs. Mr Scobie walked up behind
her short swaying body. The warm sweet perfume which
he thought must belong to Jewish girls of a certain class
overwhelmed him. He hardly knew where he was going, the
perfume and the brilliant sunshine pouring through a window on that side of the house dazzled him.

'It doesn't matter now, Lina,' he said. He was a young man
then, uneasy and inexperienced, he often told himself in
later years as he went over, in his mind, the events of that
morning.

The secret places of the upstairs part of the house frightened him.

'Show them to me some other time,' he said to Lina. She
laughed and laughed and rolled on the big smooth bed and
told him to get up on the bed and help her to find the picture.

'I want you to explain this one to me,' she said. She was
kneeling on the bed and he thought she was trying to turn
up the mattress to find the holy pictures. He bent down to
help her and Lina pulled him down so that they were suddenly in an intimate position on the edge of her own

mother's bed in the mysterious woman's room, in an atmosphere of silk and lace underwear. It was a place, even though he was grown up, he had no knowledge of and had never dreamed of entering.

He felt Lina's heart beating hard and was reminded of some small animal or a trapped bird. He felt the warmth of her body under the slippery silky things. He was frightened of her and sorry for her. He did not know what he should do in her soft eager embrace.

'Kiss me,' Lina said. 'This is the one I like best.' She pushed the picture towards him with one hand, while with the other hand she pulled him closer.

It was a picture of a woman with long golden red hair. She was reclining on a sofa. Her indolent body was naked, covered in places by the long hair.

'This is the one I like best,' Lina said. 'You must like it too, Mr Scobie. Now kiss me. Hard. Harder.' She pulled him and held him with her strong childish arms and legs.

Mr Scobie tried not to think of the next part. It was still as vivid as if it had been that morning.

The housekeeper, Lina's mother's housekeeper, Fräulein Recha, must have been coming up the stairs for she entered the room then saying, 'What are you doing in here!' in such a terrible voice.

For years it had meant a great deal for him to go to that house. He was happy there always, teaching Lina. When her mother was pleased with her progress that was his ultimate reward.

All his life he remembered and thought about the unkind letter he had received from Lina's mother telling him never to come to the house again. He did not have a chance to explain about the holy pictures. He never saw Lina again.

Often when he sat alone he tried to put into words an explanation to give to Lina's mother, that he had not meant any harm to Lina, none at all, that he had no idea how the naked red-haired lady's picture came to be there at all.

Mr Scobie supposed it was the weakness from his recent illness which made him weep when he listened to the music. He had not meant to listen to anything painful or sad. Simply the music was to be for pleasure. He dried his tears on a clean folded handkerchief.

The music was meant to recall, and he was making the effort, the fullness of a choppy sea, the restless blue-green changing surfaces gleaming in the twilight, a full running and rising sea, slapping and chopping against ageless piers and sea walls. It was meant to bring back too the excitement of being at the edge of an ocean, of being in that place where land and sea meet with exquisite colours and an extraordinary vitality of movement and sound.

The music was meant to recall too the little churches with steeples and onion spires, and wayside shrines, decorated with offerings of fruit and flowers and grain, guarding the curves of the mountain paths.

Contained and stored in the music were fountains spilling water over worn steps, and noble grey buildings, their heights shrouded in early morning European mists.

His thought was then, being in the presence of all which was ancient, immense and measureless, that he would preserve images of rapture somewhere inside him for those times ahead when he would need to be comforted.

Now in Room One in the hospital of St Christopher and St Jude the only memories existing for him were the sad and painful. He could not recall anything from those treasures he once thought he was putting away safely for later.

He glanced at the other two beds. Mr Hughes seemed to be asleep. It was hard to know whether Mr Privett was asleep. He lay on his bed with both eyes screwed up like a child pretending to be asleep. Mr Scobie often felt that Mr Privett squinted at him through half-closed lids.

'Oh don't turn off that glorious Mozart,' Miss Hailey's

voice came round the door. 'Horns really do something for me.' She held out her long-fingered hands to protest. 'Do not turn it off,' she said. 'Where I ask you, in this spiritual wilderness, is there any hope of salvation but in this music of yours? Do you know,' she stroked the door post, 'that for years I have been starved, yes starved? I mean, of course, culture starvation.' She held up both arms and thrust one leg forward and declaimed,

> Until you came there was no music
> or rather
> until you came or rather
> until thou camest no bird sang –
> Music. A portrait in sound!

Miss Hailey laughed. Either she did not notice Mr Scobie's recent tears or she chose to pretend not to see them. 'This Mozart', she continued, 'has a vitality. There is an emotional radiance of love in the music, in the actual music I mean. All right let's face it – you have the scene, for example, between Don Giovanni and the peasant girl, it is not the singing of the words '*Vorrei, e non vorrei mi trema un poco il cor . . .*' lovely though they are. It's not just the words, it isn't the plot or the fact that the Don has, in spite of his boasting, lost his amorous powers. It's what Mozart has put into the music.' Miss Hailey sighed and gathered her long black hair in two sweeps across her breast. She held her hair thus with both hands, a rather dramatic pose, she thought, indulging herself a little. 'It is this radiance in the music which stirs deep pools within the human being,' she said. 'It might, for example, make me offer a tenderness in an unlikely place and cause no end of trouble. By becoming involved and unable to escape involvement I might even cause Hyacinth, I mean Matron, to lose a valuable member of her staff. Staff is so difficult to come by these days,' Miss Hailey sighed again, 'especially the young ones.' She looked at Mr Scobie earnestly. 'One cannot be too careful,' she said, and gathering her hair in two handfuls she conveyed it to the top of her head holding it bunched; her large dark eyes peered through the long black strands.

Frankie and Robyn, on a bed-making spree, danced disco fashion down the hall.

'It could,' Miss Hailey said after watching the two girls disappear into Room Three, 'it could be simply a post-menopausal madness if I set off in pursuit of those two girls not giving a hoot about the consequences.' She laughed, a deep boom of sound. 'Perhaps we should have the German Requiem instead,' she said, 'put on the Requiem. The holiness of the Brahms is purely intellectual. It is an intellectual and a spiritual tenderness,' she said, 'and surely that cannot harm anyone.' She paused and said, 'Those two girls will be bringing the afternoon tea round any minute. You'd like a nice cup of tea wouldn't you.'

'I'm not allowed to have it,' Mr Scobie said.

'Rubbish,' said Miss Hailey.

Come on Come on
Turn me on
Tip me Flip me
Turn me on
Holla Rocka baby Huh!

Robyn and Frankie danced along the passage from the kitchen to the rooms. One step – two steps – forward step – one step – back step – forward two – back one

Tip me Flip me

'Here's your tea Mrs Murphy.'

'Here's your tea Mrs Renfrew.'

'Here's your tea Miss Nunne.'

'Here's your tea Mrs Morgan.'

'Here's your tea Mrs Tompkins.'

'Miss Hailey, here's your tea, MISS HAILEY HERE'S YOUR TEA.'

Flip me Tip me
Turn me on

'Here's your tea, Mr Hughes, Mr Privett here's your tea . . .'

One step   two step   kick step shake
One step   two step   kick step

'Mr Scobie, no tea, Robslob Matron said *NO TEA* for Scobie.'

'Rubbish!' Miss Hailey said, 'I'll get a cup, he can have half mine. By the way,' she smiled at Frankie and Robyn, 'that's a very beautiful dance. Where did you learn it or did you, by any chance, do the choreography yourselves?' She gave Mr Scobie her tea and watched him drink it gratefully.

'We'll have to watch Hailey,' Frankie nudged Robyn.

'Why? So? Why? For?'

'Well didn't you see just now. She's after you.'

'Aw Shit. Come off it. Why me?'

'Yeah! Yeah! Yeah!'

'Yeah? Aw. Yeah!'

'That's why Miami left,' Frankie nodded and rolled a cigarette. 'Here have a drag.'

'Thanks! How so Miami? Who's Miami?'

'Girl who was here before youse.'

'Geez! Why she leave then?'

'Things.'

'Aw come on. Gerroff. What things? I mean. Shit!'

'Nah. 'strue. Miami lived in the caravan and one night Hailey hid in there.'

'Geez. An' what happened?'

'Aw. Things.'

'Geez. I'd a been scared to death.'

'Me too! Hey. Get the cups in. Right?'

'Right. Yeah.'

Come on Come on
You turn me on
Tip me Flip me
Flip me Tip
Huh Huh Huh
Yair Yair Rocka hoola Yair Yair Yair

The cups crashed on to the tin trays crashing on into the sink. Frankie turned on the hot tap.

'What she do to Miami then?' Robyn asked.

'Huh Huh Huh'

'What she do to Miami then?'

'Nuthin' 'swhat she tried to do. That's why Miami left. See. Matron went mad.'

'Yeah. She still is.'

'I don't get it.'

'Aw never mind I wuz being schmart.'

'Apparently Hailey was a teacher once?'

'A Headmistress.'

'Yeah, well – Teach or Head. She got tipped out.'

'For the same reason?'

'Yeah s'pose.'

'Funny old bag. I quite like her but.'

'Well there y'are. See? She'll get you next.'

'Yeah? Oh yeah?'

One morning when Mr Hughes was sitting on the verandah he felt ill. He thought it was the Epsom salts working. He told Mrs Rawlings and she helped him out of his chair. Slowly they went indoors.

'For many years,' Miss Hailey confided, she was sitting in the chair next to Mr Scobie, 'for many years I was in love with one of my characters and then in time I came to love her, not in love with her any longer you understand, simply I loved her. There is a difference, you know, between being in love and loving, and now, of course, we have settled into an easy rhythm, a comfortable rhythm. I feel I know her so well, d'you see, and obviously she must know me after all this time.' She laughed somewhere down inside her chest. 'All our little idiosyncratics, I made up that word, it just suits us, are known to us both. Do you know,' she lowered her deep voice to a theatrical whisper, 'she likes to sleep raw, you know, in the nuddy to use young Frankie's word, very naughty isn't she, my character I mean. It's all explored thoroughly, pages three hundred to three hundred and seventy-five. Have you, by any chance finished my ms yet?' She gave the pom-poms on her bedroom slippers a coy look. She was clutching her sponge bag and towel still, having missed her turn in the shower earlier.

'Oh, I beg your pardon. Excuse me,' Mr Scobie rose to a half-standing position. 'I must, er, take a little walk.'

'Oh, yes of course,' Miss Hailey smiled. 'Don't mind me, I'm waiting for the Lt Col. to finish in the bathroom. The only thing is,' she paused and said in as delicate a way as she could, 'I think Mr Hughes has just gone indoors to the . . .'

'No. No,' Mr Scobie said, 'I usually take a little walk at this time of the day. In the street.'

'Ah! Freedom. Enjoy! Enjoy!' Miss Hailey waved her shameless sponge bag. 'I shall see you anon.'

Mr Hughes collapsed in the hall. The doctor was sent for and an ambulance and Keppie.

'Who gave Mr Hughes his Epsom Salts this morning?' Matron Price asked in a loud voice all over St Christopher and St Jude. 'In future,' she called out for the whole hospital to hear, 'no Epsom Salts are to be administered to patients except by me.' She went to the front door to look for the ambulance. It was her policy, as far as possible, in the event of collapse, to send patients away to the City and District Hospital as quickly as she could.

Keppie and the sisters-in-law came as soon as they were sent for but Mr Hughes was, by that time, already on his way to the hopital.

On the way to the hospital he listened to the bricks talking softly, whispering and muttering and chattering to themselves. So many bricks, clean and new and useful. They fidgeted and squeaked and laughed in little voices. As he listened to them he was reminded of his wife and her sisters, six sisters-in-law and how they would all gather in the kitchen or the bedroom or by the garden gate to talk and laugh, tell each other things and show things to each other. He thought he could hear them, all the time, talking talking talking.

N.A. to report. All pats. play cards in dinette. Message from Mrs Morgan Mr Boxer Morgan and Mr Rob Shady *'Cough up Matron Price or else'* its on account of Lt Col. (retired) Matron.

And Matron Mr Hughes did not come in. I thought you should know I did not even know he was out.

Signed Night Sister M. Shady (unregistered)

Missis Shady: Don't you ever read my day report? If you turn back one page you will see that it states quite clearly that Mr Hughes collapsed at 10 a.m. and was taken immediately to the City and Ditrict Hospital where he was dead on arrival. D.O.A.

Signed Matron H. Price

```
FOR SALE

1 old mans body with rare and
interesting condition only person
with established interest need
apply price reasonable
will deliver no dealers
```

Mr Privett knew that an advertisement carried disadvantages. All at once a person's privacy is invaded and threatened. It is not possible to have an advertisement without everyone knowing about it.

Mr Privett was looking for an immediate sale. He looked beyond the sale to having a small place of his own once more. He was quite agreeable to having something small.

There were only two people in Room One now. Mr Privett, Matron said, had a chill and must be kept in bed. His clothes were packed away on the bathroom shelf.

Mr Privett, surviving the slippery bars of soap on the shower-room floor and flushing Lilian's poisoned cake down the toilet, enjoyed the memory of Matron Price and Mrs Rawlings spending a morning trying to clear the drains. It was after this he had been put to bed.

'It's lucky, Dad, that you couldn't come for that drive,' his son, Jack, visiting, said. 'Would you believe! I crashed the car. Not too bad. A prang on the left side. You'd have copped the lot except you was here in bed. You're a wise one, Dad. You're best where you are – in bed.'

Mr Privett cackled till he nearly choked. He knocked over his water jug and, getting out of bed, he trod in his chamber pot upsetting it. He sang to the memory of the vanished Hep Duck and Hildegarde the Meat.

HEP DUCK DUCKY DUCK
HEP HEP HEP
HILDEGARDE THE MEAT

'You can't live on nothing,' he said to the duck and the fowl, 'that's what the ad is for. I'll make 'em pay in advance . . .'

'What exactly is your interesting condition?' The visitor, a stranger in a dark suit, pulled the chair to the old man's bed and sat down.

Mr Privett realized he must have fallen asleep over his tray of cold meat. He roused himself and saw, with pleasure that his beetroot was spilled on the counterpane.

'Oh? Yo' must have come about my advert?'

'I have,' said the stranger. 'I'll come straight to the point. I have a place down by the harbour. Everything goes on there, it's only a matter of turning off at the right place . . .'

'I said no dealers,' Mr Privett interrupted.

'I'm not a dealer.'

'Yo' a collector then? A collector of some sort?' Mr Privett asked.

'I suppose that's what you'd call me,' the stranger replied, 'though there's not much that's really rare.' He coughed. 'I do have some very old ones,' he said, 'antiques they are really. And I have plenty of damaged and broken.' He paused. 'Quite badly damaged really.' He sighed. 'Then there are the ordinary things you know, injections, medication, crutches, remedial surgery, emergency surgery, fat-free diets and . . .'

'Ruptures,' Mr Privett sat up, 'gall stones, valuable gems from gall. I don't think I've got any.' He pressed his side. 'Nothing rattles and nothing hurts,' he said.

'Yes, that sort of thing,' the visitor said, ' and then there are those that follow the path which no fowl knows and which the vulture's eye has not seen.'

'I don't know what yo' mean.'

'It's just an ancient and a rather poetical way of describing a not very rare condition. I mean, you have not thought of naming it yourself?' The visitor, with care, brushed a few specks from his dark suit.

'No, to tell yo' the truth, I was hopin' summat would turn up.'

The visitor smiled. 'Lie down and have a rest,' he said, 'there is nothing quite like a long sleep.'

The wood was not at all hard on his bones. Old Privett was surprisingly comfortable. It was like being in a wooden cradle. The gentle swaying, the result of four men walking in step, was restful. There was music too.

    HEP DUCK RATTLE TAP TAP HEP HEPPY DUCK
    HEP DUCK SHAKE DUCK RATTLE AND ROLL DUCK
    HEP HEP HEP DUCK
    HEAR THAT HILDEGARDE
    MIND YOUR MANNERS MEAT BIRD
    HEP DUCK HEP HILDEGARDE THE MEAT
    COME DOWN OFF THEM RAFTERS

The road to the harbour was long and straight. The sun was near the horizon. A few people, keeping their eyes on the bright ball of the sun, were able to see the miraculous flash of green explode into the sky and the sea at the moment of sunset.

Miss Rosemary Whyte, her mind on Christmas shopping rather than her social work studies, thought, as she was passing St Christopher and St Jude, that she knew the old folk well enough now to slip in quickly and wish them all a merry Christmas. It was still a little early for spoken wishes but she thought she would have less time later on.

She entered Room One with a cheerful, 'Hallo! Hallo! Everybody! I'm sure you remember me.' She came upon a stillness with which she was not previously acquainted. The stillness was something not given in lectures and it did not occur in examination questions either.

There was only one of the old men in the room and he was in bed. He looked tranquil. Very small like a child asleep except that his soft hair, decorating his head in wisps, was white. There was no movement of response to her cheery greeting. She stood for a moment inside the door and then, clutching her file to her embroidered breast, she darted along the passage and out of the front door, Doctors and Visitors Only.

Thank goodness she had Mummy's car. She would go straight home. It was all so unexpected. Really it was all too much.

NOTICE

To disinfect a bed after a
patient has left take a bowl
of hot water with ten per cent
lysol and a cloth and wash down

                              Matron

'Your urine has ruined one of Matron's best bedside rugs.'
Mrs Rawlings, breathing heavily, finished mopping the
floor.

'But it's not mine. I was out with my niece Joan this afternoon. It must be Mr Privett. Mr Privett must have, by accident of course, upset his . . .'

'Mr Scobie, we do not speak ill of those who have passed
on,' Mrs Rawlings said, 'and certainly not an evil accu-
sation.'

'But it's not evil, Mrs Rawlings. And Mr Privett will be
in heavenly peace at last. He is to be envied by all of us.'
Mr Scobie stood up.

'*For here we have no continuing city, but we seek one to come.*'
Epistle to the Hebrews, Mrs Rawlings, chapter thirteen
verse fourteen, *For here we have no continuing city* . . . I can play
the music for you. Beautiful music.' Mr Scobie's voice
trembled.

'Oh you and your Bible rubbish,' Mrs Rawlings said, her
mouth set in a thin line. She picked up her mop and bucket
and marched out of the room saying, 'I've no time for music.
There's something about your urine, Mr Scobie, that would
ruin everything it came in contact with.'

It was the day of his needle and he went often down the
passage to the toilet. As he passed the kitchen he was sure
he could hear Mrs Rawlings and the cook complaining
about him. Later on, he thought, he would take a little walk.
He would have to wait for the effect of the injection to wear
off. There were so many worrying things. For one thing,
Matron wanted to take him out in the morning; she had not
given up the idea of helping him with his financial affairs.
She was always talking about her idea.

'The Nursing Home account is the safest Mr Scobie dear
and we shall be able to see that you are completely settled
for the rest of your life.'

He returned to Room One and sat on the side of his bed.

He had the room to himself now. There was a chill about the room perhaps because of being overcrowded before. He wondered when Hartley would be coming. It was nearly Christmas and there had been no visit from him.

He could hear the voices of the doves outside. To and fro they spoke to each other. He liked to hear the doves even though he knew they had no mercy and were cruel like every other living creature is cruel when the need arises. He liked to hear them questioning and answering. He liked too to see them catching the jewelled light from the sun. The warm colour seemed to be burnished along their pleated feathers as they sat one by the other alongside and opposite, above and below, covering all the branches of a dead tree.

The sound of doves was all about the woodyard; he remembered the place where he went as a little boy with his father. His father liked the clean smell of the place. He said so. The red wood was cut and stacked in an orderly way which made the place peaceful. There were Moreton Bay fig trees between the yard and the road. It was like being in another world behind these trees. The ground was special too, soft and springing with the red chips and the wood dust. The yard was always clean and glowing, lit entirely from within by the red colour of the wood. They always went there after work and there would be no one there at all except the old man in the little hut beside the weighbridge.

'Collect a box of kindling,' his father said every time.

Later at home his mother brushed his sister's long fair hair.

'Are you an angel Agnes?' he asked her.

'Of course I am,' she said, and laughed.

At his place in Rosewood East the mornings unfolded cold and damp in the winter and a white mist hung in the pines along the side of his house. However wealthy he had become or how much he had travelled during his life, the small house on his own land mattered more to him than concert platforms and applause. He remembered, with a smile, his dog, Peter, and how he always looked for a place in the sun to be warm. In the mornings there was not much warmth in the sun but he always chose the best place.

'How did Joan?'

'Joan? I beg your pardon?' Mr Scobie, sitting alone on the edge of his bed, recognized Miss Hailey's voice. She was at the door of Room One.

'How was your outing with your niece, Joan?'

'Oh yes, that,' Mr Scobie said, trying to recollect recent events. 'I can't think what is the matter with Joan. You know, I simply suggested that she ought, at her time of life – she's no longer young, you see, I simply suggested that she ought, at her time of life, to give up running after that artist fellow, what's his name, he calls himself an artist but to my mind he can't paint at all – just dabs the paint and makes a mess!' Mr Scobie shook his head, frowning. 'I told her, this afternoon, she ought to get herself a nice clean little job in Woolworths and leave that worthless fellow alone. "He must be twice your age," I told her.

' "Uncle," she said to me, "just how old d'you think I am? You're impossible!" and she burst out crying and turned the car right in the middle of The Terrace where turning's not allowed, and she brought me straight back here. So you see,' he added, 'I haven't really had any outing.'

'Splendid!' Miss Hailey boomed. 'I'd like to use that if you have no objection.'

'What do you mean?'

'In my novel, of course, I'd like to use it in my novel. It would mean considerable rewriting, you know – implication, hint, suggestion, even a touch of authorial intrusion – all would have to be taken up at various points. Ah!' she put her hands up to her head. 'The endless rewriting, the linking of events, the approach to drama, the dramatic moment and the resolution. But,' she paused as if at a dramatic moment in her own life, 'it is so rewarding, the rewriting, the choosing of *le mot juste, la petite phrase*. You're absooty sure you don't mind?'

Mr Scobie replied, in spite of some uneasiness, that he did not mind.

'Oh Goody Goody Gum Drops!' Miss Hailey performed a little dance in the doorway and disappeared twirling, without grace, down the hall towards Room Three.

One morning, a few days later, Mr Scobie, reassured by the discovery of a little money carelessly overlooked by Mrs Rawlings in the inside pocket of his suit, set off for his daily walk. It was his idea to walk up The Terrace where Joan had so wildly breached traffic regulations and, from there, he would walk on to the station. There he would simply buy a ticket to Rosewood East. He could not think how he had not thought of this simple plan before.

He set off with a light heart.

'Plenty of little walks Mr Scobie,' the doctor said every time he came. 'Plenty of rest and plenty of little walks.'

Mr Scobie supposed he had walked more than the doctor ever would walk.

'Oh wait! Wait for me!' he recognized the familiar voice. Miss Hailey, with an enormous lilac shawl thrown over her gown, came loping along the pavement behind him, the pink tassles on her slippers dancing madly.

'I should so like to take a walk,' she said, struggling for breath, 'I mean, to take one with you.'

'I was thinking of going a long way,' Mr Scobie said hurrying forward. The suburban street, empty and quiet, offered no distraction and no one had come running after Miss Hailey to take her back to St Christopher and St Jude.

They walked together in silence. At the end of the street, Mr Scobie turned off into a small park; not only was it a short cut to The Terrace but it provided a certain convenience for him. His injection, he found, was still active and he was more than glad to see the welcome black and white sign beyond, half hidden in some trees.

'Excuse me,' he muttered.

'Oh but of course.' Miss Hailey, in her alert way, was quick to understand. 'Go ahead. I'll wait . . . down there on the grassy slope,' she said.

She stood with her back to the square red-brick building. She tried to look unconcerned. In her deep voice she hummed the Senta theme from *The Flying Dutchman*. 'Ah! Wagner!' she said aloud, her voice reaching over the grass to astonished shopping ladies who paused under their parasols resting on laden or unladen shopping trolleys, depending on the direction they were facing. Miss Hailey sang a little louder. She would have liked to simulate the storm. It was there in her head but it was not possible to know how it would emerge. 'The voice you know,' Miss Hailey said, more than half to herself, 'at my age, not only is it entirely unpredictable but it lacks power. In any case,' she warmed to her subject, 'a Wagnerian Storm requires full orchestration so what can the humble voice do?' She tried the horns and produced a sound so remarkable she became more ambitious. 'I wonder,' she said, 'I wonder if I could recall the electrifying ride of the Valkeries, a different opera of course.' Self conscious suddenly, as more people were passing, she lowered her singing by an octave, left the

115

Valkeries to continue their aerial flight unaided and returned to the condemned Dutchman. Singing under her breath, she produced sounds quite unlike anything within the range of human possibility.

Meanwhile Mr Scobie had slipped from the cavern of the men's toilet and, behind his companion's innocent back, was heading towards the railway station, unobtrusively fastening himself in front. He did not look behind to see if he was being followed.

Miss Hailey waited, singing for several hours. Occasionally she wondered if Mr Scobie was all right. Somewhat perplexed but with excellent manners she continued to sing outside the men's toilet. Sometimes she paced up and down keeping her balance admirably on the grassy slope. Mr Scobie, she told herself, would come out in his own good time.

ROOM ONE very quiet all night.

ROOM THREE voided sponged slept well. Mrs Tompkins bath 10 p.m. also hot milk veggies and kitchen floor.

Miss Hailey came in 4 a.m. All pats. play cards in dinette. Lt Col. Price (retired) lose bad.

  N.A. to report signed Night Sister M. Shady (unregistered)

Missis Shady: What do you mean N.A. to report. Of course room one was very quiet. Mr Hughes and Mr Privett have passed away and Mr Scobie spent the night in the police station lock-up. Don't you ever look in the rooms? And Missis Shady where is Miss Hailey's good night dress and where is her lilac shawl? I do have the good name of this hospital to consider.   *Signed Matron H. Price*

DECEMBER 22 NIGHT SISTER'S REPORT

All pats. play cards in dinette. N.A. to report. Please matron the milkman wants his grey blanket back. He used it to wrap round Miss Hailey when he found her sunbaking in the park at 4 a.m.

          Signed N/S M. Shady (unregist.)

Mr Scobie knew he should have as much rest as he could. He understood completely that he had been very ill before being taken to the general hospital. Since then, though, he had had more than enough of the convalescence offered by St Christopher and St Jude. He resolved to rest, to save his energy and to get away as soon as he could.

'I am so well now,' he told Mrs Rawlings. 'I feel I could walk for miles and miles, slowly, of course, but miles and miles just the same.'

'It's kilometres now,' Mrs Rawlings said, without a smile, 'and it's the verandah for you this morning. Matron wants you to see the doctor, so no walks this morning.' Mrs Rawlings turned Mr Scobie round in the hall and pointed to the door. 'Don't just stand there, Mr Scobie,' she said, 'go and sit on the verandah with the others like I'm telling you to.'

'Don't you like to hear the doves,' Mr Scobie said to Matron when she came round. He thought he ought to say something soothing. Noises from the kitchen had disturbed the whole hospital. There had been a terrible shouting which increased dramatically whenever the door was opened; and the door was opened frequently, it seemed, so that it could be slammed with a fierce bang. Every time the kitchen door was slammed, plaster, a fine dust and some quite large flakes, fell in Room One. The cook's voice, a raucous hooter, was raised as usual refusing to bake apples for the patients.

'I haven't got time to stand on everybody's individual cooking,' she bawled. What did they all think the place was, she wanted to know, the Ritz? And what did they think she was anyway, some kind of paragon? 'They can stuff themselves,' she shouted, 'and bake their own fuckin' apples.'

Mr Scobie felt he must help Matron Price to feel better.

'Can you hear the peaceful doves?' he asked again. He smiled at her in spite of his nerves after a very strange and difficult night and in spite of the impending visit from the doctor.

'Oh you and your doves!' Matron said. 'Don't you know that doves are cruel birds. If you put doves together in a cage they will peck each other to death.' Matron turned away to go to Miss Nunne.

'Frankie!' she called, 'where are Miss Nunne's teeth?'

Mr Scobie knew about doves. He thought he could make up a riddle. 'What do human beings do, what is it human beings do?' he began, he was thinking of adding a part about cages and doves but Matron, pinning up Miss Nunne's fallen hair, turned back quickly.

'That's enough Mr Scobie. We don't want anything disgusting,' she said.

The doctor stepped out onto the verandah and Matron said, 'Oh, excuse me! I must just get the medicine list.'

'Doctor,' Mr Scobie said, taking advantage, 'Doctor, I do so much want to go home to Rosewood East. Do you know the place? Would it be all right for me to leave and go back there?'

'Of course, of course, old chap. Anything you feel able to do you can do. He's as fit as a fiddle eh? Matron?' Dr Risley, in a playful way, thumped Mr Scobie on the chest as Matron came hurrying back. Her good humour was merely facial. She put her hand on Mr Scobie's white head with more heaviness than kindness.

'Oh we all love dear Uncle Martin!' she said. 'He's so much better now, such a lot better. Just a teeny weeny ickle bit difficult at times. A naughty uncle!' In a lower voice, out of the side of her mouth Hyacinth Price said, 'I'll just have to speak to his niece, Miss Frost.' In a voice audible for both the doctor and Mr Scobie she said that she would have to tell Joan that it was necessary to increase the nursing home fees because certain of the old folk were making life very difficult for the nursing staff and because of this it was increasingly difficult for her to keep staff. 'So there it is in a nutshell they leave like ninepins going off in all directions,' Miss Price, not too certain of her metaphor, said.

'I see,' Doctor Risley, nodding his head, walked slowly along behind the row of wicker chairs. He listened to the complaints with patience.

When Matron returned from seeing Dr Risley to the gate, Mr Scobie, feeling he was in disgrace – even though he could explain that the night in the police lock-up was all a mistake – thought he would try again to divert Matron with a riddle. He had a different one forming in his mind. It would be appropriate, he felt, just now in connection with the passing on of Mr Hughes and Mr Privett. The riddle, he felt, could not be considered to be in bad taste, it was simply thought provoking. It might help Matron into a better mood.

'I'll ask you a riddle,' he said to her.

'Oh you and your riddles,' Matron Price said, 'go on then.'

'What is it that we all know is going to happen but we don't know when or how?' Mr Scobie, looking up from his round basket chair, could not refrain from smiling. He smiled from one ear to the other and his lightly veined cheeks bulged. It was exciting to ask a riddle. He almost gave the answer straight away.

'What is it that we all know is going to happen but we don't know when or how?' Matron mumbled as people do over riddles. She smiled along the verandah.

'Come along dears,' she said to the heaped-up old ladies. 'Frankie! Robyn!' she called, 'Robyn! push Miss Nunne's teeth back. No child, not like that, the other way round. There. That's better.' She smiled and mumbled the words of the riddle once more.

'Shall I tell?' Mr Scobie asked. 'Do you give up? Do you give it up?'

'Wait a minute,' Matron said, 'what is it that we all know is going to happen? . . . Oh,' she said, 'I give up.'

'Bend your ear down here then,' Mr Scobie said. 'I'll whisper the answer in your ear and then the others can go on thinking and waiting for the answer.'

Matron, obliging, bent down. Mr Scobie reached up his face towards her ear and whispered something. At once Matron straightened up, her face red.

'Frankie! Robyn!' she called, her voice rising to a scream. 'Come out here at once and take Mr Scobie to the shower and wash his hair.'

'But I've had my shower, Matron. I'm perfectly clean. All clean and correct,' Mr Scobie said, protesting, as the two girls seized him by the arms, one on either side, to help him up and take him indoors.

'Get him away as quick as you can,' Matron shouted. 'I don't want him out here, he'll only upset Mrs Renfrew and Miss Nunne. Look, Miss Nunne's crying already.' Matron Price bent over Miss Nunne's chair. 'There dear,' she said. 'There. There and there!'

Mr Scobie could not think how anyone could suggest that he would upset the old ladies when he sat by them for so long, so patiently, listening, every day, while they told him the same things, repeating themselves, over and over. Often he sat for hours trying not to notice their unpleasant smell, the saliva trickling from their partly open mouths and the food spilled on their clothes.

'The verandah is the best place these days,' he said, trying to make conversation with Frankie and Robyn in the dreary bathroom. The water had not drained away. He could see that he would have to stand in the dirty slimy water.

'I am not at all dirty, you know,' he said to Frankie.

'Aw come on. Get all of youse things off,' she said. He felt ridiculous getting undressed in front of these two girls, children they were really. And in the middle of the day too.

The girls had trouble with the hot water tap. It seemed impossible to adjust it. Mr Scobie stood waiting and shivering.

'Get a case and put his clothes away on one of these shelves.' Matron Price entered the room. 'I'll fix that tap,' she said taking off her shoe and giving the tap a number of sharp bangs. 'There we are! That'll be all right,' she said.

'Come on, Mr Scobie, into the shower with you,' Frankie said.

'Yes come on Mr Scobie,' Robyn said.

'But it's far too hot, dears,' he said. 'I'll be scalded. I have never seen so much hot water in my life before.'

Even Frankie could see it was too hot.

'Frankee! Don't let all my Good Hot water run to waste like that,' Matron shouted over the noise of the water.

'The tap won't turn off Matron. The steam's that thick I can't see for looking,' Robyn cried.

'Well, child, save some then. Quick! Fetch some basins and the kettle!' Matron could hardly contain her anger.

'The tap's too hot to hold. I'll have to wrap it in a towel. Drat and Drat!' Matron Price, a boiled purple shape in the steam, lifted her once proud cap from where it hung about her ears and neck. 'My precious, precious hot water,' she moaned. Soon jugs and basins were steaming in every corner.

'I'll have to rake the boiler out,' the cook threatened.

'What about the Christmas baking, but?' Frankie asked.

'Well. What about it?' snapped the cook scalding her foot in a shallow pan of hot water.

'Damn and Blast! Oh Shit! and Damn! Damn! Damn!' Matron's voice climbed even higher. 'Oh Lord! For God's sake! My Water!'

'*Thou shalt not take the Name of the Lord Thy God in vain,*'
Mr Scobie felt he must help in some way.

'Christ! Get him out of here!' Matron hissed. Mr Scobie,
realizing the emergency, the seriousness of the emergency,
persisted, '*For the Lord will not hold him Guiltless that taketh his
Name in Vain.* Exodus . . .' He paused. 'I think you will need
the plumber,' he said still trying to be helpful.

'Frankie, you too Robyn, take Mr Scobie and put him to
bed,' Matron said. 'He can have his tea in bed. It'll be one
less for Rawlings to see to after tea. Hurry now! Get him
out of here.'

Mr Scobie, sitting alone in bed in Room One, could hear
the banging and the shouting. He thought he could hear
them fighting, quite violently, certainly someone was weeping. It was clear there would be no hot water for some time
and no stove. There would be no hot meal, not even a warm
drink. He sat, missing his walk, on a fine afternoon, and
praying that he would never become bedridden in such a
place. He made up his mind that he would make more effort
to get back to Rosewood East before it was too late. Without
wanting to, he remembered Matron's promised outing. He
felt afraid. He did not want to go with her to settle his affairs
in the way, whatever it was, she had in mind for him.

He thought he would send a letter to Hartley. Perhaps,
if he wrote, Hartley would come again. He took the little
writing pad, Matron's gift, from the box where he kept his
Bible and the cassettes. It did not seem right to rest the pad
on the Bible so he held it as firmly as he could against one
knee.

'Dear nephew,' he wrote, 'dear Hartley I am writing this
from my bed. I am here "in distance and in sorrow". When

can you come again? I must leave this place. It is not suitable for me at all Hartley. Today I am being kept in bed for no reason whatsoever. I am quite fit. The doctor was here today and said that I could go home.'

His ornamental and old-fashioned writing began to cover the page.

'Two days ago,' he wrote, 'I made the attempt to take the train to Rosewood East. When I got to the station with enough money for a ticket (That is All the money I have) I found that there was a suburban railway strike. Though the man in the ticket office was most kind, he couldn't sell me a ticket if there was no train. I therefore set off on foot thinking to cover some ground and pick up a train at one of the stations further on, should the trains start again, which they would be sure to do some sort of agreement being in the offing (so the ticket-office man said). I walked along the railway, Hartley, it being a fine day and the path quite good and very peaceful, of course, with no trains. My Joy at going East towards my home, towards my Youth, so to speak, carried me forward and I did not feel in the least tired.

Who will look for me here I said to myself and on I went. Who will look for me on this path. Who has seen this path. Who can know where I am going I said to myself. If you look up Job chapter twenty-eight verse seven, dear Nephew, you will see at once what I mean. Darkness fell and I walked on and on beside the railway lines. These lines were my only companion and how I loved them. In the end I sat in a small waiting room. It was a very small wayside station, I don't know the name of it. I sat there to rest and I must have slept and this, Hartley, was my undoing for some people, a nice young man and a young lady found me and, thinking I was ill, fetched the police. I told them I was perfectly fit and they need not worry about me but they would not hear of leaving me alone there. At the police station everyone was very kind. The trouble was when they kept on questioning me. Where are you staying? they kept asking me. Where are you staying? Can you remember the name of the street where you live? Are you from a hospital? Can you remember the name of the hospital? I could not remember anything.

'And do you know Hartley the only thing I seemed to have in my mind was that lovely song, I wonder if you know it, the words of the poet Wilhelm Müller set to music by Franz Schubert, so often I have accompanied the singer on the pianoforte. I sang a little for them, though my voice and my ear are not at all what they used to be.

> *Fremd bin ich eingezogen,*
> *fremd zieh' ich wieder aus,*

which in English is,

> *A stranger came I hither*
> *A stranger I depart,*

and the next verse which starts on the purest tenor note, so beautiful,

> *Ich Kann zu meiner Reisen*
> *nicht Wählen mit der Zeit*
> > *I cannot for my journey*
> > *Choose the appointed time.*

'The song, Hartley, seemed so appropriate but it did not satisfy them at all. Not one bit. I said should I sing it again but they said not to and I was given some bread and butter and a cup of tea. There was a bed for me, they said, in a little room and they gave me two blankets. I was very glad of these because the night, after the hot day, was very chilly and I do feel the cold badly. The blankets were only lent to me you understand . . .'

Mr Scobie stopped writing to rest his hand and his bent

knee. He thought about the innocence of his riddle. It was only meant to be amusing. Thought provoking of course but mostly for amusement.

What is it that we all know is going to happen but we don't know when or how?

There was an excitement about riddles, about the asking of riddles. Sometimes the answers, even if wrong and unexpected, were interesting. He wished he had thought of asking the riddle in the police station, but he had been cold and tired then. Sitting in bed he smiled remembering the slices of delicious bread and butter and the hot tea . . .

'Mr Scobie,' Mrs Rawlings interrupted his thoughts as she came hurrying into the room, 'I've got to get you up again. Matron's decided she's got the time to take you up The Terrace. She's got an hour to spare and feels it would be best to get your affairs settled once and for all. It's only a matter of your signature on some papers, that's all.' She was out of breath, struggling to carry the case of clothes.

'I'll have to neaten these up,' she said shaking out his suit. She pounded the jacket and his head alternately with a clothes brush. Quickly she unbuttoned his pyjamas. 'Just take a look at your shoes,' she said. 'You put your trousers on while I go and rub up these dreadful shoes.'

'Mrs Rawlings, I am just writing to my nephew . . .'

'Never mind that now. We can't keep Matron waiting. Hurry up now, I'll be back.'

There was the sound of a familiar voice in the hall.

'Hallo there! Nunky. G'day. Long time no see.'

'Hartley! Oh Hartley you've come at last! Oh Hartley, Mrs Rawlings will be back in a minute. My shoes. Hartley I must get away from here. Matron's going to put my money, everything I've got, into St Christopher and St Jude. She's also going to increase the charges, she wants my bank books and my title deeds. I haven't . . .'

126

Hartley drew up the chair and sat down, legs astride, facing the back of the chair. He rocked the chair.

'Steady on Nunky,' he cried, 'one thing at a time. Giddyap!' he rocked the chair violently. 'Hey – Hey – Hey! Ho – Ho – Ho! Whoa there!' he stopped rocking. 'I. Price and Hya Price. I. Price and Hya Price,' Hartley pranced with the chair once more, roaring at his own joke. Mr Scobie, partly dressed, stared at him.

'What do you mean Hartley?'

'Well Nunky, it's like this, there's Lt Col. Iris Price, wot a handle! I. Price equals I. Price – everything's such i price these days. Haw! Haw! Haw! And then there's Hyacinth, there's a ridiculous handle too, she's Hya Price. Get it? See, i price and hya price. No? eh? Well how's about a little burl in the vehicle then, oh, hullo er hem, Miss Price. Nice day, G'day Miss Price, turned out nice again hasn't it?' Hartley stood up.

Matron Price, filling the doorway, did not look pleased either with Hartley or with his joke.

'Mr Scobie,' she forced a smile which showed her bottom teeth, 'you enjoy your drive with your nephew. My little outing can easily wait till tomorrow.'

'I think I've found the very place for you Nunky,' Hartley said in the car. 'You'll be able to leave old St Jude whenever you want. I think you'll like Horace . . .'

'It's not that rich-looking house with the religious widow Hartley? The one who wanted to read the Bible?' Mr Scobie, battered by his afternoon, felt tired and worried.

'Nah, remember that day we looked at that house? Me and the boys cased the joint and got it cleaned up that very night. We done it spiritual. That's why you no see me ching chang chinaman very busy so no see me. See?' Hartley sang to himself, 'ching chang chinaman . . .'

'Oh Hartley, I hope that nice lady was not harmed.'

'Nope. She's off again, round-the-world trip, what have you, restless as a kitten that woman. Place looked untouched by yooman hand. But yours truly here,' Hartley winked and patted his pocket comfortably, driving with one hand on the wheel, 'I done all right Nunks.'

'Oh Hartley!' Mr Scobie said, 'I thought you had come back to the Lord. I thought you had given up, entirely, those wicked ways.'

'Well so I have Nuncle. No worries. Only once in a while when needs must. It's the fair sex, Nunky, always wanting this and that. I mean I'd get it other ways if there was other ways. If I had a farm for eg. I'd be a farmer. Here, hold tight!' Hartley changed gear. 'This twisted bridge!' he said. 'This end of the town needs doing over, needs straightening out. Get it?' he laughed. 'Oh my doobal entends!' he said.

'I remember this street when it was a gravel track Hartley, with trees meeting overhead making lovely arches of beautiful shade,' Mr Scobie said.

'Not to worry Uncle.' Hartley held the steering wheel with both knees while he lit a cigarette. 'No use crying over lost nephews and bygone gravel chips. Four lanes of bitumen today, six tomorrow, eight next week. Progress!

'Here we are Nunk,' Hartley swung the car into the curb. 'I know it's right on the road, a bit shabby, verandah's a bit rough but wait till you've seen the inside. Might be just what you're looking for. Come along. I can't wait to show you the place. Just wait till you see the decor.'

Mr Scobie almost fell as he was scrambling out of the car. Hartley pulled him up by the arms eagerly,

'It's beaut inside,' he said. 'It's a boarding and lodging house run by a Christian gentleman and his lady friend. I mean his wife, I should say. They have some spare rooms all done up and they're really anxious to have fellow Christian lodgers.'

'Shall you be staying here too Hartley?' Mr Scobie asked

looking at the purple and yellow paint in the hall. He felt the unheated quality of the house. It seemed bare and it shone with glazed linoleum.

'No Nunks, I shall have to be skipping off for a few weeks,' he winked and patted his pockets. 'Got a few things to see to,' he said, 'but I thought I'd fix you up first seeing as you want out of Jude so bad.'

'Yes I certainly do,' Mr Scobie said. 'The bedrooms here, are they all this yellow paint too?' he shivered.

'Yes they are Nunks. Horace, my friend Mr Briggs and I got a haul, I mean we got a bargain in paint and it was mostly this yellow. Cheery isn't it. Beggars can't be choosers as we learned at school. Hey Nuncle?'

Mr Scobie was afraid his uneasiness about the offered rooms might show. He smiled at Mr Briggs, trying to be enthusiastic.

'Horace here', Hartley said, 'has done all the work himself.' Mr Briggs' scrubbed face carried a generous smile of real pleasure.

'There's rather a lot of linoleum,' Mr Scobie said. There were two places laid on a big table in a dark uninviting room which had two tall windows right on the street. Mr Scobie felt that perhaps he was meant to live there. He did not know. The house seemed entirely unlived in. The more he saw of the house the more he could not help longing for his own house at Rosewood East.

Mr Briggs, the Christian gentleman, suddenly, like a religious camel, folded his long legs into a kneeling position and prayed aloud.

'To the Dear Lord up above,' he prayed, 'that Mr Scobie here decides to do whatever is God's Will for him to do and whatever it best for us all in the case.'

'Amen!' Hartley said. 'Amen. We'll be back in a few days, Horace, when my uncle has decided what he would like to do.' He lowered his voice. 'There's a van coming tonight H.

to pick up my stuff.' Hartley and Mr Briggs shook hands elaborately as if they were, Mr Scobie thought, passing something small like a key between them. Perhaps it was only his own imagination, Mr Scobie thought. In any case Hartley, since a child, had been something of a play actor and his present life was sadly out of an old uncle's reach.

Mr Briggs shook hands with Mr Scobie who, remembering his manners, said, 'God Bless you Mr Briggs.'

'Thank you,' Horace Briggs said, 'and the same to you.'

'Well Nunky dory,' Hartley said, 'hold tight! I'll get you back for tea.'

'When Joan sent me to this place,' Mr Scobie said as Hartley walked with him into Room One, 'I sat down on this bed like this. "I'll be quite all right here Joan," I said to her that first day when she popped her head round the door to see me, she had really just been to see Matron that time. I thought then that this room was very small and very shabby. There were, as you know three of us in here then. There was nowhere at all to put my things, you know, my Bible and my music. I felt very weak. You see Hartley Dear I'd been very ill. I did not say to Joan how I felt about the room. It seemed like a prison cell, these high walls. I tried to think about the saints. There are two of them, Hartley, you see, and I tried to feel comforted. St Christopher, I suppose you know, is the saint of the wayfarer a sort of Holy Helper and St Jude is the patron saint of all Hopeless Cases right from the first century. Well, Hartley, in spite of these two I felt very weak and ill and alone, you understand.

' "I'll be perfectly all right here Joan Dear," I said to her. I wanted to go home then but thought I was only going to be here for a few days. I didn't know she was getting rid of all my things and putting in long-term tenants at Rosewood. "I'd be all right at home," I wanted to say to her but she was busy promising Matron she'd get me a dressing gown and all sorts of things which she's never done. And then Hartley, are you listening Hartley? And then that night something terrible happened. The night sister, an awful woman, Hartley, gave me such a fright.

' "It's only a suppository dear," she said, "to help your poor old bowels." I was so ashamed . . .'

'Nunky I'll have to be going,' Hartley said watching Frankie fly past the door on nimble legs. 'Excuse the rush Nuncles.' Hartley peered into the hall as Frankie and Robyn were coming back towards the kitchen, dancing two steps forward and one back. 'I'll be back, Nunks, before I go,' Hartley turned towards Mr Scobie, 'if you can understand the French! It's the Fair Sex, Uncle, I can't keep them waiting. Orrevoire!'

'Have you seen anything of Joan, Hartley?' Mr Scobie tried to detain his nephew. He caught the sleeve of his jacket.

'No Uncle, like I said, I've been out of town, as they say, till things quietened down after one or two jobs. No use sitting near trouble is it, but all's well,' he patted his pocket. 'But Nunks,' Hartley seemed to brighten with an idea, 'what say you buy one of Joan's paintings. That'd fetch her round in no time. I can get them over for you, you can pick your choice. Choose your pick. Straight! I could get 'em over. What d'you like, there's still life – bread and fruit and flowers wellington boots and umberellas, there's noods, back and full front, sitting noods, reclining and twining noods and there's a whole heap of Madonnas, all colours. You name it, Joan's done it. There's all kinds of pickies . . .'

'I would Hartley dear,' Mr Scobie said, 'I'd buy them all, every painting. I'd buy every one if she would give up that fellow and her dreadful immoral life. Yes, I must call it that, immoral life. That man will ruin her . . . a married man, twice her age, he'll ruin her . . .'

'Good on yer Nunks. That's the spirit. Well Nunks,' Hartley watched the two girls as they rushed screeching down the hall. 'Well Nunks,' he said, half out of the door, 'really must hit the road. See ya. Arrivadachee!'

131

'She had become the kind of person who gave children pencil sharpeners for Christmas,' Miss Hailey often practised the composition of descriptive sentences.

'In her later years she discovered in herself a tendency to choose pencil sharpeners for children at Christmas.' The English language, like all other languages, was marvellous. One could play with it. Make all kinds of subtle changes in meaning. She loved the energy and the rhythm.

'She took to giving children pencil sharpeners ... She put down her pen and practised instead the horns from Eroica. Lately, she thought, her voice had taken on new possibilities. In her head the horns were reproduced to perfection. The sounds which emerged were far from perfect but, as Miss Hailey told herself, repeatedly, the human voice was not intended to represent hunting horns or any other horns. *Comme c'est triste le son du cor au fond des bois*, Miss Hailey sighed, not sad hunting horns but triumphant sounds, a vision in the frantic rush of living. She pitched her own horns a little higher and tried to make a positive major key instead of a minor.

The imitation horns were accompanied by soft moanings and growlings from the other inmates of Room Three.

'Fore!' The Lt Col., now a fixture in Room Three, was standing on the wardrobe practising with his golf club.

Outside the window, loud monotonous doves talked to and fro, to and fro. And, from the kitchen came a strangled rattling and a muffled cursing as if the cook, while cleaning her impassioned stove, had, temporarily, entered the secret passages of the flues and subsequently lost her way therein.

Mr Scobie, alone in Room One standing by his bed was conducting the opening movement of Eroica. The noise from Room Three interfered with his performance. Miss Hailey thought she would have to withhold her horns; she felt sure they occurred in the third movement. She would have to ask Mr Scobie later. Her forgetfulness was appal-

132

ling. She forgot simple things like where Beethoven had put his horns.

'The distribution of horns in Beethoven', she said aloud, 'will be our subject for discussion tonight.' Fortunately Mr Scobie, having performed, played and taught music and, in addition, having a natural feeling and reverence for it, one might even say he loved music, would be able to help out her failing memory.

Storing things in her mind to ask Mr Scobie gave Miss Hailey endless pleasure.

'And talking about Beethoven,' Miss Hailey said to herself, 'what about the anguish in his later work? In the last five quartets? How could I, a humble writer, describe in words adequate enough, in my novel, the evocative suggestion in the opening phrases, say, in the A Minor Quartet?'

Miss Hailey did not hear the monotonous doves through the open window of Room Three. She was unaware of the chaotic brilliance of the summer colours of the surrounding suburban gardens. She had enough chaos, external and internal, of her own. Even the Lt Col. on top of the wardrobe, swinging his iron, made no impression. She stared out of the open window vaguely conscious that the view was unfamiliar but perfectly explainable. She was not at home and yet this place was her home and had been for many years. She had not been at the place she had once called home for a very long time.

Because both hands were occupied with balancing her pith helmet, she held her pen between her teeth. There was a wildness about her. For a hoped-for meeting with Mr Scobie, later on, she had dressed herself in something half way between a Spanish dancer and a shabby nun. From her eyes it was plain she was inconsolable. She had forgotten something else, a quotation. On the unpolished, watermarked floorboards, among scattered papers beside her bed, was a reminder, *put in quote from Goethe on first Page.*

133

'*Alors! Tiens! Merde!*' Miss Hailey tapped her helmet. Wherever was it? What was it? What on earth was the lost quotation? And why was she reminding herself to put it on the first page? First page of what? What relevance did Goethe have? Whatever had she written which could require a quotation from Goethe?

'Oh my memory!' rebuking herself, she set off along the passage to rediscover the bathroom.

It was nearly time for tea. She had intended to compose a drinking song before being interrupted by the meal.

'Here listen to this,' Frankie called to Robyn as, in disco rhythm, they were taking out the trays.

> *Flop me Drop me*
> *Turn me on*
> *Huh Huh Huh*
> *Yair Yair Yair*
> *Flop me Top me*
> *I'm turned on*

'Great! I like it,' Robyn called. 'Here's your tray Mrs Renfrew, here's your tray Miss Nunne. Miss Nunne wakey wakey here's your tray. Hey, that's good, how about that!'

> *Renfrew Murphy*
> *Wakey wakey*
> *Here's your tray*
> *Wakey Wakey*
> *Hailey Scobie*
> *Old Ma Nunne*
> *Wakey Wakey*
> *Turn me on*

Both girls danced down the hall and stopped in the doorway of Room One. Mr Scobie, no longer conducting Beethoven, was ready to go to the dinette to sit obediently waiting for his tray to be put in front of him.

'Mr Scobie,' Robyn said, 'let's have a look at your cassette recorder eh?'

'Why certainly Robyn.' Mr Scobie bent down and pulled the box from under his bed.

'Mr Scobie, can you put us on that thing? I mean, can we sing our new song into that?'

'Why certainly Robyn,' Mr Scobie smiled at the girls. He quite liked them. They were both pretty he thought but dreadfully unkempt and probably dirty. He had heard that Matron got girls from an institution for the homeless. He felt it was sad they had no mother, not even an older sister, to guide them through life's many difficulties. Their hair, in little ragged curls all over their stupid heads, worried him. Matron, he thought, should attend to their grooming.

'Well, after tea,' Frankie said, 'we'd like to sing into that thing and record our new song.'

'Of course you may.' Mr Scobie smiled, taking care not to look at their hair. 'I'll have it all set up and ready for you,' he said.

'Jeeze Squeeze,' Frankie said and both girls rushed for the next trays each with its bowl of St Christopher and St Jude curry and a thick slice of bread and butter.

'Where's Hailey?' Robyn called. 'Say, Miss Hailey! MISS HAILEY TEA TIME! COME AND GET IT.'

Miss Hailey, coming back from the bathroom, collided with Mr Scobie as they approached the dinette from different directions. There was a sharp corner where the passage turned at right angles. It was the scene of many collisions. Several people, Matron included, had often fallen partly because of the shape of the passage but mostly because of the habit of St Christopher and St Jude of leaving an unattended mop and bucket just at that place; a strategic position for this equipment.

The coming of Mr Scobie to St Christopher and St Jude was like a light in Miss Hailey's life. She had said so to Matron Price several times. Here at last was someone to relieve the spiritual wilderness which was her life. She loved his music. His background, perhaps with not so much formal education (Miss Hailey having been to University and to various places of study in Europe), was similar to her own. She often wondered what his taste in literature was. When she collided with Mr Scobie she had a terrible shock. To save herself, instinctively, she had put out her free hand, the other being caught up in the twisted strings of her sponge bag; this free hand, grasping frantically, roamed down the front of Mr Scobie's innocent crashed-into body coming to rest in that, in an old man, almost forgotten region which is private. Miss Hailey, suddenly in contact, in spite of adequate clothes, was horribly aware of the soft, intimate warmth of another human person – Mr Scobie. She screamed. The discords of all music, ancient and modern, were contained in and let loose in her scream.

'I am so sorry,' Mr Scobie said, his non-combatant heart beating violently while he struggled to regain breath and balance.

As the sad hunting horn fades in some distant forest, the unmelodious sound of Miss Hailey's scream faded. She loped off to take refuge in Room Three.

'If I could please simply have my tray here on my bed,' she lifted imploring eyes to Frankie who had followed to fetch her to the dinette. 'I feel so utterly gauche,' Miss Hailey said. 'I do so hope I have not hurt and embarrassed him. Please do let me stay here. I don't think I could eat anything, but if I might have my tray quietly on my lap perhaps I could try.'

There are places on earth which, strangely enough, have been completely overlooked by man. Places which are quite close to roads and to dwellings and to human activity but which have never been walked over or through. No human foot has ever pressed the grass or the undergrowth and no human hand has broken off twigs or pushed aside branches.

While explorers, and those following explorers, have made paths and roads and railways and have put up buildings, knocking them down at times in order to rebuild them, there remain these untrodden ways, so close, but remote as if cordoned off by invisible fences and remaining quite unchanged except for the changes which occur naturally from the cycle of growth and death, decomposition and regrowth. These places are the same as they were in the original state of the world. A state which can be known about by some people from certain scientific investigation and, for others, remains unknown, simply perhaps, being thought about with imagination and a deep reverence.

It was with this imagination and reverence that Mr Scobie always looked at the small hill which rose up behind his house. He had never walked there even though it was only on the other side of the gravel road. The hill was accessible and yet inaccessible. It was covered with scrub and stunted trees. He had never seen any person there. Never had any animal emerged, though he supposed small creatures lived there as they do in any undisturbed place. Mr Scobie did not know to whom the hill belonged. Since it was outside his boundary, he could not claim it as part of his land; and he had never journeyed round its base to see what lay beyond. His concern had been for his own place, the land which belonged by title to him, and in going to and from his place. He thought about the hill and marvelled, at times, that though he made the small changes a man can make on his land, the hill was quite unchanged and that his own place would look like the hill very quickly after his own death especially if his house was knocked down and removed and the row of pines, now in their prime, were cut down.

For some days Mr Scobie could not keep his thoughts away from the little hill. Perhaps it was because of a fine sprinkling of summer rain, a surprise shower. In the smell of the rain it was as if it was raining across his paddocks and aslant the side of the hill so that rivulets of water would be running down, darkening the gravel in places where the water collected and soaked in. He thought about the rain-misted shape of the hill, the line of undergrowth against the sky which, in wet weather, often brought soft-looking grey clouds blurring the outline of the hill. He remembered the fragrance of lightly dampened earth . . .

He set off down the hall towards the front door.

'Hey Robyn!' Frankie screeched from some unseen place, 'Confucius say: Man who do breaststroke with girl on water bed make big splash.' Both girls screamed.

'Hey it's your song!' Robyn yelled. The sound of transistor music followed, a thin wailing voice singing and Frankie and Robyn left their duties in Room Three to lose themselves for a few minutes dancing down towards the kitchen.

Mr Scobie was at the gate. It was late to be going out for a walk. He hoped he could reach the railway station before dark. As he stepped through the gateway Hartley drove up.

'Hi! Giddyap there Nunky!' He made a noisy and swift turn in the middle of the three-road junction, pulling up at the kerb with an elaborate show of care. 'And where might you be going off to Nunk?'

'Miss Joseph died the other day aged ninety-five,' Mr Scobie said to Hartley.

'Did she now,' Hartley said, 'and who's Miss Joseph when she's at home may I ask?'

'It was in the paper,' Mr Scobie said. 'I saw it in the newspaper. She was my teacher when I was a boy. You see, Hartley, the strange thing is, she can only have been a few years older than I was but in those days, Hartley, she seemed to me to be like a queen, gracious and wise and beautiful and endowed with years and years of learning and knowledge and experience. She was truly . . .'

'What Ho! Nunks hop in the vehicle. I'll go ask old High Price if I can take you for skid round in my new ute. How d'you like her? Just half an hour. How d'you like the colour? Smashing green eh? Wheel trims eh? Great!'

'Oh I hope you will not smash her Hartley.' Mr Scobie laughed at his little joke and sat himself in the comfortable seat. He wondered if he could ask to be driven to the station.

Hartley drove over the curved bridge. Mr Scobie felt uneasy. He wanted to leave St Christopher and St Jude. He was not at all sure that the lodging house, run by the Christian gentleman, was right for him.

'We're nearly there Nunky,' Hartley said. 'Hold tight! Mind the bend!'

'I suppose Mr Briggs will want an answer today,' Mr Scobie said. His heart was nearly bursting with the wish to be going to his own house. 'Couldn't I just go home, Hartley?' he was about to form the words as they turned into the street where the lodging house was.

The whole row of houses had been demolished, even the painted and partially renovated lodging house. One or two walls, uneasily aware of their destiny, were still standing among the ruins. The sheets of roofing iron, unpainted and neglected beyond repair, were in a cadaverous heap. The old bricks, scabby as if diseased, seemed to be gasping on the uneven pile of rubble. The woodwork, some of it recognizably yellow and purple, all of it splintered, together with thick lumps of yellow plaster were in another careless pile. The rotten verandah boards had been stacked up and were smouldering. The black smoke hung like a pall over the place where the houses had once been in what had seemed an indestructible permanent row.

'Holy Cow!' Hartley said. 'Strike a light! What d'ya know!' He helped Mr Scobie from the car and they stood at the edge of the pavement. Further down the street men were knocking down surviving walls. The air was full of the dust and the grit and the smoke.

'Hartley,' Mr Scobie said, 'this moment is for me very solemn and full of meaning. Hartley it is His Will. It is God's Will that I do not live here.'

'Too Right Uncle.' Hartley lit another cigarette. 'I'm stonkered,' he said.

'It's God's Will. The Will of God,' Mr Scobie said.

'D'you think Horace knew he would have to lose his home?' Hartley said half to himself. He was very pale. He hustled Mr Scobie back into the car.

'Holy Cow!' he said. 'I suppose it comes to us all in the end.'

Back in Room One, Mr Scobie sat down on the side of his bed. Perhaps in coming often Hartley would save him from having to go out with Matron Price. Thinking of the implications of the promised outing, he said, 'I hope very much, Hartley, that you'll come again soon.'

'I'll not be for a wee while Nunky,' Hartley said in an imitation Scottish accent. 'It's the Fair Sex,' he said winking at Frankie as she flounced by the door. 'Wimmin!' Hartley sighed, 'It's all on again Nuncles. She's having me back, remember I said I had my marching orders? Well, it's all on again,' he winked with the other eye as Frankie, arm in arm with Robyn, walked slowly by the open door of Room

One. He gave a low whistle of simulated appreciation. A distant screeching indicated that his winks and his whistle had reached their appointed destination.

'Oh I see,' Mr Scobie was disappointed. 'I suppose,' he said, trying to turn Hartley away from the Divorced Woman, 'Mr Briggs will badly need your help.'

'Too Right, Uncle,' Hartley said, 'Horace most certainly will.' He was half way into the passage looking in the direction of the little screams of invitation.

'Come and see me when you can Hartley. Please,' Mr Scobie said.

'Course I will Nunky as soon as ever I get back. I'll be up country. Going Bush,' he winked, 'or there'll be trouble. But, on the dot, soon as ever I get back.'

'Goodbye Hartley. God Bless you. God's Blessings,' Mr Scobie said.

'Tah, Nunky. Just what I need. Blessings. Tah! See you.'

Mr Scobie continued to sit. He did not mind the two empty beds. He was completely unaware of Matron Price fretting, upstairs in her apartment, that there were no occupants. He simply wished, when he looked at the beds, that both of them could be removed. He was accustomed to more space. It would be nice to have a table, he thought, it was easier to read his Bible when it was opened on a table. A table made all the difference to a man's life.

No one at St Christopher and St Jude ever mentioned David Hughes or Mr Privett. It was simply as if they had never been. The day after Mr Hughes died the little rosy-cheeked woman, David's sister-in-law, came to the hospital to collect his belongings.

'They can't find anything of his,' she said to Mr Scobie

as they both, in a helpless sort of way, looked at the cleaned and smoothed, freshly made, empty bed. She gave a little package neatly folded in grease-proof paper to Mr Scobie.

'I'd made it for David,' she said, 'just a bit of home baking, a slice of honey cake, it was his favourite. You have it.'

She dwelt among untrodden ways – Mr Scobie tried to remember a poem. Wordsworth was one of his favourite poets.

She dwelt among untrodden ways, he had no book, *She lived unknown and few could know* ...

The hill behind his house, the other side of the road, accompanied the half-remembered poem in Mr Scobie's mind. A remote place yet so close all the time, to people. He himself lived under the presence of the hill. It was, he thought, ... *as an hiding place from the wind and a covert from the tempest; as rivers of water in a dry place, as the shadow of a great rock in a weary land.* 'Isaiah chapter thirty-two, verse two,' he said aloud. He thought his own land was a place where tabernacles could be made. He tried to remember what it was Peter said to Jesus.

... *Master it is good for us to be here. Let us make three tabernacles* ... Was that St Mark chapter nine? he wondered. He would look up the verse and write it out for Hartley. There was something he wanted to tell Hartley. Hartley as a little boy had been so eager, loveable ...

'Mr Scobie! Mr Scobie!' The girls were in the passage. 'In a minute Mr Scobie will you put our song on your tape? We couldn't make it the other night. Remember? We'll get it all together in a minute.'

Mr Scobie roused himself. He had forgotten his earlier promise. He groped under the bed for the cassette recorder. The girls danced off down the hall.

'Let's get this straight,' Frankie said in the kitchen. 'Matron's upstairs, Rawlings is off. She's gone to the double-feature horror movie at the Plaza. Right?'

'Right!' Robyn said.

'I'll go to the caravan. See,' Frankie said. 'I'll get my gear off and hide there and you get Hailey over there. See? Right?'

'Right,' Robyn said, 'but what'll you do with Hailey?'

'Oh I'll wear an apron, one of these plastic ones will do.

143

I don't do nuthin', just keep her cool! You phone up Matron
and tell her you think I've gone to have a lay down in the
caravan. Say I've got the curse and a headache and that I
thought a bit of peace and quiet would put me right, and
tell her you think as Hailey's gone over to the caravan and
that you thought as you should let her know.

> Rock a Stop a hoola Baby Hilarious Hey Hey Hey.
> Huh Huh Huh
> Flop me drop me
> Turn me on
> Flop me Top me
> I'm turned on
> Rock a Stop a hoola Baby
> Yair Yair Yair

The girls, clicking their fingers and winking at each other,
danced back along the passage.

Mr Scobie watched Robyn dancing. He heard her thin little
voice singing. All the time the little wheels of his cassette
recorder turned. The song would come back to her at the
touch of a button. He could not understand the words of
the song at all. He would have preferred not to watch her
dancing. Her hips, first one and then the other, seemed to
go up and down and round and round. Her head jerked as
if it would snap off from her pretty little neck.

> Rock me baby hold my hand
> You gotta hold my hand
> I wanna hold your hand
> Rock a baby hoola Rock me Huh Huh Huh
> Rock me Top me
> Flop me Turn me on
> Yair Yair Yair

She wriggled and swayed, her arms hanging or swinging as if they did not belong to her body. The head jerking became more violent.

Mr Scobie thought she would look nicer with her mouth closed. He had always been particular with his pupils over this.

'You are not playing with your mouth,' he would say gently. Lina, when she played, kept her sweet mouth closed, the lips slightly pursed.

This girl, Mr Scobie thought, watching her dance, seemed to lose all human expression. He was afraid that her eyes, with their vacant look, revealed an obsession with sexual matters. He turned away watching, instead, the monitor on his recorder while Robyn continued her singing and dancing in the tiny space between the beds.

And then quite suddenly she was gone. Surprised, he peered out into the passage. There was no sign of her. He sat down again on his bed and rewound the cassette. The girl would come back. She would want to listen to her own voice. He would give her the cassette to keep.

If he had his life all over again, he thought, he would find out what was on the other side of the little hill behind his house. It was strange to think of it now, to realize he had lived there so long and had never been over it. Always he had looked in the other direction, down and across his own land. Perhaps an unknown neighbour had a dam, a reservoir of pure water half way down on the other side of the hill. It was always possible that the hill was for sale and, in that case, the boundary of his land could be extended. As soon as he could, he would leave St Christopher and St Jude . . .

'Miss Hailey,' Robyn said in Room Three, 'Miss Hailey Matron says to tell you . . .'

145

'Just a minute Frankie dear, I'm in the middle of an inspiration and the search for *le mot juste*.'

'I'm Robyn, Miss Hailey, not Frankie, and Matron says to tell you to pop across to the caravan. She wants to see you.'

'Good Lord!' Miss Hailey said, 'am I on the mat again? Matron wants to see me? What am I supposed to have done now? I hope it's nothing serious,' she smiled at the girl, perplexed, drawing her dark eyebrows close in a frown of pretended wondering. 'How amusing!' she said. 'Are you sure dear child? I mean, I must tell you, you probably know, in any case, the caravan is out of bounds for me. Absooty out of bounds. In a word, I am gated from the caravan.'

'You'd better hurry Miss Hailey,' Robyn said, 'that's the message, get it?'

Miss Hailey obediently clambered out of her bed and put on her dressing gown and slippers. She wondered if she should take her sponge bag. Not being sure, she slipped the cord over her wrist, just in case, and set off to go out of the side door and across the already dark garden.

The caravan was in darkness but its narrow door was open. Surely it was a mistake, Miss Hailey thought, Matron Price would hardly sit there in the dark. Perhaps the door ought to be closed, after all a stray cat might get in. Miss Hailey started to close the door. As she did so, she heard a little moan. She thought it was a moan.

'Is there anyone in there?' she said in a loud whisper and stepped inside. 'Why on earth are you in the dark, whoever you are!'

Mr Scobie was afraid Robyn would go on all night listening to herself. She seemed delighted with her own voice and with the song. She danced swaying and stamping and wriggling. She sang with her own recorded voice sometimes ahead of her song and sometimes, adding more words, behind.

'Great!' she said. 'Great!' and then, quite suddenly she said, 'Excuse me, Mr Scobie, I've got to phone up Matron.' She disappeared once more only to return almost at once to continue with her dancing and singing.

'Mr Scobie,' Matron Price, enormous in angora, paused in the doorway of Room One, 'you must not keep the girls up so late. Robyn should have been in bed hours ago. Night Sister is here if you want anything. These girls of mine have to be up very early in the mornings. Put away that noise for heaven's sake. Night Sister won't want Room Three disturbed.' She hurried on down the hall.

'Who the hell left this pail here!' the customary crash and complaint came back to them. The side door slammed and heavy footsteps crunched on the gravel outside.

Inside the caravan Miss Hailey said, 'But dear child you simply cannot lie here all alone in the dark. Aren't you cold? You haven't a stitch on. What is the matter?'

Frankie made no reply. Slipping off the bunk, letting the plastic apron hang loose from her narrow shoulders, she stepped towards Miss Hailey, her long bare legs white in the shaft of light which fell from the uncurtained window of Room One.

'Good Heavens child, this is not the time or the place for dancing. You are dancing I suppose? Where is Matron Price? I thought she was out here . . .'

'Oh Miss Hailey,' Frankie purred, 'I wanted you to come out here. I think you're cute Miss Hailey. I'm real sweet on

147

you. I'd like us to be real special friends, really I would.'

'Well that's very kind of you Frankie,' Miss Hailey began.

'I haven't got no one. See,' Frankie said, 'I never had no one. Everybody needs a friend.' She slithered towards Miss Hailey.

'It's very kind of you Frankie,' Miss Hailey said again. She felt tall suddenly in the caravan; she towered in her feelings of protection. The situation was an ennobling one. She was tall and noble and protective. 'But I am far too old and ugly, dear, for a young and pretty girl like you. You have no need to feel lonely, dear, we are all very fond of you here at St Christopher and St Jude.' Miss Hailey, for a moment, was beside her rich mahogany desk back in her study, back at White Cranes. She could have been talking to one of her girls. 'You've all your life ahead of you,' she said, 'there is absolutely no need for you to panic. A lovely friend, far better than I, will come along for you.' Miss Hailey sighed and took a little step towards the girl. 'And, in any case,' she said, 'you should be tucked up in bed. You have to start work at such a frightfully early time, you poor dear child.' Tenderness lowered Miss Hailey's voice.

Frankie seemed to lose her balance and she stumbled and fell against Miss Hailey. In the awkwardness, both fell sinking in the narrow space to the floor as the beam of Matron Price's pocket torch shone whitely on their tangled bodies.

'But Tin Tin I assure you, I never, I had no idea, I swear, I thought you were in the caravan. I understood you wanted to speak to me.'

'No Christian names on duty please, Miss Hailey.'

'Oh that is too much!' Miss Hailey disconsolate, on the edge of her bed, wept.

'You know perfectly well I am never in the caravan. The caravan is simply, well, it's for Mrs Rawlings and, er, the girls to use,' Hyacinth Price said. 'You know perfectly well that if I want to see people I see them in my office.'

'Oh yes yes yes and yes I do realize. I've been an absolute fool,' Miss Hailey sobbed in her deep voice, drawing hoarse breaths, saying in between her choking sobs, 'it's Bianca and Marguerite all over again, those two awful girls! To think that I looked upon them as reliable fourth formers, solid good girls and they did that frightful thing ... And now this ...'

'Now come along Miss Hailey,' Matron Price forced a cheerful note into her voice. 'It's no good bringing in what's passed.'

'Oh it's all right for you to be cheerful Tin Tin. I can't help remembering the horrors of the past. I know things are far from perfect for you Tin Tin but you do have your own house where you can be private and comfortable. You do have everything. I too once had everything. I had my own school, with a wonderful reputation, until that unfortunate business with that girl, well those two girls actually. How was I to know that they, I mean, I did not know the setting up of compromise, well I knew about it, of course, but never for one moment did I imagine I would be a victim. My school, as you know, was everything to me and when I took that girl to Bayreuth it simply was intended to help her, to show her something of the culture of Europe; she had absolutely nowhere else to go for the hols. And just now when I saw little Frankie I simply thought – I simply felt concerned that she was not in bed.' Miss Hailey wiped her unattractive nose. 'Of course, Tin Tin,' she said, I'll always be grateful to you for coming to my rescue. But Tin Tin, I never dreamed that you would take everything, but everything. You must know, you do know, that I am a pauper. I can't leave St Christopher and St Jude. I'm trapped for life, for what's left of it and I hope there isn't much left.' She began to cry afresh and sobbed without restraint. Collecting herself, she said, 'I thought being in the same dorm all those years at school, our being friends and so on would make a difference. But nothing makes any difference to you, nothing at all Tin Tin. I mean, what about Iris?' Miss Hailey's voice rose, she became bold. 'What about your own brother Hyacinth? Tin Tin? How can you be so cruel to him. I know he needs looking after, but not in Room Three of all places. And what or who has made him like he is? I mean Tin Tin, think of Room Three it's packed with senile old women. It's not their faults, they have to be somewhere, but for Iris, I ask you Tin Tin is it right? I too, Tin Tin because of being in dread of those two girls, wealthy girls and their parents – I'm so frightened of being exposed and ridiculed and hated, I know it's a long time ago now but I still do dread, and because of this, Tin Tin, I am, like Iris, spending my life in this hell hole of a room. Room Three.'

Miss Hailey, glancing up at Matron Price, realized she had gone too far.

'I'm sorry Tin Tin,' she began to stammer. For answer Matron Price pushed her fingers into Miss Hailey's sponge bag and drew out a flask of whisky.

'You know that this is not allowed at St Christopher and St Jude,' she said with a frightening coldness. 'You know perfectly well what the rules are, you know perfectly well that this is not allowed here.' She paused and said, 'Come on, I'll help you into bed. There! There!' she said, 'don't be so upset. Look! I don't want the other patients disturbed, Come on, into bed with you.'

Miss Hailey, sobbing still, revealing shockingly hairy legs, undressed herself. Her hands seemed unable to unfasten her dressing gown cord. Matron Price helped her. In spite of her position she was surprisingly awkward. Miss

Hailey's tears demanded the physical consolation which was hard to give.

'Here!' Matron Price measured a small dose of the sponge-bag whisky into Miss Hailey's tooth mug.

'Oh thank you Tin Tin, you have one too. Please do, there's a dear, there's a spare glass on that locker. Down the hatch!' Miss Hailey smiled bravely. 'Let's have another,' she said, 'I can't tell you Tin Tin how abject I am. Utterly. I apologize for all the trouble. I simply cannot explain.'

Matron Price drank her second whisky with a grim expression as she recalled other similar events. Frankie would leave in the morning. Paid monthly, she had that afternoon collected her pay. She would leave, as they all did, without notice, leaving her room in a mess and all the other rooms in a mess; all the kitchen work not done and all the patients' showers still to be done. Hyacinth Price, herself, would have to put on one of the plastic aprons, take off her stockings and wade into the showers.

It took time, she knew from experience, to get girls. Frankie had been, in spite of her noisy ways, a bright good little worker.

'Down the hatch!' Miss Hailey's voice boomed in the troubled snore-filled darkness.

'Hush!' Matron Price whispered. 'I can't do with having Renfrew Nunne and Murphy disturbed, or the others for that matter.' She poured herself another drink.

'I am a writer,' Miss Hailey said.

'Yes I know,' Hyacinth Price replied, 'but try and keep quiet – there's a good girl.'

'We writers,' Miss Hailey said, waving her tooth mug, 'have a duty towards our readers. We are responsible to our readers just as you, Tin Tin, are responsible to your patients.'

'Granted,' Matron Price said graciously.

'Come up on the bed, Tin Tin, there's no need to sit on the floor like that,' Miss Hailey edged towards the wall. 'There we are. Cosy?'

'Mmm,' Matron Price tried to simulate cosiness. Miss Hailey's consolation would take time.

'I mean,' Miss Hailey said, 'back in history, Jenny Geddes, remember learning about her in school Tin Tin? Remember? She threw a stool at the parson and Jethro Tull invented the seed drill. Well, writers can either protest or plant a seed. Don't you agree?'

'Oh yes! But do keep your voice down.' Matron Price topped up their drinks.

'Down the hatch!' Miss Hailey growled, her nearest to a whisper. 'I must somehow work Jenny Geddes and Jethro Tull into my novel,' she said. 'I wonder if some sort of marriage? Jenny and Jethro? I like that,' she gave a deep laugh.

Room Three was awash with walking frames and crutches, flapping night-gowns and shuffling bursting slippers as dark forms, groping towards the faint light in the passage, made their way, with silent excitement, towards the dinette.

'Do you remember reading *Paradise Lost* at school Tin Tin?' Miss Hailey was oblivious to the evacuation of Room Three. 'Remember we used to read those big old books in the trunk room? I used to love the engravings,' she sighed like a ship hopelessly adrift in a fog. 'We used to stroke each others arms,' she said dreamily. 'Stroke my arm Tin Tin. Tell me you are crazy about people with black eyebrows. Go on Tin Tin stroke the inside of my arm like you used to, then I'll do yours . . . tell me you like my eyebrows . . .'

While Miss Hailey slept Matron Price felt a stirring in her sluggish conscience. The hospital of St Christopher and St

Jude was, as her father would have said, *God's Work*. All through the difficult times of her training he had consoled and supported, *it's God's Work Hyacinth*. Facing herself in moments of truth she wondered what sort of God. She hardly, in her own words, kept abreast of the events in the world outside St Christopher and St Jude. At certain stages certain prospects presented themselves. She sometimes saw herself walking, in yellow slacks and a tank top, without a bra or a corset of any kind, walking to raise money. A walkathon it was called. A walk to raise money for kidneys and hearts and for all kinds of diseases. Always, in her mind, she walked, chatting to friends, easily, round the long curve of a wide river.

'I really ought to join the march against nuclear war,' she said aloud and was surprised at her own voice. Disturbed, Miss Hailey sang.

'Dully dully durdle oo. Dully dully durdle oo,' she sang. 'Do you remember Tin Tin? Dully dully durdle oo.'

Miss Hailey dozed again.

'I do do my bit,' Matron Price reasoned with herself. 'I mean, I employ people. I employ girls to wash up instead of having machines. And look where it gets me! No one to do the heap of dishes except Rawlings or more likely myself because of Rawlings' dermatitis.'

And what about Rawlings, Felicity Rawlings taking her husband like that. Her own friend, a thief of the worst kind. Her own husband, a thief of the ordinary kind; a liar too. Wanted in several countries and hidden again in the caravan in his own wife's garden. But married a second time to her own friend, or one-time friend. School friend. There was a punishment for bigamy if it was discovered. There were possibilities of reward if she disclosed Mr Rawlings' 'hide-out'. To keep Felicity Rawlings in constant fear and dread and to work her almost to death, gave, in some measure, satisfaction. The real and undisclosed satisfaction was in knowing that Mr Rawlings was safe and well; well fed and comfortable and not being hunted, or having to suffer in some prison in some barbaric place. Matron Price did not allow herself, on ordinary nights, to contemplate the middle-aged bliss of the couple in the caravan. On this night though, while Hailey slept fitfully, she allowed herself the luxury of wondering just where Mr Rawlings was when young Frankie was in the caravan. Had Hailey seen him? Probably not. Melting quickly was one of his accomplishments.

'The trouble is,' she said aloud, 'I still love him.' She liked to supply wine for him and delicate special foods which she knew he liked. She did not forgive him for taking another woman while pretending to love her because she did not need to forgive him. Choosing chicken breasts and soft foreign cheeses she talked to herself, her pious lips forming words like *utterly* and *faithfully* and *for ever* as she declared her love across shining trays of stuffed olives, thinly sliced salami and sweet little cucumbers.

Perhaps it was the one good thing in her life, she thought, loving a worthless husband and trying to do her best for St Christopher and St Jude.

She poured herself another drink as her thoughts, taking these turns, indicated that she had not had quite enough whisky. 'Too much,' she said to herself, 'and not enough.'

Matron Price tried to edge her way off Miss Hailey's bed. She would slip off upstairs to her own house, to her own comfortable bed. It was more than possible that she would not enjoy sharing a bed with Mr Rawlings. She had been used to having a big bed all to herself for a long time.

Miss Hailey turned and, as if she had never been asleep, confided in a low voice.

'You know, Tin Tin,' she said, 'you can have no idea what it's like to be as I am. And on top of it all, can I say this to you? There is no one else I can tell it to. On top of it all,

all my life, as you know, I've been writing, you know, poems and stories and there's my novel too. All these years I've been living on the hope that one day I'd be published. That a publisher would want what I have written, that people would read me – you know, even talk about something I'd written. But ...' Miss Hailey paused, fresh tears hung shining and tremulous along her eyelashes. 'But it's clear to me now,' she continued, 'that I never will be. I'll never have my own book to hold and to handle and to give to someone. This on top of everything else is too hard to bear Tin Tin. Don't stop me calling you by that name when we're alone like this. You see, to be a writer who has never had a word accepted and published is so awful Tin Tin. So absooty awful.'

'There! There!' Matron Price soothed. 'There! There!'

Consoling Miss Hailey took several more whiskys and considerable time. 'Go to sleep. Go to sleep,' Matron Price seemed to sing. Unwillingly she cradled Miss Hailey's bony body in her fat arms; and, as Miss Hailey slept, Hyacinth Price remembered Mr Scobie's riddle. Life would be much simpler, she could see quite clearly, if Miss Hailey provided here and now, while asleep, the answer to one of the mysteries in his riddle. Miss Price knew from her upbringing and her training that one person does not wish death on another person. What she should not do and what she could do merged with miraculous simplicity in her own mind even though she knew she was powerless and that the answer would remain for ever an intellectual conception.

Miss Hailey, with a strong heart beat which shook her narrow spinster's chest, continued to sleep. She breathed long strong, well sustained, deep breaths, just the right number in every passing minute. There was no need to count and record either her pulse or her respiration.

Sitting on the edge of the bed, holding and supporting Miss Hailey, Matron Hyacinth Price reflected on the financial unhealthiness of St Christopher and St Jude. The prospect was so infinitely depressing that she allowed herself another little drink; this time straight from the small flat bottle. Later, noticing there was none left, she tossed the bottle across the littered floor of Room Three. She sang to Miss Hailey, rocking her to and fro, the frail iron bed creaking and rattling; an agony of ancient springs and rusty wire mesh.

'There, There, There and There,' she sang, 'There, There Then and There.'

Miss Hailey, half asleep said, 'Oh Tin Tin d'you remember that midnight feast in the dorm? Remember when the jellies you made in those jam jars didn't set because of being up against the hot pipes?' Laughing, she began to sing,

> *Je sweez une petite prairie fleur*
> *Growing sowvarge toos les heurs*
> *Ni personne me cultivate moi*
> *Si Je sweez sowvarge sowvarge twoi!*

Both women sang the song improvising a descant and in the end achieving, because of not keeping time with each other, the effect of a round.

'And Tin Tin,' Miss Hailey said, 'sometimes, here, when the sun is on the verandah I am so reminded of the warm tar smell of the verandah boards at school. Do you remember, Tin Tin, the top verandah where we wrote our names in blood under the eaves and the doves, presiding, seemed to listen with their heads sideways to our vows of, what did we call it – Ha! eternal fidelitude?' She sighed, 'There is of course no such word and, if there is no such word then, without the word, the thing does not exist . . .'

'Go to sleep,' Matron Price said, 'go back to sleep.'

The financial state of St Christopher and St Jude took more shape in its ugliness towards dawn. Matron Price was cold and her back ached. Against her full round breasts

Miss Hailey was sleeping sweetly. Outside the window the sky was pale and birds were singing. She thought, with a strange hungry longing, of Mr Rawlings asleep in the caravan.

'I'm a goose,' she said to herself knowing that she provided for him and did not have any part of him. 'Not even his back for warming my feet,' she said adding a cliché to her thoughts to make them less painful. The one useful thing was that Mrs Rawlings did the work of three people receiving in return only board and lodging. 'I can cut down on their keep,' Matron Price began working out sums in her head, knowing that she would not.

Slowly, with mutterings and tattered movements, the occupants of Room Three made their uneasy and uncertain ways back to their beds.

St Christopher and St Jude; it was clear, both saints were being gambled away. Why was it, Matron Price wondered, that Missis Shady and that dreadful old woman, Shady's mother, Mrs Morgan, always won at cards? She regretted deeply the accepting of Mrs Shady as Night Sister, and even more the taking in of Mrs Morgan as a patient. And now it was all too clear that Mr Boxer and Mr Rob included themselves as patients in the care of St Christopher and St Jude. Miss Price had no idea when or where they slept; probably all day curled up in one of her out-houses. Anger made her resolve to seek them out in their hiding places and order them off the premises. The hospital and the grounds belonged to her and to Iris. The place was also the only place where Mr Rawling was safe. These people were all part of the unmysterious things Mr Rawlings had done. They had no choice but to be there and she, because of her devotion, *a girl always loves for ever the first man she loves* (Matron Price firmly believed this), had no choice but to provide a sanctuary for them all.

It was essential that there should be a change of luck with

the cards. She could not let Iris go on gambling away all their money and all their possessions. As the sky lightened the beds in Room Three, all now filled with sleeping humps, became visible. Matron Price wondered why did Iris lose always. Why did he never win? St Christopher and St Jude would be whipped from above their heads, or swept from beneath their feet. She sank in clumsy disjointed thoughts and even contemplated a short neat speech during which Missis Shady and all her relatives would be sent packing.

All the patients in Room Three had their interest, as she herself put it, sewn up for life in St Christopher and St Jude. That they were doing life there was Matron Price's next grim joke to laugh over by herself. She wished life did not last so long for some people. If she lost St Christopher and St Jude she would still be responsible for the care of these people who had, at her suggestion and, in this moment of honesty she had to admit it, under pressure from her, tied up their money in the nursing home. Even if they all conveniently passed on, Hailey, tough old bird that she was, would live on. Again, in honesty, Hyacinth Price had to admit to herself that her old school friend was in fact the same age as she was and she did not consider her own age to be old. She imagined living in a tiny unit with Hailey and with Iris, unable to get away from either of them and never setting eyes on Mr Rawlings, not even knowing where or how he was; she shuddered.

Too much whisky always made her feel depressed and sick. She thought, with longing, of the half bottle of flat lemonade in her own kitchen.

There was only one course open, her mind ran on familiar lines, and that was to redouble her efforts with Mr Scobie. She was not sure exactly what he possessed. His niece had spoken, unwisely, of land, property and money. Matron Price made up her mind to have everything signed and

158

settled and so revitalize St Christopher and St Jude as quickly as possible.

Perhaps too it was a good thing that Frankie left. There was one less to be paid. Pity she had been paid. The girl might have left without her pay. They sometimes did. Robyn would have to work harder, that was all.

There was Mr Scobie to be dealt with and Missis Shady to be sacked, even though this meant doing night duty herself for a few weeks. Missis Shady to go and her mother to go with her. Matron Price, though relieved at making a decision, felt too muddled at that moment to form a plan to follow her resolution.

Beetroots boil as request also kitchen floor and bath for Mrs
Tompkins and sandwiches 10 p.m. Patient did not come in
all night. Room 3 very quiet all night. All pats. play cards in
dinette.

N.A. to report. Lt Col. I. Price (retired) lose bad.

Signed Night Sister M. Shady (unregistered)

*Missis Shady: Of course Mrs Tompkins did not come in. Don't
you ever read the newspaper? Mrs Tompkins has passed on
with a lovely death notice from St Christopher and St Jude.
'Food memories etc.' there is a misprint newspapers not being
what they were. Naturally Room Three was very quiet all
night. I myself remained on duty in there. You would see
yourself if you went round the rooms.*

Signed Matron H. Price

'Where's Robyn?' Mr Scobie asked Mrs Rawlings when she cleared away his breakfast tray.

'You may well ask,' Mrs Rawlings said pressing her lips into a thin line.

'Why, has the little bird flown?' Mr Scobie laughed. He hoped to help Mrs Rawlings to be more pleasant. He thought his joke would make her smile.

'She has too and left behind her a terrible mess and a confusion I thought I'd never live to see. And us all in a spot without anyone to do the showers and the beds and all and to see to the kitchen.'

Mr Scobie listened to Mrs Rawlings. He would have liked to say he thought the cook was too severe, that she frightened the girls. He heard all too plainly the daily noise from the kitchen.

'There's nothing but trouble,' Mrs Rawlings said. 'I doubt if Matron's had a wink of sleep.'

'*Weeping may endure for a night . . .*' Mr Scobie said. 'Look Mrs Rawlings, the Good Book has opened at this page by itself. Weeping may endure for a night, but Joy cometh in the morning, Psalm thirty verse five.' He looked up, his old face pink with the pleasure of being able to console Mrs Rawlings.

'There may be joy for some,' Mrs Rawlings said, 'I'm sure I wouldn't know.' At the door she paused. 'Young Robyn's left a message for Matron', she said, 'saying she was leaving because she would never get used to Dirty Old Men. She was that upset the poor little thing.'

Mr Scobie, remembering that he was the only old man – apart from the Lt Col. and he did not count – at St Christopher and St Jude, sat on the side of his bed with his head bowed. The nursing home was unusually quiet.

Later, Mrs Rawlings, passing the door of Room One said, 'You can get dressed Mr Scobie. There's no showers today.'

Miss Hailey did not seem to be anywhere about. No one

had fallen, cursing, over the bucket in the hall, and Mrs Rawlings, out of breath, was going to and fro, alone, with the tin trays.

'Where's Matron then?' the cook's voice rose above the disembowelling of the stove. 'Where's the old crab today?'

'It's a spot of the old trouble,' Mrs Rawlings' voice answered from somewhere along the passage. 'She'll be down later. She's on flat lemonade.'

'There's nothing in the world like a good chunder,' the cook's voice approached wisdom even sympathy and tenderness.

'Yes,' Mrs Rawlings said, 'Yes.'

Quietly Mr Scobie set out for his walk. He walked along the quiet side roads and through lost lanes grown over with grass and weeds, hung over by green branches, long leaved and sighing, and interwoven with trailing stems and shining leaves holding white and blue flower cups.

The sun was warm on his back and he heard the rich voices of the magpies. There was a little wind bringing a fragrance of damp peppermint and eucalyptus laden earth. An unexpected light shower had refreshed the gardens.

He stopped from time to time to lean on the side gate of some old house to look into the green shade of a deserted back garden. He saw lemons ripe on the trees. He smelled the sweetness of lemon flowers and of roses. He was comforted during his walk by the early morning serenity and the possession of the sun's warmth. He felt as if he was walking inside a halo of blessings.

'Who can mind an old man having a rest?' he said to himself, remembering a house where a woman offered him a cup of tea.

'Have you a spare room?' he had asked her. She lived in the house alone she told him and, yes, there was a spare room. She was expecting her son to come home at any time. The spare room in the house was her son's room.

162

'It's a nice house. I should like to lodge here.' Mr Scobie often thought of their conversation.

'Yes, I suppose it is a nice house,' she said.

'I would like to talk about the Bible with you every day,' he said.

'Aw! Go on with you!' She always laughed when she spoke.

'I really mean it.' He liked her rich laugh.

It seemed to Mr Scobie, at the time, that the woman was pleased. He never saw her again though he often sat on her verandah and sometimes he knocked at the door, waiting for her to come out.

'I am sure she was in the house,' he explained once to Mrs Rawlings, 'but she did not come to the door. I waited an hour on her verandah.'

'Perhaps she was having a bath,' Mrs Rawlings said.

'What, at three o'clock in the afternoon?' Mr Scobie shook his head, ' A bath for an hour?'

'Well you never know with some people,' Mrs Rawlings replied. 'I mean, there's some I know don't ever get dressed till the evening. There's some with very funny ways and habits.'

'*Do not neglect the Spiritual Endowment you possess*, Timothy chap . . .'

'Oh you and your Bible rubbish!' Mrs Rawlings' flat heavy voice ended the conversation.

It was better not to think about Mrs Rawlings. After resting on the quiet verandah of the house, Mr Scobie went over to the door and knocked twice. After some delay the door opened.

'Hosanna!' Mr Scobie said, 'Hosanna!'

'Wha' d'ya want,' the door began to close.

'Is the Lady of the House in please?' Mr Scobie smiled with ancient white-haired hope.

'Wha' d'ya want? Wah' d'ya want 'er for?'

Mr Scobie stepped back hesitating. The disagreeable not-young man was unexpected.

'I have come to see the Lady about the spare room,' he was suddenly nervous, unable to trust his bowels.

'Can't you read?' the man stepped out and pointed to the window where there was a small hand-printed notice.

'Apartment and board,' Mr Scobie read aloud, 'only student need apply.' His face was radiant. 'So you have a room after all.' He was excited. 'I am a student,' he cried, unable to hide his joy. 'I am a student of Life and the Bible is my Book. The Lady in this house knows and loves the Bible as I do myself. It is my life . . .

'*See! I will not forget you . . . I have carved you on the palm of my hand* . . . Isaiah chapter forty-nine, verse sixteen . . .' Mr Scobie was in need of breath.

'On your way old man! There's nothing for you here.' The man raised an arm and advanced, 'On your way!'

'Of course it's because I'm old.' Mr Scobie, walking along the pavement, tried not to think of the pale face and the cruel eyes. For a time he did not feel the sun or hear the birds.

He thought he would try to walk up to the station. It seemed that his house in Rosewood East was not so far away after all. Everything would be as he left it. Simply it was a matter of getting back there.

He wished for some tea and a slice of bread and butter. St Christopher and St Jude did not give him tea during the day. He had tried to tell Mrs Rawlings.

'Mrs Rawlings,' he said pleasantly, 'though I don't have my tea any more I still have to get up to use the chamber at four every morning.'

'Well that's nothing to be proud of,' Mrs Rawlings replied. 'And you ought to think about other people more and not disturb them with your light when they're trying to get the bit of sleep they need to keep them going. It's only what they deserve after all, it's not asking much, is it, just to want a fair night's sleep.'

Remembering Mrs Rawlings as he walked, Mr Scobie thought he had never heard her speak at such length before. At the time he wanted to tell her that a person should never be criticized for something he cannot help.

'I know Sir Roger de Coverly said it,' he told Mrs Rawlings, 'but he was only a made up person and the real author's name escapes me.'

'Is that so,' Mrs Rawlings said folding small sheets and shaking them as if with pent-up anger.

Mr Scobie did try, one night, getting up in the dark. In the middle of the suburban pavement the remembered shame engulfed him. He managed everything without a light and then upset it all over the floor and over the small rug. Thinking about it, he recalled that the shouts from the poker game in the dinette were so loud that the Night Sister did not hear the noise he made.

In the morning Mrs Rawlings and the cook were screaming at the Night Sister before she left, accusing her of not doing her share of the cleaning up. He thought he heard them fighting in the kitchen. Certainly one of them was crying.

At the station, Mr Scobie bought a ticket for Rosewood East.

'Return?' the man in the ticket office asked.

'Oh No, single,' Mr Scobie said, 'I shall not be coming back.' He thought he would try his riddle or a variation of it. Perhaps he would be able to give a smile to the sad official.

'Where is it we all are going, but don't know when or how ...' he began.

'Next!' the man in the office reached for the money from the passenger behind Mr Scobie. There were quite a number of people waiting in a line to buy their tickets. Mr Scobie stepped as quickly as he could out of the way.

'Over the bridge,' the clerk said, 'trains every twenty minutes. You've just missed one. Next please?'

'When I reach Rosewood East,' Mr Scobie said, talking to himself, as he climbed the wooden steps of the foot-bridge, 'I'll ask at the post office and find out who is living in my house.'

On the foot-bridge he stopped for breath. From the high place he looked along the empty railway tracks. The sight of them, purposeful between the platforms, then between the yards, and then, all at once, between embankments of sun-scorched grass, excited him.

He wanted to stand, high up, and shout, 'You there! You can have all my money and part of my pension. I shall not need it all. You can have it if I can have my home back. D'you hear me?' he wanted to shout, 'I'll pay something every week from my pension . . .'

Of course he could not shout. People would think he was mad and, in any case, he had no breath for shouting. He made his way down the other side. He waited on the platform. He looked anxiously along the tracks. Both ways. He waited for the train, wishing for it to come. He tried not to think of St Christopher and St Jude. In his thoughts he seemed to be always dragged back there as if it were not possible to leave. Like the time when he took his dinner back to the kitchen.

'Could I have a bit of butter on my vegetables please?' he asked Mrs Rawlings and the cook. They were serving the food with big wooden spoons.

'Butter's bad for the arteries Mr Scobie,' Mrs Rawlings said, still moving her spoon back and forth, 'I'm afraid I can't give you any because it'll clog up your arteries and you'll be in proper trouble. Think of your heart!'

'It's bad for your liver too,' the cook said, 'they've just found out all the terrible things butter can do to your body, specially old people. Matron's thinking of not having any more butter in for the patients at all.'

'But, all my life, I've eaten lots of butter . . .' Mr Scobie said.

'Well yes,' the cook interrupted him, 'and just you look at you!'

The cook's voice reverberated in his head as a fast train, going in the other direction, rattled through the small station.

He wondered what was wrong with Matron Price. Her old trouble, they said. He knew women had some peculiar illnesses. Internal troubles. He thought her size alone was enough to make her ill. How could a person of that size breathe properly? All that weight of flesh on her chest. The cook and Mrs Rawlings were big like this too. He thought how they would have to change their clothes more often because of the fatty grease their bodies must give off. His own body, Mr Scobie reflected, gave off nothing. He could wear the same singlet, the same shirt and the same nightshirt for weeks, months even, and they would still be clean.

Feeling afraid, he wished again that the train would come. There were not many people on the platform. He was glad he had thought of buying the ticket before the money had been found and cleared out of his pocket. He knew he must get away from St Christopher and St Jude before his money was swallowed up.

He knew his fear was partly because he was hungry. He was always hungry now; empty. He thought about the meat soup, thick with potatoes and carrots and onions, he would make in his own kitchen. The St Christopher and St Jude soup was made with dried peas and lentils and was always burned. There was always a smell of burned lentils or burned sago from the hospital kitchen.

He heard his stomach rumbling with emptiness.

He thought he saw Mrs Rawlings on the other platform. She was dressed in her good clothes. She was walking slowly up and down. Mr Scobie, hoping she would not look across to where he was, moved and sat as far as possible into the corner of the open shelter. It was not much of a hiding place. There was nowhere for a man to hide himself. He thought Mrs Rawlings must be going to town. He wondered why, she hardly ever went out. Perhaps to visit a doctor. Was she ill too? It was a possibility. She seemed to have very little time for herself. He hoped her train would come first and take her away quickly. Perhaps if her mind was on some doctor or dentist or even a lawyer she would not see him.

In the distance he could see his train approaching. It was a long way off. How small it looked and how slowly it came. He knew it would disappear, because of a long curve, and then reappear. When it reappeared there would be a long stretch of railway line still to cover before it reached the station.

Meanwhile the train going in the other direction slid alongside the far platform.

Mr Scobie's relief was immeasurable. He sat smiling to himself in the shelter. His own train would not be long now. Already he had heard the long drawn-out hoot of the siren.

Mrs Rawlings' train, without wasting time, pulled out of the station and began to gather speed.

To his horror Mr Scobie saw that Mrs Rawlings was still on the platform.

How could she have missed the train when she was standing right beside it? Perhaps she had suddenly changed her mind. Women, Mr Scobie thought, often changed their minds. Quite unreasonably. Or had she, perhaps, remembered something?

Mrs Rawlings, with her heavy feet, walked to the gate marked *exit*. Again, Mr Scobie allowed himself the pleasure of relief. This relief did not last long as Mrs Rawlings reappeared. She was talking to someone. An official, Mr Scobie saw at once with dismay. He tried to tell himself the man was an acquaintance, a relative of Mrs Rawlings. Of course he must be her brother. She would surely have a brother and this must be where he worked. She had simply come up to the station to see her brother. Mad about trains she watched them from the platform and then found her brother to give him a little parcel of home-baking from St Christopher and St Jude. The same kind of thing that the little sister-in-law brought for David Hughes before he died.

Mrs Rawlings and the man seemed to be looking across in his direction.

Just before Mr Scobie's train came into the station, he saw Mrs Rawlings climbing the steps of the foot-bridge. As usual she was not smiling. The lineaments of her substantial body seemed even more severe.

Mr Scobie felt safe for he was sure that Mrs Rawlings would not get over the bridge and down all the steps in time. Many people, on reaching the middle of a railway bridge, missed their train.

It was a pity that so few people were travelling. He chose the seat on the platform side, hiding himself in the corner, facing the engine, pressing himself back so that anyone going by would not see, at a glance, that he was there. He tried to breathe quietly and calmly. No one else entered his compartment. This was a pity and yet he was glad because he preferred the idea of the pleasure of the train journey undisturbed. He could look forward quietly to his arrival at Rosewood East noting things of interest on the way. He supposed the key to his house would still be under the stone by the door. Mostly he did not lock his house. The back door on the verandah did not have a key. He supposed everything would be as it was when he was taken away. He wondered whether the market gardens were still alongside the railway. He looked forward to that part of the ride.

He wished the train would start. It was standing longer than usual. He wondered what the cause of the delay could be. He leaned forward slightly.

'You'll have to come back with me Mr Scobie.' He was face to face with Mrs Rawlings. She was standing on her square feet only a few inches from him.

Taken by surprise, he felt as if she had pushed his head back and exposed his throat.

'Oh, but I have my ticket Mrs Rawlings,' he said, his energy draining. 'I shall not be coming back.'

'Think of your heart,' Mrs Rawlings said. 'You're due for your needle tomorrow. How will you get that if you go away?'

'I think the train is about to leave,' Mr Scobie said. 'If you stand so close you might get hurt,' his voice was shaking. 'Thank you for all you have done for me Mrs – Mrs Rawlings. Good morning to you or is it, er, afternoon now?' He gave a nervous little laugh and tried to look at his watch.

'Come along!' Mrs Rawlings said. 'The Guard can't let the train go till you are off it. So come along. It's for your own good. Heaven knows what will happen to you . . .'

'*There is a path which no fowl knoweth* . . . Job chapter twenty-eight verse seven.' Mr Scobie smiled at Mrs Rawlings. 'It's all in the Good Book,' he added.

'Oh you and your Bible nonsense.' Mrs Rawlings put a massive hand on his thin arm. 'You are coming off this train this minute or else I'll have you lifted off.' She did not loosen her grip. 'You realize,' she said, 'that you are holding up the train.'

Sadly he left his corner seat and, with slow steps, they made their way back over the bridge. The train left immediately. He heard the rumble of it leaving the station and then the long melancholy cry of the horn. He heard it gather speed and he heard the distant settling into its regular satisfying sound. The rhythm of the train stayed in Mr Scobie's head long after it was possible to hear the real sounds of departure.

'That wasn't a very nice thing to do Mr Scobie, now was it?' Mrs Rawlings said when she came to collect his tray. 'With Matron upstairs ill and half her staff left sudden it's not very nice is it to make extra worries for her? What you did won't make her feel any better will it?'

Mr Scobie sat on the edge of his bed. The ticket, still in his hand, gave him comfort. He bowed his head, humble before Mrs Rawlings.

'Aren't you going to eat any dinner?' she asked. 'After all the trouble's been taken to put some aside for you on top of all the extra work too.'

She marched from the room, the untouched tray held high to her offended breast.

Mr Scobie, looking at the two empty beds, wished his bed to be smooth and empty. He did not miss Mr Hughes or Mr Privett. He did not know them. It was not anyone's fault; they were nothing to him. They had come briefly into his life and gone out of it again. He searched in his mind for reason and explanation. It was strange, he reflected, that no one ever mentioned their names. It was as if St Christopher and St Jude never spoke of the dead. People simply ceased to need to be cared for. It was as if they had never existed. Those who were still with St Christopher and St Jude went about their lives, what was left of them, in a confined way, moving as if without purpose and all in different directions, like leaves, he thought, bundling along in the wind, this way, and then, when the wind changed, the other way.

The nursing home was very quiet. Perhaps the writer woman, Miss Hailey, was asleep. Room Three mainly slept during the day. He gathered from overheard snatches of yelled conversation in the kitchen that Miss Hailey was not too good after a troubled night.

'Hallo there Mr Scobie!' Miss Rosemary Whyte, making what she called her happy H.A.P.P.Y. social-worker rounds, called to him. She entered Room One and sat on one of the empty beds facing him. 'And how are you today?' She open-ed her folder across her little girl knees.

'Dear!' Mr Scobie leaned forward. Trembling, he pulled at her sleeve. 'Please do take me with you. You've got a car haven't you?' his blue eyes seemed to overflow, 'I must get away from here. You must believe me. I'm perfectly well. I want to go home. I cannot stay another night in this place. If you can't take me, will you please arrange for a car to call for me?'

Miss Whyte appeared to be thinking. She made a little note with a new biro by Mr Scobie's name. 'Mr Scobie still wanting to leave St Christopher and St Jude.' She sat more firmly on the bed, knees apart. She felt mannish and protec-tive. 'I'll have to put my thinking cap on,' she said. She rested her chin on her hand, and elbow on one knee, and closed her eyes.

Mr Scobie sat quietly waiting for her answer.

'There's nothing for it, Mr Scobie, we'll have to elope,' she said, opening her eyes, 'there is absolutely no other way. We shall simply have to elope. Now what d'you think of that!' she smiled her brightest whitest smile for him. 'That's very good material,' she chattered on. 'I'm thinking of becoming a writer, you know. I've heaps of "copy". It's my job, I get lots and lots of interesting experiences. I started some novels ages ago. When I get time I've got lots of books to write. I'm going to be a writer.'

She closed her file and said goodbye to Mr Scobie.

'Goodbye Mr Scobie. Chin up!' she had recently learned the expression from a senior and found it most useful.

'First Norn, Second Norn and Third Norn – now let me see,'
Miss Hailey, writing with the pad on her knee, felt she
wrote with renewed rapture. Ever new images, she declared,
simply flowed from her pen, memories, thoughts, experiences, 'so much to write and so little time,' she said to herself, 'now let me see, Brunnhilde, Siegfried, Gunther,
Hagen, Gutrune, Waltraute, Alberich, Woglinde, Well-
gunde and Flosshilde. Gotterdammerung!'

'Language!' Mrs Rawlings said. 'Watch the language! We
can't have Language here on the verandah. There's St Christopher and St Jude to think of. We have to think of the good
name of the hospital don't we Mr Scobie?' Mrs Rawlings
was bringing Mr Scobie to sit on the verandah. He had just
had his shower and his white hair was wet, flat on his head.
He was dressed in a hospital dressing gown and walked
with shuffling small steps. He had adopted a new way of
walking Miss Hailey noticed, like a wooden doll perhaps
a mandarin doll. Miss Hailey had once had such a doll. It
had painted on clothes, a round painted black hat and a
painted cigar in his painted mouth. The doll would walk
down a sloping board if you had such a thing handy. The
doll shuffled with quick little steps. If the board, or
planchette, was held at too steep an angle, the wooden doll
fell, round black hat over heels, and rolled, without complaint, to the floor. Miss Hailey tried, unsuccessfully, to
remember the name of the doll. It was a German name,
something like Adderbei. With a sigh she gave up. She had,
after all, remembered the entire cast of an opera.

'It's all right Mrs Rawlings,' Miss Hailey said. 'I'm not
uttering obscenities. It is the name of an opera (in three acts)
by Richard Wagner. *Gotterdammerung*, Twilight of the Gods
from the epic Ring Cycle. Libretto by the composer. First
produced in Bayreuth in 1876. The ghastly thing is, though,
I cannot, for the life of me, remember the umlaut. I don't

know on which vowels the umlaut should go.' She looked hopefully at Mrs Rawlings and at Mr Scobie.

'I do so want to know about the umlaut,' she sighed.

'You want to know what?' Mrs Rawlings said. 'You want to know whatter what?'

'Were you ever in Bayreuth?' Miss Hailey asked Mr Scobie when they were alone, side by side, held firmly in their basket chairs by grey blankets folded and pulled across and tucked in by Mrs Rawlings. She did this tucking in so thoroughly, every time, it was useless to try to get out of the chairs.

'Were you ever in Bayreuth?' Miss Hailey asked again. 'I mean for Wagner of course. I sometimes took some of my more accomplished girls from school, not all at once you understand, just one girl, or two sometimes – and not every time. My personal secretary was too, how shall I put it, too jealous. She preferred to make the pilgrimage *tête à tête*. A ridiculously impassioned woman. It is a relief to me that she is no longer with me . . .'

'I can't remember,' Mr Scobie said, 'I cannot remember the name of the woman in the post office at Rosewood East. I can remember her face so well and the cardigan she always kept pulled round her shoulders as though she had slipped it on in a hurry meaning to change it later. It was beige.'

'How maddening!' Miss Hailey was sympathetic, 'Not the cardigan, I mean not remembering the name.'

'There were girls there too,' Mr Scobie said, 'I cannot remember their names either though their sweet faces, rather pale but clear skinned, are before me all the time. Such quiet gentle girls serving in the shop, packing up groceries and selling postage stamps, with no bad or evil thoughts in them at all. I taught them both the pianoforte.'

'I do understand,' Miss Hailey said quietly. She was seeing beauty in Mr Scobie's eyes. She caught a look of what she called soul beauty. It did not matter now that he had never mentioned her manuscript. So often she had waited with an eyebrow arched in his direction hoping he would speak of it. Now, she thought, she had discovered something more valuable, someone to cherish with real conversation. 'Dare I hope,' she said to herself, fluttering with internal drama, 'for friendship, real friendship?' She liked too the idea that he was twenty-five years older than she was. Because of the difference in their ages there was a touch of the exquisite. He possessed a delicate wisdom and she could remain perpetually youthful. Impetuous! She smiled. She looked at Mr Scobie with her keen eyes and knew that his music and her music were two entirely different things. In her mind she formed a clear picture of him. She saw him, in a small car, going from house to school and back to house; she saw him as visiting music teacher giving piano lessons, patiently counting and beating time, gently touching a bare rounded arm and lifting a fragile wrist with his forefinger, encouraging, correcting, praising and, all the time, endlessly tender.

He has probably never heard of Bayreuth, Miss Hailey thought, with indulgence, towards him. All the same, she told herself, he will have had his own criterion and reached it on small town concert platforms and in the schoolrooms set aside for music. She knew his cassette music was limited to the popular classics. Of course she liked his music she hastened to add in her thoughts. Heaven Forbid if she could never hear Eroica and Beethoven's Fifth again. Since Mr Scobie had been in the hospital there had been an unexpected feast of music. It flowed frequently along the passage to Room Three.

It occurred to Miss Hailey that one of the true meanings of friendship was protection. She leaned towards Mr Scobie.

'Do not,' she said, 'expect too much from that little social worker. I have learned from experience,' she continued, 'we are only material for their questionnaires, their statistics and their examination results. For myself,' her voice became louder, 'I have respect for the man who comes from the Department of Public Health. He is concerned with things like taps and drains and they have a certain optimism, don't you think? He does not come here, when he comes, purely out of, how shall I put it, *Schadenfreude*. Also, he has beautiful eyes.'

Miss Hailey and Mr Scobie sat for a time in silence. It must be nearly time for the regular dustbin investigation, she thought. She began forming in her mind a plan. She would place herself in a strategic position near the dustbins and wait for the Public Health official. Without putting Mr Scobie on a pedestal of European performance she could stress how life in St Christopher and St Jude was an ordeal for him and for her. This would bring the conversation to the point of a confession about their new-found friendship. A relationship of the intellectual and the spiritual which could not thrive in the surroundings provided by St Christopher and St Jude ... Miss Hailey's racing thoughts were halted abruptly by the memory of something unpleasant and sinister.

'I'll say this to you *sotto voce*,' she said to Mr Scobie. 'Has Matron taken you for a ride yet?' She paused, looking at him earnestly. 'Has she taken you for a ride?'

'I think I will take my walk now,' Mr Scobie said to Mrs Rawlings as she brought the next patient damp and shivering from the shower. 'Can I have my clothes please?'

'Matron says that Doctor Risley wants you to rest up, not walk,' Mrs Rawlings said, panting. She bound Miss Nunne into her chair.

'But I never felt better,' Mr Scobie said. 'You can't keep

me a prisoner you know', he tried to make it sound like a joke. As always, he felt he must lighten Mrs Rawlings' lot; she seemed even more laden with sorrow.

As if Mrs Rawlings felt his attempt towards her heavy heart, she said quite kindly, 'Now just you sit and relax here in the sun and, who knows, Matron might find time to take you out in the car tomorrow.' She tucked in his grey rug.

Gradually the straggling row of cane chairs was filled with old ladies.

Come along Aunty Dear – come along Aunty Dear come to the shower – come to the toilet – come to the dinette – come along back to bed Aunty –

'I am quite warm enough, a little too warm,' Mr Scobie tried to untuck his rug, but Mrs Rawlings, bending down slowly, secured it under the chair with a large safety pin.

Outside, beyond the white painted fence and the wild struggling hedges, were all the quiet streets and the hidden overgrown back lanes. Somewhere, in the near distance a bulldozer was at work. Several old houses in the suburb were being demolished to make way for blocks of luxury flats.

Sitting, wound up in the rug, with elderly women on either side, some of them asleep only an hour after break-fast, he felt afraid he might never be able to walk, feeling the sun on his back, again. He wished to be out in the lanes, walking.

Every now and then he heard the trains in the distance. He thought he would like to see the station again, especially in the morning, the handrails of the foot-bridge, high up, painted yellow on a lime-washed sky. The Rosewood East line went off quite quickly, after the market gardens and the vineyards, into the bush. Vividly he recalled a mysteri-ous depth of varying greens misty in the early morning. Wishing to be on the track at the foot of the little hill behind his house was like a pain coming back.

'I am missing my walk very much,' he said to Matron Price who, in her rounds of St Christopher and St Jude, was creating disturbance. Little cries and moans echoed wherever she walked.

'Are you Dear? Well it's only that we have to watch the old Ticker you know.' Matron moved on swiftly. 'And how's dalling little old Aunty Beatty today?' She bent over Miss Nunne who, waking up, began crying and holding on to Matron. Both made unintelligible noises of endearment. Miss Nunne, not able to speak, included some sounds of distress.

'There! There and There!' Matron said. 'Frankie!' she called, forgetting. 'Frankie! Take Miss Nunne and Mrs Birch to the toilet – quickly now.'

Mrs Rawlings appeared, water running off her plastic apron.

'Oh drat!' Matron Price said. 'Don't you bother Rawlings. You've got enough to do. I'll take them myself.'

'Where are my clothes?' Mr Scobie asked Mrs Rawlings. 'I'd rather get dressed,' he said. 'I don't like spending the whole day in a dressing gown.'

'Oh, don't let Matron hear you say that,' Mrs Rawlings said, 'not after she's rushed into town to buy that lovely gown for you. It was a real bargain. The only one left and you without one. She's put it on your account. Joan, your niece, remember your niece? She was going to get you a dressing gown but she never did. She must've forgot.'

'Oh doesn't Mr Scobie look nice!' Matron appeared in the doorway of Room One. 'I saw the advert', she said, 'and I thought, "Just the Thing for Mr Scobie". He does look nice doesn't he?' She appealed to Mrs Rawlings.

'A fair treat!' Mrs Rawlings said.

They seemed so pleased that Mr Scobie felt he did not want to spoil their pleasure. Women seemed to think a dressing gown so special.

'I am quite clean,' he told Mrs Rawlings, after Matron had gone. 'Once a week would be quite enough for my shower. Too much water takes all the natural oils out of my skin.'

'Oh,' said Mrs Rawlings, manipulating him along to the bathroom, 'there's nothing like plenty of soap and water to put everything to rights. Come on be quick, the hot water's nearly all gone.'

Mr Scobie, shivering, did as he was told, and afterwards was taken back to Room One.

'Must be a cyclone or something like it,' Mrs Rawlings looked at the darkened sky. 'Just look at that rain! All at the wrong time of the year too!'

The rain streamed down the window and rattled through the foliage immediately outside.

'It's too wet for the verandah, that's for sure,' Mrs Rawlings said. 'Why don't you play your music these days,' she said, 'it can't disturb anyone much this hour of the day while the stove's being raked and the showers going.'

'Do you like music then? Mrs Rawlings?' Mr Scobie was surprised at her question. He could not imagine her choosing anything because she liked it. Perhaps he had been wrong in seeing her as simply putting up with her life, accepting anything and everything, unable to change any of it.

'Well it helps to pass the time if it's not too loud,' she said, pulling the cassette player from under the bed.

'My! Take a look at that dust will you,' she flicked at it with the corner of her apron.

'Choppin Bashe and Mendalsonn,' she said.

'No, Mrs Rawlings it's Chopin, Bach and Mendelssohn.'

'Well whatever. Why don't you put a tape in. Here's one with singing and a piano if the picture's got anything to do with it.'

Mr Scobie wanted to tell Mrs Rawlings that he loved the intimate bond between the singer and the pianist. It was something he had known himself. It could happen anywhere; in great concert halls and in recording studios or, as in his case, in halls made of weatherboard or pressed tin. It did not matter either what the stage was like. The performance contained this bond whether the stage was all red plush and gilt or a ricketty wooden platform in the assembly rooms of an appreciative group of people raising money for a worthwhile cause.

The same bond existed, he thought, within the music. There were matching phrases, repeated phrases, questioning and answering phrases, phrases which contained all the qualities of leading and sustaining. There were phrases which explained and comforted. He knew and remembered the slight movements of the head, the quick glance, the expressive tilt of the chin as the notes of the piano ran towards or followed after the singing voice. He loved this promise between the music and the performance. This was where the real truth of human life lay, in promise and in performance and in the seeking between people for what was needed in the keeping of the promise.

Often in his life he had played the piano with all the care needed to accompany the singer. He saw the cassette in Mrs Rawlings' red hands. In his head he heard the purest tenor singing, like silver,

> *Fremd bin ich eingezogen*
> > *Fremd zieh ich wieder aus —*
> > > *A stranger came I hither*
> > > *A stranger I depart —*
> *Ich kann zu meiner Reisen*
> *nicht Wählen mit der Zeit —*
> > *I cannot for my journey*
> > *choose the appointed time —*

'No thank you,' he said, 'I won't have the music just now.'

'Well what about the Bible then?' Mrs Rawlings said. 'It's far too cold and wet for the verandah. Winter all of a sudden. And like as not,' she shook her head towards the dark window, 'it'll be blazing hot again tomorrow.' Looking at Mr Scobie, she pressed her mouth in a thin line. 'Well, what about another book then?' she tried again. 'What's this? *Songs of Innocence* by William Blake. That sounds all right. You couldn't go wrong with a title like that.' She opened the little book, banged the dust out of it and put it on his lap.

'There,' she said, 'just you have a quiet little read till dinner time.'

Mr Scobie read because Mrs Rawlings told him to. It was a poem of nightfall, a poem of the twilight.

> The sun descending in the west
> The evening star does shine
> The birds are silent in their nest
> And I must seek for mine.

182

The moon like a flower,
In Heaven's high bower
With silent delight –
Sits and smiles on the night.

He looked up to tell Mrs Rawlings, 'Agnes, she was my sister, you know, Agnes gave me this book when I was a boy. She was the teacher in the Sunday School . . .' but Mrs Rawlings had gone.

'Fare well green fields and happy groves,' he read. He could only partly read because the words were blurred by his tears. He turned the page, more words. Blurred. He could not read their meaning. His heart, he thought, must surely break with sorrow.

Saying Wrath, by his meekness
And, by his health, sickness
Is driven away
From our immortal day.

He closed the book. It lay in his thin lap.

'Pensive?' Miss Hailey, on her way to the dinette, paused in the doorway of Room One. 'What is the book? Blake? Oh Jolly Decent!' she twirled her sponge bag on her wrist. She smiled.

'Miss Hailey! Dinner!' a familiar roar, the voice of the cook came down the passage.

'Miss Hailey!'

'Coming!' Miss Hailey called, 'Coming!' liking the music of her voice. She paused. 'Are you come to luncheon Mr Scobie?' she asked tenderly, 'or are you having a tray?'

'I think it's a tray,' he said.

The meal was all over by twelve noon as the cook and the new girl, Betty, wanted to be finished early. Betty was racing on long noisy legs to bring the trays in as quickly as possible.

There was some kind of argument going on. Mr Scobie could hear voices raised in anger from the kitchen. It sounded as if, as well as shouting, someone was hammering.

'What is wrong?' Mr Scobie asked Betty.

'Aw! she said, 'it's one hell of a row over the fish. It's Matron and Mrs Rawlings and the man from the fish. Can't agree about the price and Matron's saying he's gotta take it back if he won't look at it and bring his price down. She'll not be robbed by a fish she says and he's saying he'll have it back even if he has to smash the fridge to get it. It's froze in there, see, he brought it last week and Matron's never paid. Just hark at them! Going for each other. It's my half day. My first one. Looks as if I'll miss my bus.'

There was another crash from the kitchen and, from the other direction, the sound of an old woman screaming. It seemed, to Mr Scobie, to be an appalling noise of pain. The bell in Room Three was ringing and he heard Miss Hailey's deep voice calling.

'Are you there Hyacinth? Hyacinth! are you there?' Other voices called and cried. The noise in the kitchen moved swiftly, passing the door of Room One, in the direction of Room Three.

'Damn and Blast this bucket! Who ever left this mop and bucket here!' Mr Scobie heard the bucket kicked aside. The sound was so familiar that he did not pay much attention.

'She should never have walked in those bed socks!' He heard Matron Price; her loud voice seemed to fill St Christopher and St Jude. 'Who the hell put those socks on her! No patient is to walk about in bed socks. No socks!'

In a softer voice, Matron asked, 'Whatever did you try by yourself for; by yourself – Miss Nunne? Whyever didn't you ring the bell?' she said. 'It's here, dear, the bell, pinned to your nighty. Now stop moaning if you can, dear, we'll get you off to the District right away. It's all right dear, I expect you've broken your hip or something. There! There then There! Miss Nunne, Aunty Dear, don't cry like that. You'll soon be all right. Mrs Rawlings has phoned for a lovely ambulance. There! There!'

Mr Scobie, hearing Matron's voice and Miss Nunne moaning, felt upset. He needed to go to the toilet. He walked out into the passage.

'Betty!' screamed the cook. 'Take Mr Scobie to the dunny willya. We don't want him falling around on his arse and breaking whatever he's got there to break.'

'It's all right,' Mr Scobie said to Betty who, eyes full of fear, a result of the initiation to the unaccustomed sights of Room Three, came rushing to him. 'I can manage perfectly well on my own,' he said. 'Thank you very much all the same.'

'Sure now?' she asked and, without a backward glance, she fled, her cart-horse legs kicking out as she ran.

Mr Scobie peered round the bathroom door and found the case which, he was sure, contained his clothes. He heard them calling the fish man to come to Room Three to help lift the stout old woman. She must be, Mr Scobie reflected, a good fourteen or fifteen stone in weight and very bulky to handle. It seemed as if the whole place was filled with crying or shouting women. The Lt Col., posting himself by the front door, called out from time to time, 'Are you receiving me. Roger. Roger. Am on recce. Hyacinth. No sighting of relief vehicle yet. Over and out.'

With difficulty, Mr Scobie dragged the case to Room One. He took out his folded crumpled clothes. He was not sure how long it was since he had worn them. They seemed the worse for being kept in the case, damp and shabbier than he remembered. Everything was there, even his cap.

Quickly he searched his pockets. The ticket to Rosewood East was still there and a few coins.

With difficulty Mr Scobie dressed himself. He hovered over the open case packing his loosely folded pyjamas, the Blake poems, his cassettes and his Bible. The dressing gown seemed too big and the cassette player would have to be sent on. He found his writing pad and pencil. Tearing off a sheet of paper he wrote,

> 'Please deliver to Mr M. Scobie care of
> P. O. Rosewood East'
> (at your convenience).

He was excited and yet calm. He placed the paper on the cassette player. He thought he should leave at once. The sky was darker with the storm. He could hear the wind rushing. Outside the window, the leaves and branches tossed as if being torn at by the fury of the wind.

He never minded getting wet so what did it matter if, on the way to the station, he was caught in a squall of rain. Once home it would be a simple matter to dry clothes by the wood stove.

He thought he could hear the train and the accompanying long drawn-out sound of mourning and of triumph. Distant and near, followed by the dull rumbling drumming of the wheels steady and monotonous on and on with the matching rhythm of travel and hoped-for arrival.

It would not be long before he was part of that rhythm.

He thought he could smell his own home here in St Christopher and St Jude. It was the storm bringing a fragrance as if from wet, sun-scorched grass, from dripping pines and from the soaked pathless scrub of the hill.

It was disturbing to find among his few possessions something which he did not immediately recognize. A floppy cardboard book tied together with pieces of different coloured tape. Quickly he put his hand, palm down, over the extraordinary picture on the outside of the cover. He turned it over and placed it next to the cassette player on the bed. Of course, he remembered, it was that Miss, whatever was her name, the lady writer, it was her manuscript. It had never been returned to her. He wondered what to write on another piece of paper to put with the manuscript. He wrote,

> I am sorry I do not read works of fiction.
> signed M. Scobie

and spent some time wondering whether it was suitable. Tearing up that page, he wrote on another page, 'Please return to Miss . . .' whatever was her name? '. . . her name eludes me' he wrote and carefully placed this paper on the cardboard novel.

Outside, the wind was more boisterous. The little well-bred leaf faces on the vines scraped and banged on the window. They seemed to rush towards one another and then to rush away trembling and shaking. A sudden shower of hail-stones hit the glass. The sound was frightening. Mr Scobie sat on the side of his bed. He was ready to leave. He looked out at the darkening afternoon. He would wait, he thought, for a few minutes till this fierce little storm blew over.

'When Father died, that was many years ago, he wept, — many years ago of course,' Mr Scobie told Mrs Rawlings when she came hurrying later into Room One. 'I remember him crying. He had his hands over his face but he cried like a child,' he said. 'He wanted to feel the soft rain on his face. He knew, you see, that he wouldn't ever be out in the rain

187

or in the sun again. I know there's nothing new in this, but that's how it is with people and how it was with him. He knew he was dying. He kept telling us, "I'm dying", he kept saying it. Of course he was an old man by then. He left home, you see, in spite of kneeling with mother to witness before the Lord. He left us, in poverty, at that time. He couldn't help himself, you know, and years later, when I was a grown man, he returned, old before his time and very ill. An illness for which there was no cure. Mother was an angel. She devoted herself to him in spite of what he had done. My sister, Agnes too, though by this time she was broken down by what her own life had done to her.' Mr Scobie smiled, 'You know Mrs Rawlings, Hartley, that's my nephew, Agnes' son, was a dear little boy. Very loveable. My Father said he wanted to see rain drops falling through green leaves. He wanted to smell the blossom of the orange and the grapefruit when it was wet . . .'

'That was very wrong of you Mr Scobie.' Mrs Rawlings stood in the doorway of Room One, her big arms folded round her bosom. 'That was very wrong of you Mr Scobie,' she said, 'to go and get dressed up and everything while we were so busy with an emergency.' Mrs Rawlings sounded offended.

Mr Scobie, having no wish to hurt her, hastened to explain. 'Oh. But I am going home today, Mrs Rawlings. When this rain goes off a bit I'm going up to the station. See, I've even packed my case. Everything has fitted in so nicely. There's even room for the player, but it makes the case far too heavy. I have packed and arranged everything.'

'So you have Mr Scobie,' Mrs Rawlings said, 'but I am sorry to have to be the one to tell you that you are not going out today. Home or anywhere else. So just you unpack and get back into your nice pyjamas and dressing gown. I'll be along to help you in just a minute. You old folk, you're all the same. A great trial to yourselves and to others! Now just you start getting ready for bed while I hot up the water for the teas.'

'Oh Badders! Bad show there!' Miss Hailey paused by the door on her way to the bathroom, her sponge bag dangling from her wrist. 'Rawlings always going for her life, always out of breath, I couldn't help overhearing what she said. I feel sort of, well you know, sort of sorry for Rawlings,' Miss Hailey paused, 'but she's like everyone else. Why do they talk about, inverted commas, Old Folk, close inverted commas, as if we're something different. Actually,' she gave a shy laugh. 'Ectually I'm the same age as she is though you wouldn't believe it because of fate, call it what you will, the shape of destiny, *Weltschmerz* and the ability to feel it, *toute la tristesse du monde*, I am the same age as those two – Felicity Rawlings, Simmonds she was then, and Hyacinth Price. Used to sit together in class, I think I've told you this. Form IV was an absolute riot I can tell you. Felicity lived up to her name then. Remind me to tell you some time of how we ragged the ass. dep. princip. and the ass. mat. all thought up, I might add, by one, Felicity Simmonds.' Miss Hailey loosened the string of her twirling sponge bag. She laughed.

'But to be perfectly honest old chap,' she said, lowering her voice, 'it's one hell of a night out there. You simply cannot venture forth in this. Why, the rain is simply streaming down, you can see for yourself. You'd have to be in soaking wet clothes for *hours*.' She paused and said, with a self-conscious tremble in her voice, 'and you know, old bean, I really do care what happens to you.'

Mr Scobie and Miss Hailey were rescued from the moment by the unmusical voice of the cook, 'Miss Hailey! MISS HAILEY! Where the hell does that woman get to! MISS HAILEY your bloody tea's goin' stiff on the plate. MISS HAILEY TEA!'

'Coming! Coming!' Miss Hailey sang in her best cadence. 'Chin up!' she said softly over her shoulder to where the bowed figure of Mr Scobie sat. 'I suppose,' she added, still in as gentle a voice as possible, 'I suppose we, safely inside St Christopher and St Jude, should be noble for a few minutes and put our minds to the people who are, at this very moment, bearing the full brunt of this cyclone or whatever it is and wherever it is.'

'Of course the best thing would be if Hartley or Joan were to come and I could be driven home by car,' Mr Scobie said to Mrs Rawlings when she returned. 'That way, there would be no problem about my cassette player. I could take it with me.' Mrs Rawlings began to pull off Mr Scobie's shoes and socks.

'I suppose Hartley might come today,' Mr Scobie said.

'Whatever makes you think that Mr Scobie?' Mrs Rawlings attacked his trousers with both hands.

'You mean because he hasn't been to see me this long time?' Mr Scobie said, he was shivering.

'No,' Mrs Rawlings said, 'though there's something in that. I meant not on a day like this,' she said. 'Just you take a look at the rain. After a freak storm like this, the roads 'll be terrible. I shouldn't think he'll come today.'

'No,' Mr Scobie agreed, 'though Hartley is very unpredictable,' he said letting Mrs Rawlings help him into his pyjamas. 'He was a lovely child. I loved him very much. Joan too, but something seems to have gone wrong, I can't understand how or why both of them live the way they do. I mean take Hartley . . .'

'Oh, your trouble is,' Mrs Rawlings told him, 'your trouble is that you're not able to move with the times.' She pulled back the white counterpane. 'Now, into bed with you. You'll soon warm up in bed.'

'I wish Hartley would come,' Mr Scobie said, 'though of course, with this weather, I wouldn't want any harm to come to him.'

'No of course not,' Mrs Rawlings said, hurrying out of the room.

Thinking of Hartley's previous visits, there was always the chance that he might come, though, as he sat in bed shivering, Mr Scobie felt sure that Hartley would not come. He thought he would not see him again, though he did not want to think this. Certainly he would never say it. He heard Betty, whose half day had been cancelled, galloping down the hall and back to the kitchen, gathering in the trays.

When Lina walked, he remembered, she made no sound, she seemed to move softly over the carpet to take her place at the piano, ready for her lesson.

'Ready Lina? one two and one . . .' he listened for her first notes . . .

'Mrs Rawlings done this chop for you,' Betty brought him a tray, 'tea's done but she says to tell you she done this for you and there's bread and butter and a jelly . . .'

'You don't happen to know my niece Joan, by any chance, do you?' Mr Scobie, still shivering, let her place the tray on his knees.

'No I don't. What's she like? Nice?' Betty pulled her hair straight using her faint reflection in the window pane as a mirror. Mr Scobie smiled up at her.

'Well yes, I suppose she is, in her own way. Though the last time I saw her, I'm not sure if it was the last time, I was speaking to her about her mother, my sister Agnes, and I said something like if Agnes hadn't married she and I could still be living together . . .'

'Wow!' Betty said, polishing the toe caps of her shoes on the corner of Mr Scobie's bed quilt.

'I could never understand Joan,' Mr Scobie said, he shook his head. 'I said to her once that it was a pity her mother, that's my sister, Agnes, had died. And d'you know what? Joan rounded on me. I'll never forget her words . . .'

'Betty! Where the hell is that girl!' the cook's raucous scream interrupted the conversation. 'Betty! I can't stand here all night waitin' for you to decide whether to wash up or not. Betty!'

Mr Scobie looked at the chop. It was long and greasy. There was perhaps one mouthful of meat on it if he could get it off.

He remembered Joan's voice, ' "Uncle! You are impossible. How could you wish for Mother to go on living. I know she's your sister and I'm sorry. How d'you think we feel? Hartley and me? Of course she's ill and she can't eat that bread and butter you've made for her. She's too ill to eat. She's in pain. Can't you understand Uncle! Look at her all yellow like that. How can you wish for her to go on living. Uncle! Leave her in peace. Please Uncle!" '

He remembered Joan crying. Once you had seen someone cry you always felt differently about them. Sadly he thought he had learned, in his life, that it seemed necessary to see and feel real grief before being able to feel real compassion. Joan, when she cried, was red and swollen about the face and eyes for quite some time afterwards.

He had cried too.

He thought he could hear someone crying in the hall, somewhere down the passage. There was always someone calling or crying, always someone hurrying falling over that bucket in the hall, kicking the bucket, he laughed softly, wasn't that what people said, 'kicked the bucket', he could make a fine riddle from that too.

Perhaps someone would bring a steak knife for the chop. While he tried to cut the meat, the tray kept sliding from his knees.

'Why are you in the dark Mr Scobie? Why haven't you got your light on? Have you eaten your tea? What? Well! I never! Aw!' Mrs Rawlings, tray in hands, reached the hall.

'Matron! Matron! Are you there. Come quick! It's Mr Scobie he's . . .'

'Why is it so dark?' Mr Scobie tried to ask them. He blinked, 'Oh, you have put the light on.'

'It's all right Mr Scobie, you've had a funny old turn. Now, just let Mrs Rawlings and me prop you up. Here, let me put in these pillows. There, that's better.'

'Why ever didn't he cut it up with the steak knife?'

He wondered why they were worrying so much about the chop.

'Here, Dear,' Matron was saying to him, 'along this line, here, Dear, just your funny old name, here's the pen, no, not there, here.'

Mr Scobie fumbled with the pen and the paper, letting both slip from his hands.

'Your name, Dear! Please! Try and write your name.' Matron Price, bending over the old man, sounded exasperated.

'I am a tiresome old man,' Mr Scobie smiled weakly. 'I'm sorry I'm such a tiresome old man,' he said. 'To tell the truth I feel only half alive, no pain, just this shivering and the darkness and my breath so short though that has eased. I am thankful for that.' He paused. 'Now what was Job's question?' he asked. '*Oh that I knew where I might find Him.*'

'Never mind about naughty old Job now Mr Scobie, Dear. Come along, try and hold the pen. Mrs Rawlings will help you. Guide his hand Rawlings.'

'Oh, I couldn't do that Matron.'

'Oh! Go on Rawlings. Of course you can. You've never

refused before. You've always done it before. You can do it this time. Help him to write. Now!'

'The answer,' Mr Scobie said, 'the answer to Job.'

'Forget about Job Mr Scobie, dear, he was a naughty old man.' Matron Price glared at Mrs Rawlings.

'Go on Rawlings, help him to sign, or else . . .'

'The answer to Job,' Mr Scobie had a fit of coughing which sent the pen and paper to the floor. He lay back gasping and smiling. 'The answer to Job,' he said,

> If I take the wings of the morning,
> and dwell in the uttermost parts of the sea;
> Even there shall thy hand lead me,
> and thy right hand shall hold me.

'It's Psalm one hundred and thirty-nine,' he said, and he wept. 'It's so beautiful,' he said, 'it always makes me cry in my weakness. Before such beauty I have to weep.' Mr Scobie smiling and weeping turned his white head to look first at Matron Price and then at Mrs Rawlings.

'I'll bet that niece of his,' the cook's voice came from the doorway of Room One, 'whatsaname Joan or Jean Frost, whatever she calls herself, will be here first off in the morning with a dirty big taxi truck to get all his stuff away. She'll take everything though Lord knows there's not much.' She gave a series of disapproving grunts.

'Here! help me to sit him up again Rawlings,' Matron Price arranged the pillows. Mr Scobie began to write.

> Where Mercy Love and Pity dwell,
> There God is dwelling too.

'I expect I have gone off the lines,' he said. 'I'm sorry, but I think you can just about read my terrible handwriting.'

'That's very nice, thank you Mr Scobie,' Matron Price was trying not to be impatient. 'But it's your signature, your name, I want on this very important piece of paper. Put your name in your lovely handwriting, Martin Scobie, that's all you need to write. I only want you to sign your name, dear, Your Name!'

Mr Scobie could no longer hold the pen. It slipped from between his fingers. He was not able to hold the pen.

'It would be presumptuous to imagine that the magpies are rejoicing after the rain. Certainly they sound as if they are singing songs of praise.' Miss Hailey was sitting next to Mr Scobie's empty chair on the verandah. On the other side, in another wicker chair, sat Miss Rosemary Whyte who, making an early start, had called in on St Christopher and St Jude. She had her folder open and was writing the date carefully on Miss Hailey's page. She had no reply about the magpies but now, since Miss Hailey had mentioned them, she realized they were kicking up a frightful din.

Miss Hailey looked along the line of basket chairs which were gradually being filled as the old people were brought out, one by one, after their showers.

Miss Whyte, her biro poised with hope, listened to Miss Hailey.

'*Quomodo sedet sola civitas*,' Miss Hailey said, turning away from Miss Whyte, as if addressing the empty chair. 'How does the city stand or is it sit, in parenthesis, the rejoicing city, desolate ... hmm ... er ... how is she become a desolation?' She continued to look hopefully at the empty chair.

'How is she become a desolation?' she asked knowing that there was no one to answer her with another quotation or with a biblical reference. 'Zephaniah chapter two, verse fifteen,' she said, supplying it for herself and turning to face Miss Whyte who, for want of something to write, noted it on Miss Hailey's page.

'Before his death, I am, of course, referring to Mr Scobie – though at St Christopher and St Jude it is not the custom to mention the old folk', Miss Hailey imitated the prim voice of Matron Price, 'when they have passed on. Mr Scobie, as I said, before his death, seemed to have stopped his theological utterances. He seemed, to use my own phrase, not his way of putting things at all, he seemed to be utterly and confoundedly and perpetually down in the dumps. He hardly said a word!'

Miss Rosemary Whyte consulted Mr Scobie's page.

'He wanted to leave St Christopher and St Jude,' she said.

'Well he has now, hasn't he?' Miss Hailey said. Miss Whyte made a note on the file.

'When was it?' she asked brightly.

'Matron Price will have the exact date and time,' Miss Hailey said. 'It's no use asking me a thing like that. I don't even know what day it is today. You must remember,' she added, 'I'm bonkers, or in more modern colloquial speech, a nut case.'

Miss Whyte flipped back to Miss Hailey's page.

The rain had been only temporary. Now, after the storm, the sunny places on the verandah were already warm and pleasant. Very soon it would be too wet and cold every day, too cold to be out of doors. Miss Hailey shuddered remembering the endless dreary winter days in Room Three.

Matron Price came out.

'Mail for Miss Hailey,' she held out a large white envelope.

'For me!' Miss Hailey said. 'But no one ever writes to me.'

'Well someone has. Better open it and see. Here let me do it for you.' Matron Price slit the envelope with her scissors.

Inside was a golden shining card. On a golden background of grasses and brilliant petals there was a vague but beautiful outline of a girl's face, half hidden in long flowing fair hair.

'Like an advertisement for shampoo,' Miss Hailey said, laughing. She stared at the card. She frowned drawing her handsome eyebrows together increasing the deep frown fold of flesh which had developed – to her dismay when she bothered to notice it on the infrequent times she looked at herself in a mirror – across the bridge of her arched nose.

The card suggested sunshine and happiness and love.

'Well, who's it from then?' Matron Price asked. Miss

Hailey read the message aloud, '*To dear Miss Hailey, to my Friend with love and peace.*' She paused and said, 'It's signed *Frances.*' She said, 'I don't know anyone called Frances, Hyacinth, I mean Matron. Did we know a Frances at school?'

'Can't say that I remember one. Did you have one at your school?' Matron Price, while she had her scissors handy, bent down and cut off what remained of Mrs Murphy's hair.

'No. I can't think of one. Ah yes! There was a sort of one. Franchesca della Blanca Bianca or a name like that. She was a princess, a beautiful child. But this wouldn't be from her.' Miss Hailey studied the card. 'The handwriting', she said, 'is so unformed and childish. I am not being critical, please don't think that, but do you see those little circles, like little o's over the i's instead of plain dots and the curling up loops on the y of Hailey, even Hailey has an ornamental extravagantly looped capital H – well, that is the handwriting of a young person.'

'Looks as if this Frances is completely uneducated,' Matron Price peered at the writing, 'though, in itself, this card's nice enough.'

'It's beautiful!' Miss Hailey said. 'But about the handwriting,' she continued, 'my princess wrote in a more definite and formal style. You see, I was so particular at White Cranes about handwriting. And, in any case, she would have to know that I am here. And she doesn't know. She was reabsorbed quite early from her school career back into her father's palace where, I believe, a highly advantageous marriage lay in waiting for her.' Miss Hailey paused. 'The odd thing is that, as far as I know, no one knows I am here,' she said.

'Matron? Have you got a minute? Kitchen's in strife.' Mrs Rawlings stepped out on to the verandah and then went back indoors immediately.

'Coming!' Matron called. 'Never a dull moment is there!'

she said to Miss Rosemary Whyte, wondering, in passing, where she had seen her before.

'I suppose everything that can be said has been said about magpies,' Miss Hailey, holding her card carefully, said to Miss Whyte, 'about their voices I mean. They sing. It's more than singing, it's carolling. Their voices cascade like a waterfall, their song is like a gentle silvery liquid, it caresses the morning – but all this has become a cliché, don't you agree? Everyone who has written about magpies has been obliged to use the same descriptions when putting these extraordinary birds into words. It seems to me that they rejoice but perhaps that is quite wrong. Before this card came I suggested that the magpies were rejoicing, now, because of how I feel, you see, because of having this card, I really do think that the morning is filled with joy.' She traced the golden girl on the card with her sensitive finger tips.

Miss Whyte, feeling that she had been sitting for a long time on the verandah of St Christopher and St Jude, agreed.

'Oh! Yes!' she said. She wondered what to write on Miss Hailey's page. She scribbled the word 'magpies' and made a note that Miss Hailey liked them. 'Is into magpies,' she wrote.

'Ah! Here comes Dr Risley,' Miss Hailey said.

Dr Risley stepped over the low gate and strode up the path and, with an athletic leap almost beyond him, he cleared the thick vegetation landing on the verandah boards beside the chairs.

He sat in Mr Scobie's chair. He greeted Miss Whyte.

'Well, well, well Miss Hailey,' he said, 'and how are we this morning? Appetite all right? Bowels all right? Waterworks all right?'

'Yes perfectly thank you Doctor. I am very fit and well,' Miss Hailey said, reddening at being questioned in this way in front of a young and pretty woman like Rosemary Whyte.

'Better listen to the old ticker then, if you'd unbutton,' Dr Risley said.

'Oh! yes of course. Oh Rather!' Miss Hailey quickly un-fastened her gown.

'That's my girl!' the doctor pulled his stethoscope from his bag. Miss Whyte, deciding not to visit any more old ladies, crept with stealth from the verandah and made for her mother's car which was parked, facing in a get-away direction, further down the street.

'Now, now, now, Doctor Risley!' Matron Price steamed out on to the verandah shaking a fat finger at the doctor. 'If you persist in examining my patients without my pres-ence at the bedside, so to speak, you have only yourself to blame if you are accused of assault and rape and worse.'

Dr Risley enjoyed the joke with Matron Price. Their huge laughter, a mixture blended like a tobacco of the rich and the earthy, outdid the magpies. Miss Hailey, obediently breathing in and breathing out, her thin chest exposed to the unsympathetic light of the morning, blushed; her awk-wardness red, in patches, on both sides of her neck.

'Fine. Fine. Fine.' Dr Risley gave a few final taps with his blunt fingers. 'Dress up m'dear,' he said. And, with Matron beside him, he moved along the slowly increasing row of huddled wrapped-up bodies.

It was true Miss Hailey thought, that though Mr Scobie never mentioned her novel, he surely must have read it. He must, she thought, have been going to write his comments on the piece of paper which he had placed on the manuscript.

It was not long since his death, just a few hours, and here she was missing him so much. Yet if she was honest, and she wanted to be honest, always, with herself, she had to admit that she did not really know him. She thought of herself, still with painful honesty, as a lonely and frightened woman clutching on to a straw where Mr Scobie was concerned.

'What a dreadful cliché!' she said aloud and laughed shyly. She gave herself up to missing Mr Scobie. There simply was, as it was before he came there, no one in the place to talk to or to listen to. His music, in the days when he was still playing his cassettes, had been wonderful. She missed that too.

The long morning on the verandah became the long afternoon. Mrs Rawlings came out from time to time to take the old ladies in one by one.

'Where's Betty?' Miss Hailey asked her for want of some sort of conversation.

'She's gone. Left last night,' Mrs Rawlings, panting under the leaning weight of Mrs Murphy, said. 'Didn't even leave a note or ask for her pay. Just cleared off.'

'I expect', Miss Hailey said, 'that awful fight between the cook and the fish man and Miss Nunne's ghastly fall and then poor Mr Scobie dying like that was a bit much for the girl.' Miss Hailey waited for Mrs Rawlings to speak, and then added, 'She seemed very pleasant, Betty, but she was very young.'

'I wouldn't know, I'm sure.' Mrs Rawlings, with her burden had reached the front door where she paused, heaving and grunting, until both she and Mrs Murphy seemed to flow together through the door disappearing, as if swallowed, into the passage beyond.

It was a comfort to Miss Hailey, as she sat on alone to think about the sender of the love and peace card. It was almost as if someone was saying 'sorry sorry' to her. She found a diversion in simply wondering who could have sent it.

Room One very Quiet All night. Nothing abnormal to report.
Room Three All pats. voided 4 a.m. All play cards in dinette.
Lt Col. Price lose bad kitchen floor and veggies.

Signed Night Sister M. Shady (unregistered)

*Missis Shady: Of course Room one was very quiet last night.
There was no one in there. Don't you ever read my day report?
Please boil beetroots and sponge in Room Three in future.*

Signed Matron H. Price

The days went by slowly one after the other. In this way weeks and months came and went.

During the day Miss Hailey sat with her manuscript in the dinette. Sometimes she changed a word or wrote something in small letters in the margin.

She heard the inspector from the Department of Public Health talking outside Matron's office. He had come, at last, he said, to inspect a wing tap which should have been put on the wash hand-basin.

'The room's occupied just now,' Matron Price told him, remembering for the first time, since his last visit, about the wing tap. 'I do hope no one's spoiling my lovely new tap at this very minute.' She gazed up at the ceiling. 'The patients here do the most awful things all the time,' she said. 'I have something nice and new done to St Christopher and St Jude, yes we still do have two saints, and before you can say 'knife' someone removes whatever I have had done and puts the horrid old one back! Anyway,' she said, laughing like a nervous horse, 'do come into my office. There should be some sherry tucked away . . .'

Miss Hailey, in desperation, was about to go across the hall and place her novel in the Public Health Inspector's arms. She rehearsed her little speech.

'For you,' she was going to say, 'I know you are a good man and a wise one therefore I leave my child, the child of my brain, I have no other, in your capable hands. Do with her what you will.' She paused. She had forgotten what else she meant to say, something about the responsibilities of his department extending a helping hand towards the literary bent of the nation.

'Ah! now I remember it all,' she said. She gathered a few loose pages and tucked them between the shabby cardboard covers. She delivered a dramatic if self-conscious little caress to the smudged and dusty naked lady on the front cover. Parting the flowered curtains of the dinette she emerged. She felt she represented the tragic and the graceful; she stood in the hall, her book held close to her chest.

The Inspector was in Matron's office, opposite, with his back to Miss Hailey.

'Let me pour you another,' Matron held up the flagon.

'It will be my third!' the Inspector warned.

'I'm sorry our glasses are so huge!' Matron Price laughed, down the scale, sounding like two excited horses. Quite an achievement she thought. 'Cheers! Bottoms up!' she cried with surreptitious frowns at Miss Hailey. With a series of nods and winks and small movements of her left hand she tried to indicate to Miss Hailey that she should remain hidden.

'Ah! There you are Miss Hailey.' Mrs Rawlings came padding down the passage in a pair of man's slippers. Her feet, she explained to the cook earlier that day, were playing up hell really something terrible. 'Miss Hailey,' she said, 'there's some visitors for you, on the verandah they are. I left 'em on the verandah as the sun's nice just now. Better out there I thought.'

'Visitors, for me?' Miss Hailey could not think who would come to see her. No one in the poetry group knew or cared where she lived. They were all so wrapped up in themselves. She tried to imagine who would come to see her. Suddenly she remembered that girl at school, at her school White Cranes, and that girl's dreadful friend. She was the one really who had worked on Eloise to bring about the terrible incident which changed everything and which was the reason for being buried in St Christopher and St Jude. And, of course, there were the dreadful parents of both girls and, indeed, the committee of parents.

'Oh how frightful!' Miss Hailey sat down again in the dinette. The persecution. It was all coming back; starting all over again. Hyacinth, who had helped her to sell her school and her land, and had hidden her all these years, was the only person who could help her now.

'Hyacinth?' Miss Hailey asked Mrs Rawlings.

'No they've come to see you,' Mrs Rawlings said. 'It's them two girls,' she pulled aside one of the floral curtains.

'What two girls,' Miss Hailey said, trembling. 'Oh No!' she said, 'not *them*! I can't see them just now, Mrs Rawlings, you see, I'm working,' she opened her manuscript on the plastic tablecloth. 'I'm writing,' she said, 'it's my book. I can't possibly be disturbed now.'

'Aw! Come on,' Mrs Rawlings said, 'what's all this nonsense? Matron's busy. You can't keep visitors waiting. Come along now.' She pulled Miss Hailey to her feet and disentangled her from the curtains of the dinette. With flopping and shuffling feet Mrs Rawlings propelled Miss Hailey along the passage to the front door.

The girls were sitting next to each other in the basket chairs. Both girls had pale faces and white thin legs. Both sat with their legs crossed over and both were smoking, passing one cigarette to and fro. One of the girls had, lying across her lap, a white-faced skinny baby dressed with simplicity in a grimy napkin.

'Hi Miss Hailey!'

'Hi Miss Hailey!'

Both girls grinned through their long hair. 'How ya doin' Miss Hailey? How ya goin' Miss Hailey?'

'Why it's Frankie and Robyn,' Miss Hailey said. She sat heavily into the empty chair facing them.

'We've come to see you Miss Hailey,' Robyn said.

'This is my baby,' Frankie raised the wizened infant and then let it flop again across her lap.

'Oh Frankie and Robyn how nice of you,' Miss Hailey exclaimed. 'And Frankie, you've got a baby! How sweet! What name have you chosen?'

206

'Miriam,' said Frankie. 'Would you like to hold her?'

'Well yes,' Miss Hailey said. 'Only I'm not experienced. I mean, she might cry, I might be awkward with her and upset her.'

'Aw, I'll take her if she cries,' Robyn said. 'I usually get to carry her when she cries, don't I Fran?' The two girls giggled and seemed to hug themselves exchanging looks with each other.

The baby was placed on Miss Hailey's lap where she lay damp and smelling just a little, Miss Hailey thought, of sour milk.

'She is sweet,' Miss Hailey said. 'See, she's smiling at me.'

'Yes,' Frankie said, 'she does smile, only at people she likes, but.' The baby, waving her arms, caught Miss Hailey's finger and held it.

'Oh that is nice,' Miss Hailey said, moving her finger and feeling pleased that the baby had not let go. 'Well,' she said, 'and how have you girls been getting on?' She was not sure what she ought to say or ask.

'Fine thank you Miss Hailey,' Frankie said. 'I'm married now,' she said with what seemed like a note of defiance in her voice.

'That's nice Frankie,' Miss Hailey said, wishing that she could think of a better word than nice.

'We, me and Mr Briggs, that's my husband, want you to be Godmother to Miriam,' Frankie said.

'Good Heavens!' Miss Hailey said. 'How does one, I mean, I haven't got anything to be a Godmother with . . .'

The two girls were looking at her with an eagerness which seemed to be shared by the baby who was still clutching Miss Hailey's finger in her tiny hand. Miss Hailey felt curious stirrings of forgotten tenderness as the funny little creature stretched and wriggled on her unaccustomed lap. They all laughed when Miriam yawned. They all had to laugh a second time when Miriam, twisting her little face, gave a small sneeze which she seemed to enjoy.

'Oh, she is very sweet,' Miss Hailey said. 'I would love to be her Godmother. Thank you so much, Frankie, for asking me. Though,' she added, 'I am not at all *au fait* with religious instruction and I simply have no money for a silver spoon and for suitable presents later on.'

'No worries,' Frankie said. 'We're real pleased aren't we Rob? The Christening's next week at Rosewood East. Horry'll pick you up. We want you to come over and stay, don't we Rob?'

'Yup,' Robyn said. Her eyes, behind her long fringe, were shining and mischievous. Miss Hailey was not at all sure what these girls wanted. She looked alertly from one to the other.

'Rosewood East,' she said, 'wasn't that where Mr Scobie used to live?'

'Right!' Frankie said. 'Did you get my card?' she asked.

'Oh the beautiful golden card. That was from you?' Miss Hailey cried. 'Oh thank you Frankie dear. I should have guessed Frankie comes from Frances.'

'Yup,' Robyn said, 'Mr Briggs, Horry, her husband likes Frances better than Frankie.'

'Well Frances is a very pretty name,' Miss Hailey said, 'so is Robyn,' she added with a graciousness springing from growing confidence.

'Go on Fran tell her about the place,' Robyn said.

'Well,' Frankie uncrossed and crossed her legs. 'Well, Hartley and Mr Briggs, that's my husband, and Hartley's sister Joan and her fella, he's the one that paints, and Robyn here and me and a few other guys have this commune going at Hartley's place.'

'I didn't know Hartley had a place,' Miss Hailey said.

'Well nor he did. Remember he was Mr Scobie's nephew? Well I went out with Hartley a few times, it was going with him I met Horry.' She smiled some sort of secret to herself, Miss Hailey noted, with indulgence. 'Well,' Frankie continued, 'when Hartley's uncle died, Hartley inherited the property and that's where we are. It's a luvly place.' She stopped speaking and Miss Hailey seemed to see in her eyes something of the loveliness of Mr Scobie's land.

'How simply delightful!' Miss Hailey said not wanting to lose the soft expression which seemed to have settled not only in Frankie's eyes but over her whole face. 'I cannot think of anything more suitable,' she said. 'Mr Scobie loved his house and land so much. I am sure he would be happy to know that it is being kept and lived in by people who really want to be there.'

'Hartley says to ask you if you want to come to live,' Frankie said.

'Yair,' Robyn said. 'Wha'dya say Miss Hailey?'

'I?' Miss Hailey was surprised. 'I mean, are you sure you would want an old thing like me? I mean, is there enough room? I'm not young any more, you know.' In spite of all the difficulties she was putting forward, she felt excited and pleased.

'It's Hartley's idea to have you come. Everyone doing their thing,' Robyn said. 'That so Fran?'

'Yair,' Frankie said. 'Everyone doing their own thing.'

'Ah. Well, I am a writer,' Miss Hailey said. 'I suppose we could have poetry readings and singing. We could write our own songs and plays,' she added.

'Yair. S'right!' Frankie said. 'And we're goin' to live off the land, keep hens and grow veggies, make our own furniture and our own clothes.' Frankie stood up and turned around, striking a pose, 'I made this,' she said showing Miss Hailey her not very clean skirt.

'It's very pretty Frankie, I mean Frances,' Miss Hailey said. 'What a clever girl you are.'

'Do ya think you'll come then Miss Hailey?' Robyn asked.

'Oh yes of course. I'd love to,' Miss Hailey said.

'There's not many rooms at present but Mr Briggs, Horry, he's building on some more rooms, we're in tents just now,' Frankie was saying.

'*Master it is good for us to be here. Let us make three tabernacles,*' Miss Hailey spoke in a dreamy voice, interrupting Frankie. 'I'm sorry Frankie,' she said, 'I am sorry something came into my mind.' She smiled at Frankie. 'Please do go on; what were you going to say?'

'There's going to be a lovely big family room along the back of the house and some little rooms, there'll be one for you. That's about it,' Frankie said.

Miss Hailey could see it all, the gently sloping land, the neat house with the added buildings, the row of pine trees, an everlasting legacy from Mr Scobie, and, above all, she could see people hurrying about laughing and talking and living happily together. She clasped her shapely hands, above Miriam's little body, as if in prayer.

'An idyll!' she said softly, closing her eyes.

'This baby,' Frankie said, 'my baby, Miriam here, is Hartley's. My next one will be Horry's.'

Miss Hailey gazed at Miriam. 'Oh I see,' she said, 'it seems a reasonable plan.' And then she said, with real pleasure, 'This baby, this is, in a sense, Mr Scobie's grandchild!'

'Miriam here was a natural birth,' Frankie said. 'Robyn here helped me didn't you Robbo?' Frankie jerked her head in Robyn's direction.

'You must be a clever girl too Robyn dear,' Miss Hailey said. 'Fancy! at your age knowing how to conduct the mysteries of childbirth.'

'Seezy!' Robyn said. Both girls laughed.

'Sorl arranged then?' Frankie picked up her baby. Both girls stood up. Miss Hailey noticed how thin they were. 'So you'll come for sure Miss Hailey?'

'Oh rather!' Miss Hailey said, 'of course I'll come if you'll have me.'

'My novel lacks an idyll,' Miss Hailey, alone on the verandah said, 'tonight I shall write an idyll. It is not the easiest thing to write but I shall do it.' She paced up and down the weathered boards. Her dressing-gown skirts, trailing, caught a few splinters. She stood at the verandah rail, her keen eyes gazed across the familiar gardens which, at this moment, she did not see or recognize.

'I shall write this,' she said, and she began, with solemn movements, to dance.

Miss Hailey danced a pine tree dance. She danced a dance of the majesty of the pines and of their transfiguration in the changing light of the morning sun. She included in the dance a mysterious hill. She tiptoed round its base indicating with expressive fingers and an arching of her eyebrows that, though life was active at the foot of the hill, no one knew the secrets of the hill itself. She danced the promised vision of an open door leading in to a small but neat house. She changed her dancing to a kind of hornpipe depicting three coloured tents nestling close to the house. The movements of the dance became more explicit as the actions of everyday life were enacted, first there was the feeding of the hens, then the planting of the vegetables. Stretching up she picked ripe fruit from imagined branches. She danced a rustic and natural childbirth setting the whole scene in a primitive wash-house. Because this part of the dance, with all its meaningful movements, was so satisfying she danced a second natural childbirth demonstrating the effort and the exhaustion and the rewarding joy of the new mother when a child is born. She danced a celebration of the new life, that of the child, and of the people engaged in their new found way of living. The celebration included her own joy at being about to take part in the new life. Her dance began to include more movements of excitement. She whirled round madly and, with a final fling of exuberance to end the dance, she flung her sponge bag into the massed foliage of oleander and other flowering bushes which crowded the high edges of the verandah.

Miss Hailey, out of breath but ecstatic, gripped the rail with both hands. 'Hailey's Dance. An Idyll,' she murmured.

'Miss Hailey! MISS HAILEY! Just who do you think you are! I do not cook myself to have it go cold and spoiled.'

'Coming,' Miss Hailey sang the word. She went indoors in a soft radiance of happiness. She was chosen and therefore special. 'Coming, Coming,' she sang. 'I shall have to do that dance again,' she thought, 'I left out, completely, a whole lot of things. I left out the painting of sunsets and the sewing of clothes and the making of furniture but, above all, I left out the sunsets,' she sighed. There would be sunsets and sunrises, one after the other, day after day, people would paint them and she would write about them.

She went on down the hall.

'Happiness', she said to herself, 'is the hardest thing of all to write about.' The stored horns from Eroica, accompanying her thoughts burst from her unexpectedly as she rounded the bend in the passage and fell over the mop and bucket.

Recovering her balance she parted the curtains of the dinette and took her place at the plastic-covered table.

'The curried vegetables of St Christopher and St Jude,' she said, 'provide a culinary mystery which remains forever unmatched.'

Miss Hailey did not attempt further conversation with those old ladies moveable enough to sit in the dinette for their tea. Absentmindedly she asked the cook for a glass of iced coffee and failed to hear that lady declare to the whole hospital, the saints included, that she, personally, had no idea why Some People thought that they had the right to ask for extras when it was clear that both she and Mrs Rawlings was run offa their feet, 'and me with my head in the flues, what do you want next your ladyship?'

'What a nerve! I do agree,' Miss Hailey said, hearing part of the discourse, but not realizing that she was the subject of it. She failed to notice too that old Mrs Renfrew made several remarks to the effect that she, herself, had only asked for tea seeing as Mrs Rawlings and the cook were so busy. Mrs Renfrew, noticing Miss Hailey's lack of concentration, and being acquainted with it, took the opportunity of eating Miss Hailey's bowl of tinned pears and junket in addition to her own portion.

During the meal Miss Hailey was acutely aware that her novelist's mind was at work. That hill overlooking Mr Scobie's property but which was not part of it, that hill represented all that side of human life which remains forever unexplored. Of course this unexplored area differed from one person to the next so that it was possible, for example, in a novel to explore humanity as a whole by having reflections of different emotions and experiences from several characters.

She had not, in her dance, been able to represent the hill clearly enough. Mr Scobie himself had said very little about it and then only in the early days. Later, he had hardly spoken. She remembered with a private sadness the way he had of looking up at her when she stopped in the doorway of Room One to speak to him. His eyes, as she remembered them, were a clear light blue with a perplexed expression in them. She thought she remembered kindness and wisdom behind the perplexed look.

The hill, perhaps it would be easier after the meal with pen and paper. She sighed. It would not really be easier on paper. Writing she knew, even when it was what she wanted most to do, was an act of the will and, as such, required tremendous determination and discipline. She was afraid of failing to be determined and disciplined.

'Perhaps it is better', she thought, 'to rest from these thoughts.' It gave her pleasure to think of Hartley's commune. In her mind she had various pictures of all these people active and happy together in a sun-filled corner of the earth. It was years since she had looked forward to anything. The excitement and the pleasure of looking forward were almost too much.

'It's all right Hyacinth I dropped something earlier today in these bushes. I'm just looking for it. So stupid of me. Really I am an Egg!'

In the darkness it was only possible to know that someone was crawling below the edge of the verandah when the black masses of oleander and hibiscus trembled and shook. The voice of Miss Hailey coming from the heart of the vegetation made the fact clearer.

'No Hyacinth it's not a burglar, it's only me. I lost something out here today. *Allez vous en foutre!*' she muttered.

'Miss Hailey,' Matron Price said, 'can I remind you about our little rule about Christian names.'

'Oh Lord! Tin Tin I mean Matron I'm sorry but it's pretty hard to see down here in the dark. Also, I might put my hand on a spider or a worm or something perfectly horrid.' The bushes quivered and rustled as Miss Hailey penetrated more deeply into the woody undergrowth.

'I'm sorry about the name,' Miss Hailey said, 'the maddening thing is that it's in here somewhere.' Her voice broke in a sob. 'Oh! if only I could find it.'

'I'll help you,' Matron Price slid off the edge of the veran-dah.

'Be careful Tin Tin,' Miss Hailey sobbed, 'that's a very thorny bush.' In spite of the moonless night Miss Price was able to see the white gleam of Miss Hailey's pith helmet.

'I've got my torch here.'

'Oh thank heaven for that,' Miss Hailey said, 'shine it over here quickly. Please!'

Both women were on their hands and knees in the leaf mould. They scrambled forward together, Miss Hailey making little noises and moans half in pleasure and half in pain.

'Ah! Here it is!' Miss Hailey, with a long drawn-out howl of triumph, held up her sponge bag. 'Three rousing cheers,' she said, 'let's go down on the bottom lawn Tin Tin. This calls for a little celebration.' Holding the sponge bag over her head, as a life-saver might hold the head of a drowning man, Miss Hailey did a kind of kicking back stroke through the twigs and leafy branches until she emerged, rather tat-tered, on the path. Miss Price followed quickly.

'You know Tin Tin I'm desperately afraid of being revolting when I am old. Really old I mean,' Miss Hailey passed the flask to Matron Price.

'I expect you will be.' Matron Price remedied this remark by adding, 'I expect I shall be too. We'll both be revolting.' She took a generous mouthful. 'We have no choice!'

'It's a hideous thought,' Miss Hailey said, taking her turn with the flask. 'It's absooty awful.'

'Let's not think on it,' Matron gulped again.

'Oh Tin Tin, Shakespeare, of all things, from you,' Miss Hailey cried.

'Good Heavens!' Miss Price hiccuped softly in a ladylike manner. 'Never!' she said. 'Couldn't stand him!'

'You know Tin Tin,' Miss Hailey said, 'I have often thought you were like Helen of Troy.'

'Oh! Go on with you!' Miss Price said, pleased. 'Of course I am nothing like her.'

'Well, you are immortal Tin Tin,' Miss Hailey said. 'Just think of all the times you kick the bucket in the passage but you don't go orf, I mean, you don't pass on, pass away, shuffle off this mortal coil, you know what I mean.' She laughed. Miss Price, taking advantage of Miss Hailey's mirth, swallowed an extra dose from the precious flask.

'It would be nicer in the caravan,' Miss Hailey said a little later, 'could we, do you think?'

'No, can't go there,' Miss Price replied in a low voice, 'our honeymoon couple are in there.' She gave a husky laugh. Miss Hailey laughed too. Both began to rock with what seemed like silent laughter.

After a time Miss Hailey asked, 'Haven't *they* come for Mr Rawlings yet?'

'No, not yet,' Miss Price said coldly.

'Oh Tin Tin! Sorry. Sorry. It must be perfectly frightful for you, I mean being married to him for such a short time and then discovering he had married Felicity as well. You are truly the most noble of women!' Miss Hailey said. 'I mean that – Helen of Troy!'

After a short silence Miss Hailey's voice drifted over the black shadowed, damp grass.

'I suppose this is what they mean when, in books, they write about this questionable tranquillity, the post-coital melancholy.' Miss Hailey sighed.

'I wouldn't know,' Miss Price replied.

'Oh Tin Tin, you know perfectly well what I'm talking about.' Miss Hailey leaned towards Miss Price, who said, 'I wouldn't know, as you know, I never actually went on with my training beyond the ordinary required level. There were books I never read and lectures I simply never attended. I never liked reading. Is there,' she changed her position slightly, 'by any chance a ciggy, a cigarette in your bag? I could do with a smoke now.'

Miss Hailey, frowning, fumbled in her sponge bag. 'Have you heard the one about the two prostitutes?' she said. 'One says, "do you smoke after sex?" and the other one says, "I don't know, I've never looked." Ah! Here's a cig.' She passed it to Miss Price who, striking matches, said, 'That joke is so old. It's got hairs on its chest, it's been done to death! Done to death!'

They passed the crumbling cigarette to and fro taking turns to smoke it.

'Oh,' Miss Hailey said, after a few minutes, 'I don't know why I told that awful joke just now. I suppose I somehow felt the need,' she began to weep, 'I suppose I somehow felt the need to introduce the vulgar and the banal to avoid the realization of the lack of any real tenderness. Life,' she continued, as tears found their way down the deep lines in her cheeks, 'life has offered me much but it has been mainly suffering. Wouldn't you agree Tin Tin? But I did, piously, take up my cross, you will agree, and I have been bearing it here with St Christopher and St Jude. I suppose, Tin Tin, the same could be said of you.'

'There! There! There!' Miss Price, discovering the flask to be empty, hurled it over the straggling hedge. There was a curious satisfaction in hearing it smash on the road beyond. Perhaps, she thought, that was why people did throw bottles and litter of all sorts everywhere.

'There! There!' Awkwardly she patted Miss Hailey's thin shoulder.

There were no lights showing from the caravan. It stood in what seemed the blackest darkness a short distance from the lawn where they were sitting. Miss Price, for a moment, thought about Mr Rawlings and the second Mrs Rawlings and the strangling complication of their lives. Her thoughts, crowding, sank to lower levels, to Mrs Shady, to Mrs Morgan and to their sinister relatives. She thought of Iris. Unfortunate was not a strong enough word . . . Miss Hailey's voice interrupted her thoughts.

'Since you know all about everything in this place,' she said aggressively, 'everything, including the incoming and the outgoing mail, I don't need to tell you that my novel has been rejected for the forty-second time.'

'There! There!' Matron Price patted Miss Hailey again.

'Thank you Tin Tin,' Miss Hailey said. 'I suppose,' she continued, 'there is a consolation in that, if it never appears, it can never be looked upon by the kind of people who will declare that I never wrote it myself. There are so many people,' she said, 'uninventive people, insensitive and unintelligent people Tin Tin, I can imagine former colleagues of mine reploughing the entire works of Dickens or Trollope trying to discover the source of my image, my metaphor, my symbol and even my better dialogue.'

After a brief silence Miss Hailey asked, 'Tin Tin, where is it?'

'Where is what, Dear?'

'Tin Tin, the flask. You know perfectly well what I mean. You had it last. It's my turn now. We always keep to turns.'

'I haven't got it, Dear,' Miss Price said truthfully.

'Ah well it'll turn up, it must be somewhere here in the grass, it's so dark tonight.' Miss Hailey gave a long moaning sigh. 'All that I said just now,' she said, 'I must confess Tin Tin, all that is only the bitter and the hurt side of me. Those same people, my former friends and colleagues would be quite likely, from sheer generosity, to say kind words about my book if they read it. I should not deny that they are sensitive and intelligent and perceptive . . .'

After another short silence during which the night

seemed darker than ever, Miss Hailey said, 'You know Tin Tin, I simply cannot take my old age to those young people.'

'Which people Dear?'

'Well you know, Tin Tin, Hartley, Mr Briggs, Frankie, Robyn, a whole lot of people.'

'Whatever do you mean, Dear?'

'Well you know Tin Tin Mr Scobie's nephew and that Mr Briggs, his cousin or some such by marriage, and you remember that lovely girl, Frankie? Well, they've got some sort of camp going, a commune, it's called.'

'Oh yes, I did hear something about it,' Matron Price said, dismissing the subject. She stroked Miss Hailey's innocent hand. 'Can you spell archipelago, Dear?' she asked.

'Yes of course,' Miss Hailey said, 'here goes. A.R.C.H.I.-P.E.L.A.G.O. Jolly good eh? Why do you want it spelled?'

'Well,' Miss Price smiled all round the word, 'Well – Dear, I've always thought to myself, just a little thought of my very own, that this bottom lawn, all by itself in this long finger of garden between the three roads was like a sort of peninsula. Don't you think, Heather, that being down here is almost like being on a holiday, away from it all, you know, like in the Greek Islands? The Islands of Greece?' She smiled again, still stroking Miss Hailey's hand. 'Being on a peninsula', she continued, 'is sort of remote, isn't it? And since you can spell archipelago you could write a postcard saying, *the archipelago are very beautiful.*'

'But who would we send the card to?' Miss Hailey was on her hands and knees searching the grass. 'It's very damp here,' she said, 'we shall catch cold.'

'Why to Frances, of course, Dear,' Matron's voice was silvery and flute like. 'Frances sent you a beautiful card didn't she?'

'You're so right Tin Tin,' Miss Hailey stood up and straightened her helmet. 'I do owe her a letter, a reply, an acknowledgement, and, in a sense, I do have to let them know, I mean there's little Miriam, the promise I made about her. I promised. I'll have to let them know', her voice trembled, 'that I will not be coming after all.'

'There! There! Dear I knew you would see it the right way,' Matron Price guided Miss Hailey towards the dark front door of St Christopher and St Jude.

'*To bed to bed cries Sleepy Head*,' she said as they fell over each other on the path.

'*Tarry awhile says Slow*,' Miss Hailey cried, 'Oh Tin Tin fancy you remembering Walter de la Mare! That's Walter de la Mare! Remember at school we used to say he was porny.'

'Good Lord!' Miss Price said. 'Did we Heather, I wouldn't know. Anyway, whoever it was, I couldn't stick him. But I always mean what I say.'

'Oh yes you do,' Miss Hailey said. 'Do you mean that we'll go upstairs? Upstairs to your house?'

'*And on the beach undid his corded bales* (Matthew Arnold),' Miss Hailey said, taking off her helmet and her shoes. 'This is sanctuary indeed, a far away unknown region, *Ultima Thule*,' she sank into a round, apricot-coloured armchair. Miss Price handed her a glass encased in silver.

'This is Nectar. Nectar of the Gods Hyacinth,' Miss Hailey's dark eyes shone through the steam. 'It has honey in it, there's honey in this,' she said. 'I shall fall under the influence of this drink. I shall succumb to my temptress!'

They sat sipping the hot drinks Miss Price had made with her own private electric kettle.

'Oh Hyacinth this is nice,' Miss Hailey said. 'You always had such good taste,' she looked round the spacious bed-

220

room with approval. 'All those gorgeous curtains and those elegant mirrors!'

'Well,' Miss Price said, 'Mr Rawlings has good taste, even if he does not come up here any more.'

For some time neither of them spoke and then Miss Hailey said, 'It has always been my opinion that there's no point in living unless you are doing something towards the future. A future, of course, in which you don't expect any part but which might contain something of what you have tried to do. I mean,' she added, 'things like painting or making clay pots or even planting pine trees. I felt this about my school and the girls who would go on with their lives after leaving school, taking with them some of the qualities and the ideals beyond the ordinary things of education.' She gazed thoughtfully into her golden drink. Miss Price, on the other side of the valiant little gas fire, drew her skirt up and back above her knees and warmed her thighs so that the flesh above her stocking tops became mottled; a pinkish-purple marbling appearing quickly on the white skin. It had been colder than she realized out on that lawn.

'I suppose,' Miss Hailey continued with a quick and handsome smile of recognition in the direction of the thighs, 'I suppose I shall go on writing even if I have no success. I suppose a writer can really only write with the ever present thought that, like an orchard planted, he can only leave it behind for those coming after.'

Matron Price, lost in the hot steam of a second glass from her own personal supply of whisky and honey and lemon, began to make in her head a list something like a grocery list. It was a kind of preparation for the long night ahead of her when she would listen to Miss Hailey's endless talking, her endless breathing and her endless heart-beat. If she planned her thoughts it was just possible that she would manage to avoid the more gloomy ones. First on her list she put the long white hands and feet of Mr Rawlings; the narrow, sensitive hands and feet of a thief, she told herself firmly. Second on the list she meant to include a particular way he had of looking sideways, a shifty look, followed by a sly way of talking – words slipping from his flaccid mouth contradicting previous words, before they had been properly uttered – but instead she found that she was thinking of the veal and ham pastries which he loved. Veal and ham came next on her list followed by a succession of vegetables of the sort which could be prepared in butter and served in little ramekins. Wines naturally followed. Mr Rawlings was very fond of the sweeter vintages; the moselles and the sauternes. Miss Price remembered the delight over a tawny port and a not-too-ripe stilton cheese, these must be added . . . She raised herself and prepared another drink for herself and one for Miss Hailey.

'I suppose,' Miss Hailey said sleepily, 'Mr Scobie has provided the answer.'

'Answer for what, Dear?' Miss Price folded back the apricot silk of her large bed. 'Answer for what, Dear?'

'The answer to his riddle of course,' Miss Hailey kicked off her slippers. 'After you, Hyacinth,' she said, '*toujours la politesse!*' She took her glass from Miss Price and held it gracefully beneath her knowledgeable nose.

'Down the hatch!' she said in her deep voice. 'Let's drink, Tin Tin, to Mr Scobie,' she said, 'we simply cannot waste these enchanted vapours.'

'Oh!' Miss Price's voice was chilly, 'I don't see the need.'

'Sorry, Sorry Tin Tin I am truly gauche! Well, what about my personal secretary? Do you remember her? Let's toast her. I think she deserves our best wishes wherever she is.'

'I don't think I remember her at all,' Miss Price said.

'Oh surely you do Hyacinth. She was with me for years,' Miss Hailey laughed. 'She was very jealous of you! Think! She had a battered look. Even her underwear always seemed battered.'

'I wouldn't know,' Miss Price said.

'The awful thing is,' Miss Hailey continued, 'I simply cannot think of her name at this moment. Hyacinth, her name eludes me. But you'll remember her in a minute. She was a sort of small passionate creature, an impassioned mouse. Once roused she was quickly assuaged, her passion, I mean. But so possessive, my dear. So repetitive. So predictable. An utter bore! Surely Tin Tin you remember that time in Venice? For myself I prefer something more complicated, something more provocative.' Miss Hailey yawned. 'Oh, how utterly comfortable that bed looks. Hyacinth, you are a Dear!'

'Miss Hailey, wake up Miss Hailey.' Miss Price, buttoning herself into her navy uniform dress, shook Miss Hailey. Thank God she had not wept at all during the night. Having slept unexpectedly well herself she did not know whether Miss Hailey had talked all night. She rather thought not.

'Miss Hailey,' she said, 'come along, I'll take you back down to Room Three. Come along.' Miss Price helped Miss Hailey to her feet. 'No,' she said, 'don't bother about finding your slippers now. I'll bring them down later. We shan't be a minute getting down there. Your feet won't get cold.'

'What is the time, Matron?' Miss Hailey asked. 'I must have overslept.'

'Oh, it's early yet,' Matron Price said. 'You can go on sleeping in your own bed. I've got to be down early. I've two new kitchen girls starting at six and there are three new admissions expected today. So hurry up, Dear, if you can. Hurry up do. I mustn't be late. I mean three new admissions are three new admissions!'

'Good Heavens No, you must not be late and yes three

admissions are indeed a Gift Hyacinth,' Miss Hailey said. 'Two new girls and three new patients. *Zut* !' she said. 'I'm awfully glad to be up early,' she added. 'I have at least a dozen poems to write before breakfast, one of them is a sort of pastoral dirge. You know, lately I have been, as it were, egg bound. Not a poem written. Yes, before brekker I shall write twelve poems.'

'And the card,' Miss Price reminded, 'you've the card to write, don't forget that card.' She steadied Miss Hailey at the top of the stairs.

'Heavens. What card?' Miss Hailey clutched the bannister.

'The one to Frankie of course.' Miss Price, discovering suddenly that she had a bad headache, was impatient.

'Oh yes. Rather! I remember,' Miss Hailey cried, 'the only thing is I haven't a card to send, not even a plain one without a picture. Hyacinth, I haven't got anything to send. You should know I don't have anything. Not anything.'

'Please do keep your voice down, Dear,' Miss Price said, 'I don't want the whole hospital to hear us coming downstairs.'

'Oh no of course not,' Miss Hailey growled, attempting a whisper. 'But I must have a card, a nice one, to send.'

'Yes yes.' Matron Price hustled her along the passage. The familiar voices of Mrs Rawlings and the cook could be heard in common consent on a favourite subject.

'I told 'im straight, I sed, Doctor my feet have been right through the mincer . . .' The voices were lost in the fierce attack on the innocent stove. Crashing noises as of metal pieces falling on the tiled floor followed as the day began to take shape in St Christopher and St Jude.

Through the open front door of the hospital Miss Hailey saw the pale-yellow light of the rising sun. It was as if the morning was being washed in this tender colour. As she was guided by Miss Price into the dark familiar airlessness of

Room Three, Miss Hailey, in her mind, saw the bright new tents, three of them, clustered together near the door of Mr Scobie's old house at Rosewood East. The tents, she thought, would be sheltered by the little hill behind his place and by his row of pine trees. Probably Frankie and Robyn, Mr Briggs and Hartley and the other people would be seeing the same sunrise. People, when they were camping under canvas, usually woke early.

'She's as mingy as they come,' the cook's end of a kitchen conversation followed Mrs Rawlings down the hall.

'The front door must have been open all night Matron,' Mrs Rawlings paused by the door of Room Three.

'Is that so Rawlings?' Matron Price said. 'Well just see that it is closed now.'

Hot milk prepared for Lt Col. I. Price (retired) 10 p.m. also kitchen floor and veggies.

ROOM 3 voided 4 a.m. Sponged. Slept well. All patients play cards in dinette. Lt Col. I. Price lose bad but enjoy himself and Mrs Morgan.

Message from Mr Boxer Morgan and Mr Rob Shady

    Cough up Matron or else Signed B. Morgan and R. Shady
Matron Mother I mean Mrs Morgan says even if St Christopher and St Jude is not yours any more you can still be matron as we shall need one.

Signed Night Sister M. Shady (unregistered)

Miss Shady: What do you do all night? Don't you ever read my Day Report? If you look back in this book, one page only, you will see that there are three new patients in Room One.

Mr Peter White 85 years. Hemiplegia (left side) admitted 4 p.m. Condition satisfactory. Treatment prescribed: Epsom Salts daily

Mr John Strange 85 years. Hypertension. Admitted 4 p.m. Condition satisfactory. Treatment prescribed: Epsom Salts daily.

Mr Timothy Ward 85 years. Hypertension. Altered mental state. Admitted 4 p.m. Condition satisfactory. Treatment: Epsom Salts daily.

Religion and next of kin on bathroom door.

Signed Matron H. Price